Goosebumps®

HAIR-RAISING COLLECTION

WELCOME TO DEAD HOUSE

STAY OUT OF THE BASEMENT

MONSTER BLOOD

R.L.STINE

SCHOLASTIC INC.

New York   Toronto   London   Auckland

Sydney   Mexico City   New Delhi   Hong Kong

Goosebumps book series created by Parachute Press, Inc.

ISBN 978-0-545-42937-5

Welcome to Dead House, ISBN 978-0-439-56847-0,
Copyright © 1992 by Scholastic Inc.

Stay Out of the Basement, ISBN 978-0-439-56845-6,
Copyright © 1992 by Scholastic Inc.

Monster Blood, ISBN 978-0-439-56839-5,
Copyright © 1992 by Scholastic Inc.

12 11 10 9 8 7 6 5 4 3 2 1   11 12 13 14 15 16/0

Printed in the U.S.A.   40
First edition printing, November 2004

CONTENTS

WELCOME TO DEAD HOUSE

1

Josh and I hated our new house.

Sure, it was big. It looked like a mansion compared to our old house. It was a tall redbrick house with a sloping black roof and rows of windows framed by black shutters.

It's so dark, I thought, studying it from the street. The whole house was covered in darkness, as if it were hiding in the shadows of the gnarled, old trees that bent over it.

It was the middle of July, but dead brown leaves blanketed the front yard. Our sneakers crunched over them as we trudged up the gravel driveway.

Tall weeds poked up everywhere through the dead leaves. Thick clumps of weeds had completely overgrown an old flower bed beside the front porch.

This house is creepy, I thought unhappily.

Josh must have been thinking the same thing. Looking up at the old house, we both groaned loudly.

Mr. Dawes, the friendly young man from the local real estate office, stopped near the front walk and turned around.

"Everything okay?" he asked, staring first at Josh, then at me, with his crinkly blue eyes.

"Josh and Amanda aren't happy about moving," Dad explained, tucking his shirttail in. Dad is a little overweight, and his shirts always seem to be coming untucked.

"It's hard for kids," my mother added, smiling at Mr. Dawes, her hands shoved into her jeans pockets as she continued up to the front door. "You know. Leaving all of their friends behind. Moving to a strange new place."

"Strange is right," Josh said, shaking his head. "This house is gross."

Mr. Dawes chuckled. "It's an old house, that's for sure," he said, patting Josh on the shoulder.

"It just needs some work, Josh," Dad said, smiling at Mr. Dawes. "No one has lived in it for a while, so it'll take some fixing up."

"Look how big it is," Mom added, smoothing back her straight black hair and smiling at Josh. "We'll have room for a den and maybe a rec room, too. You'd like that — wouldn't you, Amanda?"

I shrugged. A cold breeze made me shiver. It was actually a beautiful, hot summer day. But the closer we got to the house, the colder I felt.

I guessed it was because of all the tall, old trees.

I was wearing white tennis shorts and a sleeveless blue T-shirt. It had been hot in the car. But now I was freezing. Maybe it'll be warmer in the house, I thought.

"How old are they?" Mr. Dawes asked Mom, stepping onto the front porch.

"Amanda is twelve," Mom answered. "And Josh turned eleven last month."

"They look so much alike," Mr. Dawes told Mom.

I couldn't decide if that was a compliment or not. I guess it's true. Josh and I are both tall and thin and have curly brown hair like Dad's, and dark brown eyes. Everyone says we have "serious" faces.

"I really want to go home," Josh said, his voice cracking. "I hate this place."

My brother is the most impatient kid in the world. And when he makes up his mind about something, that's it. He's a little spoiled. At least, I think so. Whenever he makes a big fuss about something, he usually gets his way.

We may look alike, but we're really not that similar. I'm a lot more patient than Josh is. A lot more sensible. Probably because I'm older and because I'm a girl.

Josh had hold of Dad's hand and was trying to pull him back to the car. "Let's go. Come on, Dad. Let's go."

I knew this was one time Josh wouldn't get his way. We were moving to this house. No doubt

3

about it. After all, the house was absolutely free. A great-uncle of Dad's, a man we didn't even know, had died and left the house to Dad in his will.

I'll never forget the look on Dad's face when he got the letter from the lawyer. He let out a loud whoop and began dancing around the living room. Josh and I thought he'd flipped or something.

"My Great-Uncle Charles has left us a house in his will," Dad explained, reading and rereading the letter. "It's in a town called Dark Falls."

"Huh?" Josh and I cried. "Where's Dark Falls?"

Dad shrugged.

"I don't remember your Uncle Charles," Mom said, moving behind Dad to read the letter over his shoulder.

"Neither do I," admitted Dad. "But he must've been a great guy! Wow! This sounds like an incredible house!" He grabbed Mom's hands and began dancing happily with her across the living room.

Dad sure was excited. He'd been looking for an excuse to quit his boring office job and devote all of his time to his writing career. This house — absolutely free — would be just the excuse he needed.

And now, a week later, here we were in Dark Falls, a four-hour drive from our home, seeing our new house for the first time. We hadn't even gone inside, and Josh was trying to drag Dad back to the car.

"Josh — stop pulling me," Dad snapped impatiently, trying to tug his hand out of Josh's grasp.

Dad glanced helplessly at Mr. Dawes. I could see that he was embarrassed by how Josh was carrying on. I decided maybe I could help.

"Let go, Josh," I said quietly, grabbing Josh by the shoulder. "We promised we'd give Dark Falls a chance — remember?"

"I already gave it a chance," Josh whined, not letting go of Dad's hand. "This house is old and ugly and I hate it."

"You haven't even gone inside," Dad said angrily.

"Yes. Let's go in," Mr. Dawes urged, staring at Josh.

"I'm staying outside," Josh insisted.

He can be really stubborn sometimes. I felt just as unhappy as Josh looking at this dark, old house. But I'd never carry on the way Josh was.

"Josh, don't you want to pick out your own room?" Mom asked.

"No," Josh muttered.

He and I both glanced up to the second floor. There were two large bay windows side by side up there. They looked like two dark eyes staring back at us.

"How long have you lived in your present house?" Mr. Dawes asked Dad.

Dad had to think for a second. "About fourteen years," he answered. "The kids have lived there for their whole lives."

"Moving is always hard," Mr. Dawes said sympathetically, turning his gaze on me. "You know, Amanda, I moved here to Dark Falls just a few months ago. I didn't like it much either, at first. But now I wouldn't live anywhere else." He winked at me. He had a cute dimple in his chin when he smiled. "Let's go inside. It's really quite nice. You'll be surprised."

All of us followed Mr. Dawes, except Josh. "Are there other kids on this block?" Josh demanded. He made it sound more like a challenge than a question.

Mr. Dawes nodded. "The school's just two blocks away," he said, pointing up the street.

"See?" Mom quickly cut in. "A short walk to school. No more long bus rides every morning."

"I *liked* the bus," Josh insisted.

His mind was made up. He wasn't going to give my parents a break, even though we'd both promised to be open-minded about this move.

I don't know what Josh thought he had to gain by being such a pain. I mean, Dad already had plenty to worry about. For one thing, he hadn't been able to sell our old house yet.

I didn't like the idea of moving. But I knew that inheriting this big house was a great opportunity for us. We were so cramped in our little house.

6

And once Dad managed to sell the old place, we wouldn't have to worry at all about money anymore.

Josh should at least give it a chance. That's what I thought.

Suddenly, from our car at the foot of the driveway, we heard Petey barking and howling and making a fuss.

Petey is our dog, a white, curly-haired terrier, cute as a button, and usually well-behaved. He never minded being left in the car. But now he was yowling and yapping at full volume and scratching at the car window, desperate to get out.

"Petey — quiet! Quiet!" I shouted. Petey usually listened to me.

But not this time.

"I'm going to let him out!" Josh declared, and took off down the driveway toward the car.

"No. Wait — " Dad called.

But I don't think Josh could hear him over Petey's wails.

"Might as well let the dog explore," Mr. Dawes said. "It's going to be his house, too."

A few seconds later, Petey came charging across the lawn, kicking up brown leaves, yipping excitedly as he ran up to us. He jumped on all of us as if he hadn't seen us in weeks and then, to our surprise, he started growling menacingly and barking at Mr. Dawes.

"Petey — stop!" Mom yelled.

"He's never done this," Dad said apologetically. "Really. He's usually very friendly."

"He probably smells something on me. Another dog, maybe," Mr. Dawes said, loosening his striped tie, looking warily at our growling dog.

Finally, Josh grabbed Petey around the middle and lifted him away from Mr. Dawes. "Stop it, Petey," Josh scolded, holding the dog up close to his face so that they were nose-to-nose. "Mr. Dawes is our friend."

Petey whimpered and licked Josh's face. After a short while, Josh set him back down on the ground. Petey looked up at Mr. Dawes, then at me, then decided to go sniffing around the yard, letting his nose lead the way.

"Let's go inside," Mr. Dawes urged, moving a hand through his short blond hair. He unlocked the front door and pushed it open.

Mr. Dawes held the screen door open for us. I started to follow my parents into the house.

"I'll stay out here with Petey," Josh insisted from the walk.

Dad started to protest, but changed his mind. "Okay. Fine," he said, sighing and shaking his head. "I'm not going to argue with you. Don't come in. You can *live* outside if you want." He sounded really exasperated.

"I want to stay with Petey," Josh said again,

watching Petey nose his way through the dead flower bed.

Mr. Dawes followed us into the hallway, gently closing the screen door behind him, giving Josh a final glance. "He'll be fine," he said softly, smiling at Mom.

"He can be so stubborn sometimes," Mom said apologetically. She peeked into the living room. "I'm really sorry about Petey. I don't know what got into that dog."

"No problem. Let's start in the living room," Mr. Dawes said, leading the way. "I think you'll be pleasantly surprised by how spacious it is. Of course, it needs work."

He took us on a tour of every room in the house. I was beginning to get excited. The house was really kind of neat. There were so many rooms and so many closets. And my room was huge and had its own bathroom and an old-fashioned window seat where I could sit at the window and look down at the street.

I wished Josh had come inside with us. If he could see how great the house was inside, I knew he'd start to cheer up.

I couldn't believe how many rooms there were. Even a finished attic filled with old furniture and stacks of old, mysterious cartons we could explore.

We must have been inside for at least half an

hour. I didn't really keep track of the time. I think all three of us were feeling cheered up.

"Well, I think I've shown you everything," Mr. Dawes said, glancing at his watch. He led the way to the front door.

"Wait — I want to take one more look at my room," I told them excitedly. I started up the stairs, taking them two at a time. "I'll be down in a second."

"Hurry, dear. I'm sure Mr. Dawes has other appointments," Mom called after me.

I reached the second-floor landing and hurried down the narrow hallway and into my new room. "Wow!" I said aloud, and the word echoed faintly against the empty walls.

It was so big. And I loved the bay window with the window seat. I walked over to it and peered out. Through the trees, I could see our car in the driveway and, beyond it, a house that looked a lot like ours across the street.

I'm going to put my bed against that wall across from the window, I thought happily. And my desk can go over there. I'll have room for a computer now!

I took one more look at my closet, a long, walk-in closet with a light in the ceiling, and wide shelves against the back wall.

I was heading to the door, thinking about which of my posters I wanted to bring with me, when I saw the boy.

He stood in the doorway for just a second. And then he turned and disappeared down the hall.

"Josh?" I cried. "Hey — come look!"

With a shock, I realized it wasn't Josh.

For one thing, the boy had blond hair.

"Hey!" I called and ran to the hallway, stopping just outside my bedroom door, looking both ways. "Who's here?"

But the long hall was empty. All of the doors were closed.

"Whoa, Amanda," I said aloud.

Was I seeing things?

Mom and Dad were calling from downstairs. I took one last look down the dark corridor, then hurried to rejoin them.

"Hey, Mr. Dawes," I called as I ran down the stairs, "is this house haunted?"

He chuckled. The question seemed to strike him funny. "No. Sorry," he said, looking at me with those crinkly blue eyes. "No ghost included. A lot of old houses around here are said to be haunted. But I'm afraid this isn't one of them."

"I — I thought I saw something," I said, feeling a little foolish.

"Probably just shadows," Mom said. "With all the trees, this house is so dark."

"Why don't you run outside and tell Josh about the house," Dad suggested, tucking in the front of his shirt. "Your Mom and I have some things to talk over with Mr. Dawes."

11

"Yes, master," I said with a little bow, and obediently ran out to tell Josh all about what he had missed. "Hey, Josh," I called, eagerly searching the yard. "Josh?"

My heart sank.

Josh and Petey were gone.

2

"Josh! Josh!"

First I called Josh. Then I called Petey. But there was no sign of either of them.

I ran down to the bottom of the driveway and peered into the car, but they weren't there. Mom and Dad were still inside talking with Mr. Dawes. I looked along the street in both directions, but there was no sign of them.

"Josh! Hey, Josh!"

Finally, Mom and Dad came hurrying out the front door, looking alarmed. I guess they heard my shouts. "I can't find Josh or Petey!" I yelled up to them from the street.

"Maybe they're around back," Dad shouted down to me.

I headed up the driveway, kicking away dead leaves as I ran. It was sunny down on the street, but as soon as I entered our yard, I was back in the shade, and it was immediately cool again.

"Hey, Josh! Josh — where are you?"

13

Why did I feel so scared? It was perfectly natural for Josh to wander off. He did it all the time.

I ran full speed along the side of the house. Tall trees leaned over the house on this side, blocking out nearly all of the sunlight.

The backyard was bigger than I'd expected, a long rectangle that sloped gradually down to a wooden fence at the back. Just like the front, this yard was a mass of tall weeds, poking up through a thick covering of brown leaves. A stone birdbath had toppled onto its side. Beyond it, I could see the side of the garage, a dark, brick building that matched the house.

"Hey — Josh!"

He wasn't back here. I stopped and searched the ground for footprints or a sign that he had run through the thick leaves.

"Well?" Out of breath, Dad came jogging up to me.

"No sign of him," I said, surprised at how worried I felt.

"Did you check the car?" He sounded more angry than worried.

"Yes. It's the first place I looked." I gave the backyard a last quick search. "I don't believe Josh would just take off."

"I do," Dad said, rolling his eyes. "You know your brother when he doesn't get his way. Maybe he wants us to think he's run away from home." He frowned.

"Where is he?" Mom asked as we returned to the front of the house.

Dad and I both shrugged. "Maybe he made a friend and wandered off," Dad said. He raised a hand and scratched his curly brown hair. I could tell that he was starting to worry, too.

"We've *got* to find him," Mom said, gazing down to the street. "He doesn't know this neighborhood at all. He probably wandered off and got lost."

Mr. Dawes locked the front door and stepped down off the porch, pocketing the keys. "He couldn't have gotten far," he said, giving Mom a reassuring smile. "Let's drive around the block. I'm sure we'll find him."

Mom shook her head and glanced nervously at Dad. "I'll kill him," she muttered. Dad patted her on the shoulder.

Mr. Dawes opened the trunk of the small Honda, pulled off his dark blazer, and tossed it inside. Then he took out a wide-brimmed, black cowboy hat and put it on his head.

"Hey — that's quite a hat," Dad said, climbing into the front passenger seat.

"Keeps the sun away," Mr. Dawes said, sliding behind the wheel and slamming the car door.

Mom and I got in back. Glancing over at her, I saw that Mom was as worried as I was.

We headed down the block in silence, all four of us staring out the car windows. The houses we passed all seemed old. Most of them were even bigger than our house. All of them seemed to be in better condition, nicely painted with neat, well-trimmed lawns.

I didn't see any people in the houses or yards, and there was no one on the street.

It certainly is a *quiet* neighborhood, I thought. And shady. The houses all seemed to be surrounded by tall, leafy trees. The front yards we drove slowly past all seemed to be bathed in shade. The street was the only sunny place, a narrow gold ribbon that ran through the shadows on both sides.

Maybe that's why it's called Dark Falls, I thought.

"Where is that son of mine?" Dad asked, staring hard out the windshield.

"I'll kill him. I really will," Mom muttered. It wasn't the first time she had said that about Josh.

We had gone around the block twice. No sign of him.

Mr. Dawes suggested we drive around the next few blocks, and Dad quickly agreed. "Hope I don't get lost. I'm new here, too," Mr. Dawes said, turning a corner. "Hey, there's the school," he announced, pointing out the window at a tall red-brick building. It looked very old-fashioned, with white columns on both sides of the double front doors. "Of course, it's closed now," Mr. Dawes added.

My eyes searched the fenced-in playground behind the school. It was empty. No one there.

"Could Josh have walked this far?" Mom asked, her voice tight and higher than usual.

"Josh doesn't walk," Dad said, rolling his eyes. "He runs."

"We'll find him," Mr. Dawes said confidently, tapping his fingers on the wheel as he steered.

We turned a corner onto another shady block. A street sign read "Cemetery Drive," and sure enough, a large cemetery rose up in front of us. Granite gravestones rolled along a low hill, which sloped down and then up again onto a large flat stretch, also marked with rows of low grave markers and monuments.

A few shrubs dotted the cemetery, but there weren't many trees. As we drove slowly past, the gravestones passing by in a blur on the left, I realized that this was the sunniest spot I had seen in the whole town.

"There's your son." Mr. Dawes, pointing out the window, stopped the car suddenly.

"Oh, thank goodness!" Mom exclaimed, leaning down to see out the window on my side of the car.

Sure enough, there was Josh, running wildly along a crooked row of low, white gravestones. "What's he doing *here*?" I asked, pushing open my car door.

I stepped down from the car, took a few steps onto the grass, and called to him. At first, he didn't react to my shouts. He seemed to be ducking and

17

dodging through the tombstones. He would run in one direction, then cut to the side, then head in another direction.

Why was he doing that?

I took another few steps — and then stopped, gripped with fear.

I suddenly realized why Josh was darting and ducking like that, running so wildly through the tombstones. He was being chased.

Someone — or something — was after him.

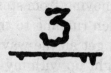

Then, as I took a few reluctant steps toward Josh, watching him bend low, then change directions, his arms outstretched as he ran, I realized I had it completely backward.

Josh wasn't being chased. Josh was *chasing*.

He was chasing after Petey.

Okay, okay. So sometimes my imagination runs away with me. Running through an old graveyard like this — even in bright daylight — it's only natural that a person might start to have weird thoughts.

I called to Josh again, and this time he heard me and turned around. He looked worried. "Amanda — come help me!" he cried.

"Josh, what's the matter?" I ran as fast as I could to catch up with him, but he kept darting through the gravestones, moving from row to row.

"Help!"

"Josh — what's wrong?" I turned and saw that

19

Mom and Dad were right behind me.

"It's Petey," Josh explained, out of breath. "I can't get him to stop. I caught him once, but he pulled away from me."

"Petey! Petey!" Dad started calling the dog. But Petey was moving from stone to stone, sniffing each one, then running to the next.

"How did you get all the way over here?" Dad asked as he caught up with my brother.

"I had to follow Petey," Josh explained, still looking very worried. "He just took off. One second he was sniffing around that dead flower bed in our front yard. The next second, he just started to run. He wouldn't stop when I called. Wouldn't even look back. He kept running till he got here. I had to follow. I was afraid he'd get lost."

Josh stopped and gratefully let Dad take over the chase. "I don't know what that dumb dog's problem is," he said to me. "He's just *weird*."

It took Dad a few tries, but he finally managed to grab Petey and pick him up off the ground. Our little terrier gave a halfhearted yelp of protest, then allowed himself to be carried away.

We all trooped back to the car on the side of the road. Mr. Dawes was waiting by the car. "Maybe you'd better get a leash for that dog," he said, looking very concerned.

"Petey's never been on a leash," Josh protested, wearily climbing into the backseat.

"Well, we might have to try one for a while,"

Dad said quietly. "Especially if he keeps running away." Dad tossed Petey into the backseat. The dog eagerly curled up in Josh's arms.

The rest of us piled into the car, and Mr. Dawes drove us back to his office, a tiny, white, flat-roofed building at the end of a row of small offices. As we rode, I reached over and stroked the back of Petey's head.

Why did the dog run away like that? I wondered. Petey had never done that before.

I guessed that Petey was also upset about our moving. After all, Petey had spent his whole life in our old house. He probably felt a lot like Josh and I did about having to pack up and move and never see the old neighborhood again.

The new house, the new streets, and all the new smells must have freaked the poor dog out. Josh wanted to run away from the whole idea. And so did Petey.

Anyway, that was my theory.

Mr. Dawes parked the car in front of his tiny office, shook Dad's hand, and gave him a business card. "You can come by next week," he told Mom and Dad. "I'll have all the legal work done by then. After you sign the papers, you can move in anytime."

He pushed open the car door and, giving us all a final smile, prepared to climb out.

"Compton Dawes," Mom said, reading the white business card over Dad's shoulder. "That's an unusual name. Is Compton an old family name?"

Mr. Dawes shook his head. "No," he said, "I'm the only Compton in my family. I have no idea where the name comes from. No idea at all. Maybe my parents didn't know how to spell Charlie!"

Chuckling at his terrible joke, he climbed out of the car, lowered the wide black Stetson hat on his head, pulled his blazer from the trunk, and disappeared into the small white building.

Dad climbed behind the wheel, moving the seat back to make room for his big stomach. Mom got up front, and we started the long drive home. "I guess you and Petey had quite an adventure today," Mom said to Josh, rolling up her window because Dad had turned on the air conditioner.

"I guess," Josh said without enthusiasm. Petey was sound asleep in his lap, snoring quietly.

"You're going to love your room," I told Josh. "The whole house is great. Really."

Josh stared at me thoughtfully, but didn't answer.

I poked him in the ribs with my elbow. "Say something. Did you hear what I said?"

But the weird, thoughtful look didn't fade from Josh's face.

The next couple of weeks seemed to crawl by. I walked around the house thinking about how I'd never see my room again, how I'd never eat breakfast in this kitchen again, how I'd never watch TV in the living room again. Morbid stuff like that.

I had this sick feeling when the movers came one afternoon and delivered a tall stack of cartons. Time to pack up. It was really happening. Even though it was the middle of the afternoon, I went up to my room and flopped down on my bed. I didn't nap or anything. I just stared at the ceiling for more than an hour, and all these wild, unconnected thoughts ran through my head, like a dream, only I was awake.

I wasn't the only one who was nervous about the move. Mom and Dad were snapping at each other over nothing at all. One morning they had a big fight over whether the bacon was too crispy or not.

In a way, it was funny to see them being so childish. Josh was acting really sullen all the time. He hardly spoke a word to anyone. And Petey sulked, too. That dumb dog wouldn't even pick himself up and come over to me when I had some table scraps for him.

I guess the hardest part about moving was saying good-bye to my friends. Carol and Amy were away at camp, so I had to write to them. But Kathy was home, and she was my oldest and best friend, and the hardest to say good-bye to.

I think some people were surprised that Kathy and I had stayed such good friends. For one thing, we look so different. I'm tall and thin and dark, and she's fair-skinned, with long blonde hair, and a little chubby. But we've been friends since pre-school, and best best friends since fourth grade.

When she came over the night before the move, we were both terribly awkward. "Kathy, you shouldn't be nervous," I told her. "You're not the one who's moving away forever."

"It's not like you're moving to China or some-thing," she answered, chewing hard on her bubble gum. "Dark Falls is only four hours away, Amanda. We'll see each other a lot."

"Yeah, I guess," I said. But I didn't believe it. Four hours away was as bad as being in China, as far as I was concerned. "I guess we can still talk on the phone," I said glumly.

She blew a small green bubble, then sucked it back into her mouth. "Yeah. Sure," she said, pre-tending to be enthusiastic. "You're lucky, you know. Moving out of this crummy neighborhood to a big house."

"It's *not* a crummy neighborhood," I insisted. I don't know why I was defending the neighbor-hood. I never had before. One of our favorite pas-times was thinking of places we'd rather be growing up.

"School won't be the same without you," she sighed, curling her legs under her on the chair. "Who's going to slip me the answers in math?"

I laughed. "I always slipped you the *wrong* answers."

"But it was the thought that counted," Kathy said. And then she groaned. "Ugh. Junior high. Is your new junior high part of the high school or part of the elementary school?"

I made a disgusted face. "Everything's in one building. It's a small town, remember? There's no separate high school. At least, I didn't see one."

"Bummer," she said.

Bummer was right.

We chatted for hours. Until Kathy's mom called and said it was time for her to come home.

Then we hugged. I had made up my mind that I wouldn't cry, but I could feel the big, hot tears forming in the corners of my eyes. And then they were running down my cheeks.

"I'm so miserable!" I wailed.

I had planned to be really controlled and mature. But Kathy was my best friend, after all, and what could I do?

We made a promise that we'd always be together on our birthdays — no matter what. We'd force our parents to make sure we didn't miss each other's birthdays.

And then we hugged again. And Kathy said, "Don't worry. We'll see each other a lot. Really." And she had tears in her eyes, too.

She turned and ran out the door. The screen door slammed hard behind her. I stood there staring out into the darkness until Petey came scampering in, his toenails clicking across the linoleum, and started to lick my hand.

The next morning, moving day, was a rainy Saturday. Not a downpour. No thunder or lightning. But just enough rain and wind to make the long drive slow and unpleasant.

The sky seemed to get darker as we neared the new neighborhood. The heavy trees bent low over the street. "Slow down, Jack," Mom warned shrilly. "The street is really slick."

But Dad was in a hurry to get to the house before the moving van did. "They'll just put the stuff anywhere if we're not there to supervise," he explained.

Josh, beside me in the backseat, was being a real pain, as usual. He kept complaining that he was thirsty. When that didn't get results, he started whining that he was starving. But we had all had a big breakfast, so that didn't get any reaction, either.

He just wanted attention, of course. I kept trying to cheer him up by telling him how great the house was inside and how big his room was. He still hadn't seen it.

But he didn't want to be cheered up. He started wrestling with Petey, getting the poor dog all worked up, until Dad had to shout at him to stop.

"Let's all try really hard not to get on each other's nerves," Mom suggested.

Dad laughed. "Good idea, dear."

"Don't make fun of me," she snapped.

They started to argue about who was more exhausted from all the packing. Petey stood up on his hind legs and started to howl at the back window.

"Can't you shut him up?" Mom screamed.

I pulled Petey down, but he struggled back up and started howling again. "He's never done this before," I said.

"Just get him quiet!" Mom insisted.

I pulled Petey down by his hind legs, and Josh started to howl. Mom turned around and gave him a dirty look. Josh didn't stop howling, though. He thought he was a riot.

Finally, Dad pulled the car up the driveway of the new house. The tires crunched over the wet gravel. Rain pounded on the roof.

"Home sweet home," Mom said. I couldn't tell if she was being sarcastic or not. I think she was really glad the long car ride was over.

"At least we beat the movers," Dad said, glancing at his watch. Then his expression changed. "Hope they're not lost."

"It's as dark as night out there," Josh complained.

Petey was jumping up and down in my lap, desperate to get out of the car. He was usually a good traveler. But once the car stopped, he wanted out immediately.

I opened my car door and he leaped onto the driveway with a splash and started to run in a wild zigzag across the front yard.

"At least *someone's* glad to be here," Josh said quietly.

Dad ran up to the porch and, fumbling with the unfamiliar keys, managed to get the front door open. Then he motioned for us to come into the house.

Mom and Josh ran across the walk, eager to get in out of the rain. I closed the car door behind me and started to jog after them.

But something caught my eye. I stopped and looked up to the twin bay windows above the porch.

I held a hand over my eyebrows to shield my eyes and squinted through the rain.

Yes. I saw it.

A face. In the window on the left.

The boy.

The same boy was up there, staring down at me.

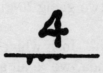

4

"Wipe your feet! Don't track mud on the nice clean floors!" Mom called. Her voice echoed against the bare walls of the empty living room.

I stepped into the hallway. The house smelled of paint. The painters had just finished on Thursday. It was hot in the house, much hotter than outside.

"This kitchen light won't go on," Dad called from the back. "Did the painters turn off the electricity or something?"

"How should I know?" Mom shouted back.

Their voices sounded so loud in the big, empty house.

"Mom — there's someone upstairs!" I cried, wiping my feet on the new welcome mat and hurrying into the living room.

She was at the window, staring out at the rain, looking for the movers probably. She spun around as I came in. "What?"

"There's a boy upstairs. I saw him in the window," I said, struggling to catch my breath.

Josh entered the room from the back hallway. He'd probably been with Dad. He laughed. "Is someone already living here?"

"There's no one upstairs," Mom said, rolling her eyes. "Are you two going to give me a break today, or what?"

"What did *I* do?" Josh whined.

"Listen, Amanda, we're all a little on edge today — " Mom started.

But I interrupted her. "I saw his face, Mom. In the window. I'm not crazy, you know."

"Says who?" Josh cracked.

"Amanda!" Mom bit her lower lip, the way she always did when she was really exasperated. "You saw a reflection of something. Of a tree probably." She turned back to the window. The rain was coming down in sheets now, the wind driving it noisily against the large picture window.

I ran to the stairway, cupped my hands over my mouth, and shouted up to the second floor, "Who's up there?"

No answer.

"Who's up there?" I called, a little louder.

Mom had her hands over her ears. "Amanda — please!"

Josh had disappeared through the dining room. He was finally exploring the house.

"There's someone up there," I insisted and, impulsively, I started up the wooden stairway, my sneakers thudding loudly on the bare steps.

"Amanda — " I heard Mom call after me.

But I was too angry to stop. Why didn't she believe me? Why did she have to say it was a reflection of a tree I saw up there?

I was curious. I had to know who was upstairs. I had to prove Mom wrong. I had to show her I hadn't seen a stupid reflection. I guess I can be pretty stubborn, too. Maybe it's a family trait.

The stairs squeaked and creaked under me as I climbed. I didn't feel at all scared until I reached the second-floor landing. Then I suddenly had this heavy feeling in the pit of my stomach.

I stopped, breathing hard, leaning on the banister.

Who could it be? A burglar? A bored neighborhood kid who had broken into an empty house for a thrill?

Maybe I shouldn't be up here alone, I realized.

Maybe the boy in the window was dangerous.

"Anybody up here?" I called, my voice suddenly trembly and weak.

Still leaning against the banister, I listened.

And I could hear footsteps scampering across the hallway.

No.

Not footsteps.

The rain. That's what it was. The patter of rain against the slate-shingled roof.

For some reason, the sound made me feel a little

31

calmer. I let go of the banister and stepped into the long, narrow hallway. It was dark up here, except for a rectangle of gray light from a small window at the other end.

I took a few steps, the old wooden floorboards creaking noisily beneath me. "Anybody up here?"

Again no answer.

I stepped up to the first doorway on my left. The door was closed. The smell of fresh paint was suffocating. There was a light switch on the wall near the door. Maybe it's for the hall light, I thought. I clicked it on. But nothing happened.

"Anybody here?"

My hand was trembling as I grabbed the doorknob. It felt warm in my hand. And damp.

I turned it and, taking a deep breath, pushed open the door.

I peered into the room. Gray light filtered in through the bay window. A flash of lightning made me jump back. The thunder that followed was a dull, distant roar.

Slowly, carefully, I took a step into the room. Then another.

No sign of anyone.

This was a guest bedroom. Or it could be Josh's room if he decided he liked it.

Another flash of lightning. The sky seemed to be darkening. It was pitch-black out there even though it was just after lunchtime.

I backed into the hall. The next room down was

going to be mine. It also had a bay window that looked down on the front yard.

Was the boy I saw staring down at me in *my* room?

I crept down the hall, letting my hand run along the wall for some reason, and stopped outside my door, which was also closed.

Taking a deep breath, I knocked on the door. "Who's in there?" I called.

I listened.

Silence.

Then a clap of thunder, closer than the last. I froze as if I were paralyzed, holding my breath. It was so hot up here, hot and damp. And the smell of paint was making me dizzy.

I grabbed the doorknob. "Anybody in there?"

I started to turn the knob — when the boy crept up from behind and grabbed my shoulder.

5

I couldn't breathe. I couldn't cry out.

My heart seemed to stop. My chest felt as if it were about to explode.

With a desperate, terrified effort, I spun a-round.

"Josh!" I shrieked. "You scared me to death! I thought — "

He let go of me and took a step back. "Gotcha!" he declared, and then started to laugh, a high-pitched laugh that echoed down the long, bare hallway.

My heart was pounding hard now. My forehead throbbed. "You're not funny," I said angrily. I shoved him against the wall. "You really scared me."

He laughed and rolled around on the floor. He's really a sicko. I tried to shove him again but missed.

Angrily, I turned away from him — just in time to see my bedroom door slowly swinging open.

I gasped in disbelief. And froze, gaping at the moving door.

Josh stopped laughing and stood up, immediately serious, his dark eyes wide with fright.

I could hear someone moving inside the room.

I could hear whispering.

Excited giggles.

"Who — who's there?" I managed to stammer in a high little voice I didn't recognize.

The door, creaking loudly, opened a bit more, then started to close.

"Who's there?" I demanded, a bit more forcefully.

Again, I could hear whispering, someone moving about.

Josh had backed up against the wall and was edging away, toward the stairs. He had an expression on his face I'd never seen before — sheer terror.

The door, creaking like a door in a movie haunted house, closed a little more.

Josh was nearly to the stairway. He was staring at me, violently motioning with his hand for me to follow.

But instead, I stepped forward, grabbed the doorknob, and pushed the door open hard.

It didn't resist.

I let go of the doorknob and stood blocking the doorway. "Who's there?"

The room was empty.

35

Thunder crashed.

It took me a few seconds to realize what was making the door move. The window on the opposite wall had been left open several inches. The gusting wind through the open window must have been opening and closing the door. I guessed that also explained the other sounds I heard inside the room, the sounds I thought were whispers.

. Who had left the window open? The painters, probably.

I took a deep breath and let it out slowly, waiting for my pounding heart to settle down to normal.

Feeling a little foolish, I walked quickly to the window and pushed it shut.

"Amanda — are you all right?" Josh whispered from the hallway.

I started to answer him. But then I had a better idea.

He had practically scared me to death a few minutes before. Why not give *him* a little scare? He deserved it.

So I didn't answer him.

I could hear him take a few timid steps closer to my room. "Amanda? Amanda? You okay?"

I tiptoed over to my closet, pulled the door open a third of the way. Then I laid down flat on the floor, on my back, with my head and shoulders hidden inside the closet and the rest of me out in the room.

"Amanda?" Josh sounded very scared.

"Ohhhhh," I moaned loudly.

I knew when he saw me sprawled on the floor like this, he'd totally freak out!

"Amanda — what's happening?"

He was in the doorway now. He'd see me any second now, lying in the dark room, my head hidden from view, the lightning flashing impressively and the thunder cracking outside the old window.

I took a deep breath and held it to keep from giggling.

"Amanda?" he whispered. And then he must have seen me, because he uttered a loud "Huh?!" And I heard him gasp.

And then he screamed at the top of his lungs. I heard him running down the hall to the stairway, shrieking, "Mom! Dad!" And I heard his sneakers thudding down the wooden stairs, with him screaming and calling all the way down.

I snickered to myself. Then, before I could pull myself up, I felt a rough, warm tongue licking my face.

"Petey!"

He was licking my cheeks, licking my eyelids, licking me frantically, as if he were trying to revive me, or as if to let me know that everything was okay.

"Oh, Petey! Petey!" I cried, laughing and throwing my arms around the sweet dog. "Stop! You're getting me all sticky!"

But he wouldn't stop. He kept on licking fiercely.

The poor dog is nervous, too, I thought.

"Come on, Petey, shape up," I told him, holding his panting face away with both my hands. "There's nothing to be nervous about. This new place is going to be fun. You'll see."

6

That night, I was smiling to myself as I fluffed up my pillow and slid into bed. I was thinking about how terrified Josh had been that afternoon, how frightened he looked even after I came prancing down the stairs, perfectly okay. How angry he was that I'd fooled him.

Of course, Mom and Dad didn't think it was funny. They were both nervous and upset because the moving van had just arrived, an hour late. They forced Josh and me to call a truce. No more scaring each other.

"It's hard *not* to get scared in this creepy old place," Josh muttered. But we reluctantly agreed not to play any more jokes on each other, if we could possibly help it.

The men, complaining about the rain, started carrying in all of our furniture. Josh and I helped show them where we wanted stuff in our rooms. They dropped my dresser on the stairs, but it only got a small scratch.

The furniture looked strange and small in this big house. Josh and I tried to stay out of the way while Mom and Dad worked all day, arranging things, emptying cartons, putting clothes away. Mom even managed to get the curtains hung in my room.

What a day!

Now, a little after ten o'clock, trying to get to sleep for the first time in my new room, I turned onto my side, then onto my back. Even though this was my old bed, I couldn't get comfortable.

Everything seemed so different, so wrong. The bed didn't face the same direction as in my old bedroom. The walls were bare. I hadn't had time to hang any of my posters. The room seemed so large and empty. The shadows seemed so much darker.

My back started to itch, and then I suddenly felt itchy all over. The bed is filled with bugs! I thought, sitting up. But of course that was ridiculous. It was my same old bed with clean sheets.

I forced myself to settle back down and closed my eyes. Sometimes when I can't get to sleep, I count silently by twos, picturing each number in my mind as I think it. It usually helps to clear my mind so that I can drift off to sleep.

I tried it now, burying my face in the pillow, picturing the numbers rolling past . . . 4 . . . 6 . . . 8 . . .

I yawned loudly, still wide awake at two-twenty.

I'm going to be awake forever, I thought. I'm never going to be able to sleep in this new room.

But then I must have drifted off without realizing it. I don't know how long I slept. An hour or two at the most. It was a light, uncomfortable sleep. Then something woke me. I sat straight up, startled.

Despite the heat of the room, I felt cold all over. Looking down to the end of the bed, I saw that I had kicked off the sheet and light blanket. With a groan, I reached down for them, but then froze.

I heard whispers.

Someone was whispering across the room.

"Who — who's there?" My voice was a whisper, too, tiny and frightened.

I grabbed my covers and pulled them up to my chin.

I heard more whispers. The room came into focus as my eyes adjusted to the dim light.

The curtains. The long, sheer curtains from my old room that my mother had hung that afternoon were fluttering at the window.

So. That explained the whispers. The billowing curtains must have woken me up.

A soft, gray light floated in from outside. The curtains cast moving shadows onto the foot of my bed.

Yawning, I stretched and climbed out of bed. I felt chilled all over as I crept across the wooden floor to close the window.

As I came near, the curtains stopped billowing and floated back into place. I pushed them aside and reached out to close the window.

"Oh!"

I uttered a soft cry when I realized that the window *was* closed.

But how could the curtains flutter like that with the window closed? I stood there for a while, staring out at the grays of the night. There wasn't much of a draft. The window seemed pretty airtight.

Had I imagined the curtains billowing? Were my eyes playing tricks on me?

Yawning, I hurried back through the strange shadows to my bed and pulled the covers up as high as they would go. "Amanda, stop scaring yourself," I scolded.

When I fell back to sleep a few minutes later, I had the ugliest, most terrifying dream.

I dreamed that we were all dead. Mom, Dad, Josh, and me.

At first, I saw us sitting around the dinner table in the new dining room. The room was very bright, so bright I couldn't see our faces very well. They were just a bright, white blur.

But, then, slowly, slowly, everything came into focus, and I could see that beneath our hair, we had no faces. Our skin was gone, and only our gray-green skulls were left. Bits of flesh clung to my bony cheeks. There were only deep, black sockets where my eyes had been.

The four of us, all dead, sat eating in silence. Our dinner plates, I saw, were filled with small bones. A big platter in the center of the table was piled high with gray-green bones, human-looking bones.

And then, in this dream, our disgusting meal was interrupted by a loud knocking on the door, an insistent pounding that grew louder and louder. It was Kathy, my friend from back home. I could see her at our front door, pounding on it with both fists.

I wanted to go answer the door. I wanted to run from the dining room and pull open the door and greet Kathy. I wanted to talk to Kathy. I wanted to tell her what had happened to me, to explain that I was dead and that my face had fallen away.

I wanted to see Kathy *so* badly.

But I couldn't get up from the table. I tried and tried, but I couldn't get up.

The pounding on the door grew louder and louder, until it was deafening. But I just sat there with my gruesome family, picking up bones from my dinner plate and eating them.

I woke up with a start, the horror of the dream still with me. I could still hear the pounding in my ears. I shook my head, trying to chase the dream away.

It was morning. I could tell from the blue of the sky outside the window.

"Oh, no."

The curtains. They were billowing again, flapping noisily as they blew into the room.

I sat up and stared.

The window was still closed.

7

"I'll take a look at the window. There must be a draft or a leak or something," Dad said at breakfast. He shoveled in another mouthful of scrambled eggs and ham.

"But, Dad — it's so weird!" I insisted, still feeling scared. "The curtains were blowing like crazy, and the window was *closed*!"

"There might be a pane missing," Dad suggested.

"Amanda is a pain!" Josh cracked. His idea of a really witty joke.

"Don't start with your sister," Mom said, putting her plate down on the table and dropping into her chair. She looked tired. Her black hair, usually carefully pulled back, was disheveled. She tugged at the belt on her bathrobe. "Whew. I don't think I slept two hours last night."

"Neither did I," I said, sighing. "I kept thinking that boy would show up in my room again."

"Amanda — you've really got to stop this,"

45

Mom said sharply. "Boys in your room. Curtains blowing. You have to realize that you're nervous, and your imagination is working overtime."

"But, Mom — " I started.

"Maybe a ghost was behind the curtains," Josh said, teasing. He raised up his hands and made a ghostly "oooooooh" wail.

"Whoa." Mom put a hand on Josh's shoulder. "Remember what you promised about scaring each other?"

"It's going to be hard for all of us to adjust to this place," Dad said. "You may have dreamed about the curtains blowing, Amanda. You said you had bad dreams, right?"

The terrifying nightmare flashed back into my mind. Once again I saw the big platter of bones on the table. I shivered.

"It's so damp in here," Mom said.

"A little sunshine will help dry the place out," Dad said.

I peered out the window. The sky had turned solid gray. Trees seemed to spread darkness over our backyard. "Where's Petey?" I asked.

"Out back," Mom replied, swallowing a mouthful of eggs. "He got up early, too. Couldn't sleep, I guess. So I let him out."

"What are we doing today?" Josh asked. He always needed to know the plan for the day. Every detail. Mainly so he could argue about it.

"Your father and I still have a lot of unpacking

to do," Mom said, glancing to the back hallway, which was cluttered with unopened cartons. "You two can explore the neighborhood. See what you can find out. See if there are any other kids your age around."

"In other words, you want us to get lost!" I said.

Mom and Dad both laughed. "You're very smart, Amanda."

"But I want to help unpack *my* stuff," Josh whined. I knew he'd argue with the plan, just like always.

"Go get dressed and take a long walk," Dad said. "Take Petey with you, okay? And take a leash for him. I left one by the front stairs."

"What about our bikes? Why can't we ride our bikes?" Josh asked.

"They're buried in the back of the garage," Dad told him. "You'll never be able to get to them. Besides, you have a flat tire."

"If I can't ride my bike, I'm not going out," Josh insisted, crossing his arms in front of his chest.

Mom and Dad had to argue with him. Then threaten him. Finally, he agreed to go for "a short walk."

I finished my breakfast, thinking about Kathy and my other friends back home. I wondered what the kids were like in Dark Falls. I wondered if I'd be able to find new friends, real friends.

I volunteered to do the breakfast dishes since

Mom and Dad had so much work to do. The warm water felt soothing on my hands as I sponged the dishes clean. I guess maybe I'm weird. I like washing dishes.

Behind me, from somewhere in the front of the house, I could hear Josh arguing with Dad. I could just barely make out the words over the trickle of the tap water.

"Your basketball is packed in one of these cartons," Dad was saying. Then Josh said something. Then Dad said, "How should *I* know which one?" Then Josh said something. Then Dad said, "No, I don't have time to look now. Believe it or not, your basketball isn't at the top of my list."

I stacked the last dish onto the counter to drain, and looked for a dish towel to dry my hands. There was none in sight. I guess they hadn't been unpacked yet.

Wiping off my hands on the front of my robe, I headed for the stairs. "I'll be dressed in five minutes," I called to Josh, who was still arguing with Dad in the living room. "Then we can go out."

I started up the front stairs, and then stopped.

Above me on the landing stood a strange girl, about my age, with short black hair. She was smiling down at me, not a warm smile, not a friendly smile, but the coldest, most frightening smile I had ever seen.

8

A hand touched my shoulder.

I spun around.

It was Josh. "I'm not going for a walk unless I can take my basketball," he said.

"Josh — please!" I looked back up to the landing, and the girl was gone.

I felt cold all over. My legs were all trembly. I grabbed the banister.

"Dad! Come here — please!" I called.

Josh's face filled with alarm. "Hey, I didn't do anything!" he shouted.

"No — it's — it's not you," I said, and called Dad again.

"Amanda, I'm kind of busy," Dad said, appearing below at the foot of the stairs, already perspiring from uncrating living room stuff.

"Dad, I saw somebody," I told him. "Up there. A girl." I pointed.

"Amanda, please," he replied, making a face.

"Stop seeing things — okay? There's no one in this house except the four of us . . . . and maybe a few mice."

"Mice?" Josh asked with sudden interest. "Really? Where?"

"Dad, I didn't imagine it," I said, my voice cracking. I was really hurt that he didn't believe me.

"Amanda, look up there," Dad said, gazing up to the landing. "What do you see?"

I followed his gaze. There was a pile of my clothes on the landing. Mom must have just unpacked them.

"It's just clothes," Dad said impatiently. "It's not a girl. It's clothes." He rolled his eyes.

"Sorry," I said quietly. I repeated it as I started up the stairs. "Sorry."

But I didn't really feel sorry. I felt confused.

And still scared.

Was it possible that I thought a pile of clothes was a smiling girl?

No. I didn't think so.

I'm not crazy. And I have really good eyesight.

So then, what was going on?

I opened the door to my room, turned on the ceiling light, and saw the curtains billowing in front of the bay window.

Oh, no. Not again, I thought.

50

I hurried over to them. This time, the window was open.

Who opened it?

Mom, I guessed.

Warm, wet air blew into the room. The sky was heavy and gray. It smelled like rain.

Turning to my bed, I had another shock.

Someone had laid out an outfit for me. A pair of faded jeans and a pale blue, sleeveless T-shirt. They were spread out side by side at the foot of the bed.

Who had put them there? Mom?

I stood at the doorway and called to her. "Mom? Mom? Did you pick out clothes for me?"

I could hear her shout something from downstairs, but I couldn't make out the words.

Calm down, Amanda, I told myself. Calm down.

Of *course* Mom pulled the clothes out. Of *course* Mom put them there.

From the doorway, I heard whispering in my closet.

Whispering and hushed giggling behind the closet door.

This was the last straw. "What's going on here?" I yelled at the top of my lungs.

I stormed over to the closet and pulled open the door.

Frantically, I pushed clothes out of the way. No one in there.

Mice? I thought. Had I heard the mice that Dad was talking about?

"I've got to get out of here," I said aloud.

The room, I realized, was driving me crazy.

No. I was driving *myself* crazy. Imagining all of these weird things.

There was a logical explanation for everything. Everything.

As I pulled up my jeans and fastened them, I said the word "logical" over and over in my mind. I said it so many times that it didn't sound like a real word anymore.

Calm down, Amanda. Calm down.

I took a deep breath and held it to ten.

"Boo!"

"Josh — cut it out. You didn't scare me," I told him, sounding more cross than I had meant to.

"Let's get out of here," he said, staring at me from the doorway. "This place gives me the creeps."

"Huh? You, too?" I exclaimed. "What's *your* problem?"

He started to say something, then stopped. He suddenly looked embarrassed. "Forget it," he muttered.

"No, tell me," I insisted. "What were you going to say?"

He kicked at the floor molding. "I had a really creepy dream last night," he finally admitted, looking past me to the fluttering curtains at the window.

"A dream?" I remembered my horrible dream.

"Yeah. There were these two boys in my room. And they were mean."

"What did they do?" I asked.

"I don't remember," Josh said, avoiding my eyes. "I just remember they were scary."

"And what happened?" I asked, turning to the mirror to brush my hair.

"I woke up," he said. And then added impatiently, "Come *on*. Let's go."

"Did the boys say anything to you?" I asked.

"No. I don't think so," he answered thoughtfully. "They just laughed."

"Laughed?"

"Well, giggled, sort of," Josh said. "I don't want to talk about it anymore," he snapped. "Are we going for this dumb walk, or not?"

"Okay. I'm ready," I said, putting down my brush, taking one last look in the mirror. "Let's go on this dumb walk."

I followed him down the hall. As we passed the stack of clothes on the landing, I thought about the girl I had seen standing there. And I thought about the boy in the window when we first arrived. And the two boys Josh had seen in his dream.

I decided it proved that Josh and I were both

really nervous about moving to this new place. Maybe Mom and Dad were right. We were letting our imaginations run away with us.

It had to be our imaginations.

I mean, what *else* could it be?

9

A few seconds later, we stepped into the backyard to get Petey. He was as glad to see us as ever, leaping on us with his muddy paws, yapping excitedly, running in frantic circles through the leaves. It cheered me up just to see him.

It was hot and muggy even though the sky was gray. There was no wind at all. The heavy, old trees stood as still as statues.

We headed down the gravel driveway toward the street, our sneakers kicking at the dead, brown leaves, Petey running in zigzags at our sides, first in front of us, then behind. "At least Dad hasn't asked us to rake all these old leaves," Josh said.

"He will," I warned. "I don't think he's unpacked the rake yet."

Josh made a face. We stood at the curb, looking up at our house, the two second-floor bay windows staring back at us like eyes.

The house next door, I noticed for the first time,

was about the same size as ours, except it was shingle instead of brick. The curtains in the living room were drawn shut. Some of the upstairs windows were shuttered. Tall trees cast the neighbors' house in darkness, too.

"Which way?" Josh asked, tossing a stick for Petey to chase.

I pointed up the street. "The school is up that way," I said. "Let's check it out."

The road sloped uphill. Josh picked up a small tree branch from the side of the road and used it as a walking stick. Petey kept trying to chew on it while Josh walked.

We didn't see anyone on the street or in any of the front yards we passed. No cars went by.

I was beginning to think the whole town was deserted, until the boy stepped out from behind the low ledge.

He popped out so suddenly, both Josh and I stopped in our tracks. "Hi," he said shyly, giving us a little wave.

"Hi," Josh and I answered at the same time.

Then, before we could pull him back, Petey ran up to the boy, sniffed his sneakers, and began snarling and barking. The boy stepped back and raised his hands as if he were protecting himself. He looked really frightened.

"Petey — stop!" I cried.

Josh grabbed the dog and picked him up, but he kept growling.

"He doesn't bite," I told the boy. "He usually doesn't bark, either. I'm sorry."

"That's okay," the boy said, staring at Petey, who was squirming to get out of Josh's arms. "He probably smells something on me."

"Petey, stop!" I shouted. The dog wouldn't stop squirming. "You don't want the leash — do you?"

The boy had short, wavy blond hair and very pale blue eyes. He had a funny turned-up nose that seemed out of place on his serious-looking face. He was wearing a maroon long-sleeved sweatshirt despite the mugginess of the day, and black straight-legged jeans. He had a blue baseball cap stuffed into the back pocket of his jeans.

"I'm Amanda Benson," I said. "And this is my brother Josh."

Josh hesitantly put Petey back on the ground. The dog yipped once, stared up at the boy, whimpered softly, then sat down on the street and began to scratch himself.

"I'm Ray Thurston," the boy said, stuffing his hands into his jeans pockets, still staring warily at Petey. He seemed to relax a little, though, seeing that the dog had lost interest in barking and growling at him.

I suddenly realized that Ray looked familiar. Where had I seen him before? Where? I stared hard at him until I remembered.

And then I gasped in sudden fright.

Ray was the boy, the boy in my room. The boy in the window.

"You — " I stammered accusingly. "You were in our house!"

He looked confused. "Huh?"

"You were in my room — right?" I insisted.

He laughed. "I don't get it," he said. "In your room?"

Petey raised his head and gave a low growl in Ray's direction. Then he went back to his serious scratching.

"I thought I saw you," I said, beginning to feel a little doubtful. Maybe it wasn't him. Maybe. . . .

"I haven't been in your house in a long time," Ray said, looking down warily at Petey.

"A long time?"

"Yeah. I used to live in your house," he replied.

"Huh?" Josh and I stared at him in surprise. "Our house?"

Ray nodded. "When we first moved here," he said. He picked up a flat pebble and heaved it down the street.

Petey growled, started to chase it, changed his mind, and plopped back down on the street, his stub of a tail wagging excitedly.

Heavy clouds lowered across the sky. It seemed to grow darker. "Where do you live now?" I asked.

Ray tossed another stone, then pointed up the road.

"Did you like our house?" Josh asked Ray.

"Yeah, it was okay," Ray told him. "Nice and shady."

"You liked it?" Josh cried. "I think it's gross. It's so dark and — "

Petey interrupted. He decided to start barking at Ray again, running up till he was a few inches in front of Ray, then backing away. Ray took a few cautious steps back to the edge of the curb.

Josh pulled the leash from the pocket of his shorts. "Sorry, Petey," he said. I held the growling dog while Josh attached the leash to his collar.

"He's never done this before. Really," I said, apologizing to Ray.

The leash seemed to confuse Petey. He tugged against it, pulling Josh across the street. But at least he stopped barking.

"Let's do something," Josh said impatiently.

"Like what?" Ray asked, relaxing again now that Petey was on the leash.

We all thought for a while.

"Maybe we could go to your house," Josh suggested to Ray.

Ray shook his head. "No. I don't think so," he said. "Not now anyway."

"Where is everyone?" I asked, looking up and down the empty street. "It's really dead around here, huh?"

He chuckled. "Yeah. I guess you could say

59

that," he said. "Want to go to the playground behind the school?"

"Yeah. Okay," I agreed.

The three of us headed up the street, Ray leading the way, me walking a few feet behind him, Josh holding his tree branch in one hand, the leash in the other, Petey running this way, then that, giving Josh a really hard time.

We didn't see the gang of kids till we turned the corner.

There were ten or twelve of them, mostly boys but a few girls, too. They were laughing and shouting, shoving each other playfully as they came toward us down the center of the street. Some of them, I saw, were about my age. The rest were teenagers. They were wearing jeans and dark T-shirts. One of the girls stood out because she had long, straight blonde hair and was wearing green spandex tights.

"Hey, look!" a tall boy with slicked-back black hair cried, pointing at us.

Seeing Ray, Josh, and me, they grew quiet but didn't stop moving toward us. A few of them giggled, as if they were enjoying some kind of private joke.

The three of us stopped and watched them approach. I smiled and waited to say hi. Petey was pulling at his leash and barking his head off.

"Hi, guys," the tall boy with the black hair said, grinning. The others thought this was very funny for some reason. They laughed. The girl in the green tights gave a short, red-haired boy a shove that almost sent him sprawling into me.

"How's it going, Ray?" a girl with short black hair asked, smiling at Ray.

"Not bad. Hi, guys," Ray answered. He turned to Josh and me. "These are some of my friends. They're all from the neighborhood."

"Hi," I said, feeling awkward. I wished Petey would stop barking and pulling at his leash like that. Poor Josh was having a terrible time holding onto him.

"This is George Carpenter," Ray said, pointing to the short, red-haired boy, who nodded. "And Jerry Franklin, Karen Somerset, Bill Gregory . . ." He went around the circle, naming each kid. I tried to remember all the names but, of course it was impossible.

"How do you like Dark Falls?" one of the girls asked me.

"I don't really know," I told her. "It's my first day here, really. It seems nice."

Some of the kids laughed at my answer, for some reason.

"What kind of dog is that?" George Carpenter asked Josh.

Josh, holding tight to the leash handle, told him. George stared hard at Petey, studying him, as if he had never seen a dog like Petey before.

Karen Somerset, a tall, pretty girl with short

blonde hair, came up to me while some of the other kids were admiring Petey. "You know, I used to live in your house," she said softly.

"What?" I wasn't sure I'd heard her correctly.

"Let's go to the playground," Ray said, interrupting.

No one responded to Ray's suggestion.

They grew quiet. Even Petey stopped barking.

Had Karen really said that she used to live in our house? I wanted to ask her, but she had stepped back into the circle of kids.

The circle.

My mouth dropped open as I realized they had formed a circle around Josh and me.

I felt a stab of fear. Was I imagining it? Was something going on?

They all suddenly looked different to me. They were smiling, but their faces were tense, watchful, as if they expected trouble.

Two of them, I noticed, were carrying baseball bats. The girl with the green tights stared at me, looking me up and down, checking me out.

No one said a word. The street was silent except for Petey, who was now whimpering softly.

I suddenly felt very afraid.

Why were they staring at us like that?

Or was my imagination running away with me again?

I turned to Ray, who was still beside me. He

didn't seem at all troubled. But he didn't return my gaze.

"Hey, guys — " I said. "What's going on?" I tried to keep it light, but my voice was a little shaky.

I looked over at Josh. He was busy soothing Petey and hadn't noticed that things had changed.

The two boys with baseball bats held them up waist high and moved forward.

I glanced around the circle, feeling the fear tighten my chest.

The circle tightened. The kids were closing in on us.

10

The black clouds overhead seemed to lower. The air felt heavy and damp.

Josh was fussing with Petey's collar and still didn't see what was happening. I wondered if Ray was going to say anything, if he was going to do anything to stop them. But he stayed frozen and expressionless beside me.

The circle grew smaller as the kids closed in.

I realized I'd been holding my breath. I took a deep breath and opened my mouth to cry out.

"Hey, kids — what's going on?"

It was a man's voice, calling from outside the circle.

Everyone turned to see Mr. Dawes coming quickly toward us, taking long strides as he crossed the street, his open blazer flapping behind him. He had a friendly smile on his face. "What's going on?" he asked again.

He didn't seem to realize that the gang of kids had been closing in on Josh and me.

"We're heading to the playground," George Carpenter told him, twirling the bat in his hand. "You know. To play softball."

"Good deal," Mr. Dawes said, pulling down his striped tie, which had blown over his shoulder. He looked up at the darkening sky. "Hope you don't get rained out."

Several of the kids had backed up. They were standing in small groups of two and three now. The circle had completely broken up.

"Is that bat for softball or hardball?" Mr. Dawes asked George.

"George doesn't know," another kid replied quickly. "He's never hit anything with it!"

The kids all laughed. George playfully menaced the kid, pretending to come at him with the bat.

Mr. Dawes gave a little wave and started to leave. But then he stopped, and his eyes opened wide with surprise. "Hey," he said, flashing me a friendly smile. "Josh. Amanda. I didn't see you there."

"Good morning," I muttered. I was feeling very confused. A moment ago, I'd felt terribly scared. Now everyone was laughing and kidding around.

Had I imagined that the kids were moving in on us? Ray and Josh hadn't seemed to notice anything peculiar. Was it just me and my overactive imagination?

What would have happened if Mr. Dawes hadn't come along?

"How are you two getting along in the new house?" Mr. Dawes asked, smoothing back his wavy blond hair.

"Okay," Josh and I answered together. Looking up at Mr. Dawes, Petey began to bark and pull at the leash.

Mr. Dawes put an exaggerated hurt expression on his face. "I'm crushed," he said. "Your dog still doesn't like me." He bent over Petey. "Hey, dog — lighten up."

Petey barked back angrily.

"He doesn't seem to like *anybody* today," I told Mr. Dawes apologetically.

Mr. Dawes stood back up and shrugged. "Can't win 'em all." He started back to his car, parked a few yards down the street. "I'm heading over to your house," he told Josh and me. "Just want to see if there's anything I can do to help your parents. Have fun, kids."

I watched him climb into his car and drive away.

"He's a nice guy," Ray said.

"Yeah," I agreed. I was still feeling uncomfortable, wondering what the kids would do now that Mr. Dawes was gone.

Would they form that frightening circle again?

No. Everyone started walking, heading down the block to the playground behind the school. They were kidding each other and talking normally, and pretty much ignored Josh and me.

I was starting to feel a little silly. It was obvious that they hadn't been trying to scare Josh and me. I must have made the whole thing up in my mind.

I must have.

At least, I told myself, I hadn't screamed or made a scene. At least I hadn't made a total fool of myself.

The playground was completely empty. I guessed that most kids had stayed inside because of the threatening sky. The playground was a large, flat grassy field, surrounded on all four sides by a tall metal fence. There were swings and slides at the end nearest the school building. There were two baseball diamonds on the other end. Beyond the fence, I could see a row of tennis courts, also deserted.

Josh tied Petey to the fence, then came running over to join the rest of us. The boy named Jerry Franklin made up the teams. Ray and I were on the same team. Josh was on the other.

As our team took the field, I felt excited and a little nervous. I'm not the best softball player in the world. I can hit the ball pretty well. But in the field, I'm a complete klutz. Luckily, Jerry sent me out to right field where not many balls are hit.

The clouds began to part a little and the sky got lighter. We played two full innings. The other team was winning, eight to two. I was having fun.

I had only messed up on one play. And I hit a double my first time at bat.

It was fun being with a whole new group of kids. They seemed really nice, especially the girl named Karen Somerset, who talked with me while we waited for our turn at bat. Karen had a great smile, even though she wore braces on all her teeth, up and down. She seemed very eager to be friends.

The sun was coming out as my team started to take the field for the beginning of the third inning. Suddenly, I heard a loud, shrill whistle. I looked around until I saw that it was Jerry Franklin, blowing a silver whistle.

Everyone came running up to him. "We'd better quit," he said, looking up at the brightening sky. "We promised our folks, remember, that we'd be home for lunch."

I glanced at my watch. It was only eleven-thirty. Still early.

But to my surprise, no one protested.

They all waved to each other and called out farewells, and then began to run. I couldn't believe how fast everyone left. It was as if they were racing or something.

Karen ran past me like the others, her head down, a serious expression on her pretty face. Then she stopped suddenly and turned around. "Nice meeting you, Amanda," she called back. "We should get together sometime."

"Great!" I called to her. "Do you know where I live?"

I couldn't hear her answer very well. She nodded, and I thought she said, "Yes. I know it. I used to live in your house."

But that *couldn't* have been what she said.

11

Several days went by. Josh and I were getting used to our new house and our new friends.

The kids we met every day at the playground weren't exactly friends yet. They talked with Josh and me, and let us on their teams. But it was really hard to get to know them.

In my room, I kept hearing whispers late at night, and soft giggling, but I forced myself to ignore it. One night, I thought I saw a girl dressed all in white at the end of the upstairs hall. But when I walked over to investigate, there was just a pile of dirty sheets and other bedclothes against the wall.

Josh and I were adjusting, but Petey was still acting really strange. We took him with us to the playground every day, but we had to leash him to the fence. Otherwise, he'd bark and snap at all the kids.

"He's still nervous being in a new place," I told Josh. "He'll calm down."

But Petey didn't calm down. And about two weeks later, we were finishing up a softball game with Ray, and Karen Somerset, and Jerry Franklin, and George Carpenter, and a bunch of other kids, when I looked over to the fence and saw that Petey was gone.

Somehow he had broken out of his leash and run away.

We looked for hours, calling "Petey!" wandering from block to block, searching front yards and backyards, empty lots and woods. Then, after circling the neighborhood twice, Josh and I suddenly realized we had no idea where we were.

The streets of Dark Falls looked the same. They were all lined with sprawling old brick or shingle houses, all filled with shady old trees.

"I don't believe it. We're lost," Josh said, leaning against a tree trunk, trying to catch his breath.

"That stupid dog," I muttered, my eyes searching up the street. "Why did he do this? He's never run away before."

"I don't know how he got loose," Josh said, shaking his head, then wiping his sweaty forehead with the sleeve of his T-shirt. "I tied him up really well."

"Hey — maybe he ran home," I said. The idea immediately cheered me up.

"Yeah!" Josh stepped away from the tree and headed back over to me. "I'll bet you're right,

Amanda. He's probably been home for hours. Wow. We've been stupid. We should've checked home first. Let's go!"

"Well," I said, looking around at the empty yards, "we just have to figure out which way is home."

I looked up and down the street, trying to figure out which way we'd turned when we left the school playground. I couldn't remember, so we just started walking.

Luckily, as we reached the next corner, the school came into sight. We had made a full circle. It was easy to find our way from there.

Passing the playground, I stared at the spot on the fence where Petey had been tied. That troublemaking dog. He'd been acting so badly ever since we came to Dark Falls.

Would he be home when we got there? I hoped so.

A few minutes later, Josh and I were running up the gravel driveway, calling the dog's name at the top of our lungs. The front door burst open and Mom, her hair tied in a red bandanna, the knees of her jeans covered with dust, leaned out. She and Dad had been painting the back porch. "Where have you two been? Lunchtime was two hours ago!"

Josh and I both answered at the same time. "Is Petey here?"

"We've been looking for Petey!"

72

"Is he here?"

Mom's face filled with confusion. "Petey? I thought he was with you."

My heart sank. Josh slumped to the driveway with a loud sigh, sprawling flat on his back in the gravel and leaves.

"You haven't seen him?" I asked, my trembling voice showing my disappointment. "He *was* with us. But he ran away."

"Oh. I'm sorry," Mom said, motioning for Josh to get up from the driveway. "He ran away? I thought you've been keeping him on a leash."

"You've got to help us find him," Josh pleaded, not budging from the ground. "Get the car. We've got to find him — right now!"

"I'm sure he hasn't gotten far," Mom said. "You must be starving. Come in and have some lunch and then we'll — "

"No. Right *now*!" Josh screamed.

"What's going on?" Dad, his face and hair covered with tiny flecks of white paint, joined Mom on the front porch. "Josh — what's all the yelling?"

We explained to Dad what had happened. He said he was too busy to drive around looking for Petey. Mom said she'd do it, but only after we had some lunch. I pulled Josh up by both arms and dragged him into the house.

We washed up and gulped down some peanut butter and jelly sandwiches. Then Mom took the car out of the garage, and we drove around and around the neighborhood searching for our lost pet.

With no luck.

No sign of him.

Josh and I were miserable. Heartbroken. Mom and Dad called the local police. Dad kept saying that Petey had a good sense of direction, that he'd show up any minute.

But we didn't really believe it.

Where was he?

The four of us ate dinner in silence. It was the longest, most horrible evening of my life. "I tied him up really good," Josh repeated, close to tears, his dinner plate still full.

"Dogs are great escape artists," Dad said, "Don't worry. He'll show up."

"Some night for a party," Mom said glumly.

I'd completely forgotten that they were going out. Some neighbors on the next block had invited them to a big potluck dinner party.

"I sure don't feel like partying, either," Dad said with a sigh. "I'm beat from painting all day. But I guess we have to be neighborly. Sure you kids will be okay here?"

"Yeah, I guess," I said, thinking about Petey. I kept listening for his bark, listening for scratching at the door.

But no. The hours dragged by. Petey still hadn't shown up by bedtime.

Josh and I both slinked upstairs. I felt really tired, weary from all the worrying, and the running around and searching for Petey, I guess. But I knew I'd never be able to get to sleep.

In the hall outside my bedroom door, I heard whispering from inside my room and quiet footsteps. The usual sounds my room made. I wasn't at all scared of them or surprised by them anymore.

Without hesitating, I stepped into my room and clicked on the light. The room was empty, as I knew it would be. The mysterious sounds disappeared. I glanced at the curtains, which lay straight and still.

Then I saw the clothes strewn all over my bed. Several pairs of jeans. Several T-shirts. A couple of sweatshirts. My only dress-up skirt.

That's strange, I thought. Mom was such a neat freak. If she had washed these things, she surely would have hung them up or put them into dresser drawers.

Sighing wearily, I started to gather up the clothes and put them away. I figured that Mom simply had too much to do to be bothered. She had probably washed the stuff and then left it here for me to put away. Or she had put it all down, planning to come back later and put it away, and then got busy with other chores.

Half an hour later, I was tucked into my bed wide awake, staring at the shadows on the ceiling.

Some time after that — I lost track of the time — I was still wide awake, still thinking about Petey, thinking about the new kids I'd met, thinking about the new neighborhood, when I heard my bedroom door creak and swing open.

Footsteps on the creaking floorboards.

I sat up in the darkness as someone crept into my room.

"Amanda — ssshh — it's me."

Alarmed, it took me a few seconds to recognize the hushed whisper. "Josh! What do you want? What are you doing in here?"

I gasped as a blinding light forced me to cover my eyes. "Oops. Sorry," Josh said. "My flashlight. I didn't mean to — "

"Ow, that's bright," I said, blinking. He aimed the powerful beam of white light up at the ceiling.

"Yeah. It's a halogen flashlight," he said.

"Well, what do you want?" I asked irritably. I still couldn't see well. I rubbed my eyes, but it didn't help.

"I know where Petey is," Josh whispered, "and I'm going to go get him. Come with me?"

"Huh?" I looked at the little clock on my bed table. "It's after midnight, Josh."

"So? It won't take long. Really."

My eyes were nearly normal by now. Staring at Josh in the light from the halogen flashlight, I noticed for the first time that he was fully dressed in jeans and a long-sleeved T-shirt.

"I don't get it, Josh," I said, swinging around and putting my feet on the floor. "We looked everywhere. Where do you think Petey is?"

"In the cemetery," Josh answered. His eyes looked big and dark and serious in the white light.

"Huh?"

"That's where he ran the first time, remember? When we first came to Dark Falls? He ran to that cemetery just past the school."

"Now, wait a minute — " I started.

"We drove past it this afternoon, but we didn't look inside. He's there, Amanda. I know he is. And I'm going to go get him whether you come or not."

"Josh, calm down," I said, putting my hands on his narrow shoulders. I was surprised to discover that he was trembling. "There's no reason for Petey to be in that cemetery."

"That's where he went the first time," Josh insisted. "He was looking for something there that day. I could tell. I know he's there again, Amanda." He pulled away from me. "Are you coming or not?"

My brother has to be the stubbornest, most headstrong person in the world.

"Josh, you're really going to walk into a strange

cemetery so late at night?" I asked.

"I'm not afraid," he said, shining the bright light around my room.

For a brief second, I thought the light caught someone, lurking behind the curtains. I opened my mouth to cry out. But there was no one there.

"You coming or not?" he repeated impatiently.

I was going to say no. But then, glancing at the curtains, I thought, it's probably no more spooky out there in that cemetery than it is here in my own bedroom!

"Yeah. Okay," I said grudgingly. "Get out of here and let me get dressed."

"Okay," he whispered, turning off the flashlight, plunging us into blackness. "Meet me down at the end of the driveway."

"Josh — one quick look at the cemetery, then we hurry home. Got it?" I told him.

"Yeah. Right. We'll be home before Mom and Dad get back from that party." He crept out. I could hear him making his way quickly down the stairs.

This is the craziest idea ever, I told myself as I searched in the darkness for some clothes to pull on.

And it was also kind of exciting.

Josh was wrong. No doubt about it. Petey wouldn't be hanging around in that cemetery now. Why on earth should he?

But at least it wasn't a long walk. And it was an adventure. Something to write about to Kathy back home.

And if Josh happened to be right, and we did manage to find poor, lost Petey, well, that would be great, too.

A few minutes later, dressed in jeans and a sweatshirt, I crept out of the house and joined Josh at the bottom of the driveway. The night was still warm. A heavy blanket of clouds covered the moon. I realized for the first time that there were no streetlights on our block.

Josh had the halogen flashlight on, aimed down at our feet. "You ready?" he asked.

Dumb question. Would I be standing there if I weren't ready?

We crunched over dead leaves as we headed up the block, toward the school. From there, it was just two blocks to the cemetery.

"It's so dark," I whispered. The houses were black and silent. There was no breeze at all. It was as if we were all alone in the world.

"It's too quiet," I said, hurrying to keep up with Josh. "No crickets or anything. Are you sure you really want to go to the cemetery?"

"I'm sure," he said, his eyes following the circle of light from the flashlight as it bumped over the ground. "I really think Petey is there."

We walked in the street, keeping close to the curb. We had gone nearly two blocks. The school was just coming into sight on the next block when we heard the scraping steps behind us on the pavement.

Josh and I both stopped. He lowered the light.

We both heard the sounds. I wasn't imagining them.

Someone was following us.

12

Josh was so startled, the flashlight tumbled from his hand and clattered onto the street. The light flickered but didn't go out.

By the time Josh had managed to pick it up, our pursuer had caught up to us. I spun around to face him, my heart pounding in my chest.

"Ray! What are *you* doing here?"

Josh aimed the light at Ray's face, but Ray shot his arms up to shield his face and ducked back into the darkness. "What are *you two* doing here?" he cried, sounding almost as startled as I did.

"You — you scared us," Josh said angrily, aiming the flashlight back down at our feet.

"Sorry," Ray said, "I would've called out, but I wasn't sure it was you."

"Josh has this crazy idea about where Petey might be," I told him, still struggling to catch my breath. "That's why we're out here."

"What about you?" Josh asked Ray.

"Well, sometimes I have trouble sleeping," Ray said softly.

"Don't your parents mind you being out so late?" I asked.

In the glow from the flashlight, I could see a wicked smile cross his face. "They don't know."

"Are we going to the cemetery or not?" Josh asked impatiently. Without waiting for an answer, he started jogging up the road, the light bobbing on the pavement in front of him. I turned and followed, wanting to stay close to the light.

"Where are you going?" Ray called, hurrying to catch up.

"The cemetery," I called back.

"No," Ray said. "You're not."

His voice was so low, so threatening, that I stopped. "What?"

"You're not going there," Ray repeated. I couldn't see his face. It was hidden in darkness. But his words sounded menacing.

"Hurry!" Josh called back to us. He hadn't slowed down. He didn't seem to notice the threat in Ray's words.

"Stop, Josh!" Ray called. It sounded more like an order than a request. "You can't go there!"

"Why not?" I demanded, suddenly afraid. Was Ray threatening Josh and me? Did he know something we didn't? Or was I making a big deal out of nothing once again?

I stared into the darkness, trying to see his face.

"You'd be nuts to go there at night!" he declared.

I began to think I had misjudged him. He was afraid to go there. That's why he was trying to stop us.

"Are you coming or not?" Josh demanded, getting farther and farther ahead of us.

"I don't think we should," Ray warned.

Yes, he's afraid, I decided. I only imagined that he was threatening us.

"You don't have to. But *we* do," Josh insisted, picking up his speed.

"No. Really," Ray said. "This is a bad idea." But now he and I were running side by side to catch up with Josh.

"Petey's there," Josh said, "I know he is."

We passed the dark, silent school. It seemed much bigger at night. Josh's light flashed through the low tree branches as we turned the corner onto Cemetery Drive.

"Wait — please," Ray pleaded. But Josh didn't slow down. Neither did I. I was eager to get there and get it over with.

I wiped my forehead with my sleeve. The air was hot and still. I wished I hadn't worn long sleeves. I felt my hair. It was dripping wet.

The clouds still covered the moon as we reached

the cemetery. We stepped through a gate in the low wall. In the darkness, I could see the crooked rows of gravestones.

Josh's light traveled from stone to stone, jumping up and down as he walked. "Petey!" he called suddenly, interrupting the silence.

He's disturbing the sleep of the dead, I thought, feeling a sudden chill of fear.

Don't be silly, Amanda. "Petey!" I called, too, forcing away my morbid thoughts.

"This is a very bad idea," Ray said, standing very close to me.

"Petey! Petey!" Josh called.

"I know it's a bad idea," I admitted to Ray. "But I didn't want Josh to come here by himself."

"But we shouldn't *be* here," Ray insisted.

I was beginning to wish he'd go away. No one had forced him to come. Why was he giving us such a hard time?

"Hey — look at this!" Josh called from several yards up ahead.

My sneakers crunching over the soft ground, I hurried between the rows of graves. I hadn't realized that we had already walked the entire length of the graveyard.

"Look," Josh said again, his flashlight playing over a strange structure built at the edge of the cemetery.

It took me a little while to figure out what it was in the small circle of light. It was so unexpected. It was some kind of theater. An amphitheater, I guess you'd call it, circular rows of bench seats dug into the ground, descending like stairs to a low stagelike platform at the bottom.

"What on earth!" I exclaimed.

I started forward to get a closer look.

"Amanda — wait. Let's go home," Ray called. He grabbed at my arm, but I hurried away, and he grabbed only air.

"Weird! Who would build an outdoor theater at the edge of a cemetery?" I asked.

I looked back to see if Josh and Ray were following me, and my sneaker caught against something. I stumbled to the ground, hitting my knee hard.

"Ow. What was that?"

Josh shone the light on it as I climbed slowly, painfully, to my feet. I had tripped over an enormous, upraised tree root.

In the flickering light, I followed the gnarled root over to a wide, old tree several yards away. The huge tree was bent over the strange belowground theater, leaning at such a low angle that it looked likely to topple over at any second. Big clumps of roots were raised up from the ground. Overhead, the tree's branches, heavy with leaves, seemed to lean to the ground.

"Timberrr!" Josh yelled.

"How weird!" I exclaimed. "Hey, Ray — what is this place?"

"It's a meeting place," Ray said quietly, standing close beside me, staring straight ahead at the leaning tree. "They use it sort of like a town hall. They have town meetings here."

"In the cemetery?" I cried, finding it hard to believe.

"Let's go," Ray urged, looking very nervous.

All three of us heard the footsteps. They were behind us, somewhere in the rows of graves. We turned around. Josh's light swept over the ground.

"Petey!"

There he was, standing between the nearest row of low, stone grave markers. I turned happily to Josh. "I don't believe it!" I cried. "You were right!"

"Petey! Petey!" Josh and I both started running toward our dog.

But Petey arched back on his hind legs as if he were getting ready to run away. He stared at us, his eyes red as jewels in the light of the flashlight.

"Petey! We found you!" I cried.

The dog lowered his head and started to trot away.

"Petey! Hey — come back! Don't you recognize us?"

With a burst of speed, Josh caught up with him

and grabbed him up off the ground. "Hey, Petey, what's the matter, fella?"

As I hurried over, Josh dropped Petey back to the ground and stepped back. "Ooh — he stinks!"

"What?" I cried.

"Petey — he stinks. He smells like a dead rat!" Josh held his nose.

Petey started to walk slowly away.

"Josh, he isn't glad to see us," I wailed. "He doesn't even seem to recognize us. Look at him!"

It was true. Petey walked to the next row of gravestones, then turned and glared at us.

I suddenly felt sick. What had happened to Petey? Why was he acting so differently? Why wasn't he glad to see us?

"I don't get it," Josh said, still making a face from the odor the dog gave off. "Usually, if we leave the room for thirty seconds, he goes nuts when we come back."

"We'd better go!" Ray called. He was still at the edge of the cemetery near the leaning tree.

"Petey — what's wrong with you?" I called to the dog. He didn't respond. "Don't you remember your name? Petey? Petey?"

"Yuck! What a stink!" Josh exclaimed.

"We've got to get him home and give him a bath," I said. My voice was shaking. I felt really sad. And frightened.

"Maybe this isn't Petey," Josh said thoughtfully. The dog's eyes again glared red in the beam of light.

"It's him all right," I said quietly. "Look. He's dragging the leash. Go get him, Josh — and let's go home."

"*You* get him!" Josh cried. "He smells too bad!"

"Just grab his leash. You don't have to pick him up," I said.

"No. *You*."

Josh was being stubborn again. I could see that I had no choice. "Okay," I said. "I'll get him. But I'll need the light." I grabbed the flashlight from Josh's hand and started to run toward Petey.

"Sit, Petey. Sit!" I ordered. It was the only command Petey ever obeyed.

But he didn't obey it this time. Instead, he turned and trotted away, holding his head down low.

"Petey — stop! Petey, come on!" I yelled, exasperated. "Don't make me chase you."

"Don't let him get away!" Josh yelled, running up behind me.

I moved the flashlight from side to side along the ground. "Where is he?"

"Petey! Petey!" Josh called, sounding shrill and desperate.

I couldn't see him.

"Oh, no. Don't tell me we've lost him again!" I said.

We both started to call him. "What's *wrong* with that mutt?" I cried.

I moved the beam of light down one long row of gravestones, then, moving quickly, down the next. No sign of him. We both kept calling his name.

And then the circle of light came to rest on the front of a granite tombstone.

Reading the name on the stone, I stopped short.

And gasped.

"Josh — look!" I grabbed Josh's sleeve. I held on tight.

"Huh? What's wrong?" His face filled with confusion.

"Look! The name on the gravestone."

It was Karen Somerset.

Josh read the name. He stared at me, still confused.

"That's my new friend Karen. The one I talk to on the playground every day," I said.

"Huh? It must be her grandmother or something," Josh said, and then added impatiently, "Come on. Look for Petey."

"No. Look at the dates," I said to him.

We both read the dates under Karen Somerset's name. 1960–1972.

"It can't be her mother or grandmother," I said, keeping the beam of light on the stone despite my trembling hand. "This girl died when she was twelve. My age. And Karen is twelve, too. She told me."

"Amanda — " Josh scowled and looked away.

But I took a few steps and beamed the light onto the next gravestone. There was a name on it I'd never heard before. I moved on to the next stone. Another name I'd never heard.

"Amanda, come on!" Josh whined.

The next gravestone had the name George Carpenter on it. 1975–1988.

"Josh — look! It's George from the playground," I called.

"Amanda, we have to get Petey," he insisted.

But I couldn't pull myself away from the gravestones. I went from one to the next, moving the flashlight over the engraved letters.

To my growing horror, I found Jerry Franklin. And then Bill Gregory.

All the kids we had played softball with. They all had gravestones here.

My heart thudding, I moved down the crooked row, my sneakers sinking into the soft grass. I felt numb, numb with fear. I struggled to hold the light steady as I beamed it onto the last stone in the row.

RAY THURSTON. 1977–1988.

"Huh?"

I could hear Josh calling me, but I couldn't make out what he was saying.

The rest of the world seemed to fall away. I read the deeply etched inscription again:

RAY THURSTON. 1977–1988.

I stood there, staring at the letters and numbers. I stared at them till they didn't make sense anymore, until they were just a gray blur.

Suddenly, I realized that Ray had crept up beside the gravestone and was staring at me.

"Ray — " I managed to say, moving the light over the name on the stone. "Ray, this one is . . . *you!*"

His eyes flared, glowing like dying embers.

"Yes, it's me," he said softly, moving toward me. "I'm so sorry, Amanda."

13

I took a step back, my sneakers sinking into the soft ground. The air was heavy and still. No one made a sound. Nothing moved.

Dead.

I'm surrounded by death, I thought.

Then, frozen to the spot, unable to breathe, the darkness swirling around me, the gravestones spinning in their own black shadows, I thought: What is he going to do to me?

"Ray — " I managed to call out. My voice sounded faint and far away. "Ray, are you really dead?"

"I'm sorry. You weren't supposed to find out yet," he said, his voice floating low and heavy on the stifling night air.

"But — how? I mean . . . I don't understand. . . ." I looked past him to the darting white light of the flashlight. Josh was several rows away, almost to the street, still searching for Petey.

"Petey!" I whispered, dread choking my throat, my stomach tightening in horror.

"Dogs always know," Ray said in a low, flat tone. "Dogs always recognize the living dead. That's why they have to go first. They always know."

"You mean — Petey's . . . dead?" I choked out the words.

Ray nodded. "They kill the dogs first."

"No!" I screamed and took another step back, nearly losing my balance as I bumped into a low marble gravestone. I jumped away from it.

"You weren't supposed to see this," Ray said, his narrow face expressionless except for his dark eyes, which revealed real sadness. "You weren't supposed to know. Not for another few weeks, anyway. I'm the watcher. I was supposed to watch, to make sure you didn't see until it was time."

He took a step toward me, his eyes lighting up red, burning into mine.

"Were you watching me from the window?" I cried. "Was that you in my room?"

Again he nodded yes. "I used to live in your house," he said, taking another step closer, forcing me back against the cold marble stone. "I'm the watcher."

I forced myself to look away, to stop staring into his glowing eyes. I wanted to scream to Josh to run and get help. But he was too far away. And I was frozen there, frozen with fear.

"We need fresh blood," Ray said.

"What?" I cried. "What are you saying?"

"The town — it can't survive without fresh blood. None of us can. You'll understand soon, Amanda. You'll understand why we had to invite you to the house, to the . . . Dead House."

In the darting, zigzagging beam of light, I could see Josh moving closer, heading our way.

Run, Josh, I thought. Run away. Fast. Get someone. Get *anyone*.

I could think the words. Why couldn't I scream them?

Ray's eyes glowed brighter. He was standing right in front of me now, his features set, hard and cold.

"Ray?" Even through my jeans, the marble gravestone felt cold against the back of my legs.

"I messed up," he whispered. "I was the watcher. But I messed up."

"Ray — what are you going to do?"

His red eyes flickered. "I'm really sorry."

He started to raise himself off the ground, to float over me.

I could feel myself start to choke. I couldn't breathe. I couldn't move. I opened my mouth to call out to Josh, but no sound came out.

Josh? Where was he?

I looked down the rows of gravestones but couldn't see his light.

Ray floated up a little higher. He hovered over me, choking me somehow, blinding me, suffocating me.

I'm dead, I thought. Dead.

Now I'm dead, too.

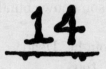

14

And then, suddenly, light broke through the darkness.

The light shone in Ray's face, the bright white halogen light.

"What's going on?" Josh asked, in a high-pitched, nervous voice. "Amanda — what's happening?"

Ray cried out and dropped back to the ground. "Turn that off! Turn it off!" he screeched, his voice a shrill whisper, like wind through a broken windowpane.

But Josh held the bright beam of light on Ray. "What's going on? What are you doing?"

I could breathe again. As I stared into the light, I struggled to stop my heart from pounding so hard.

Ray moved his arms to shield himself from the light. But I could see what was happening to him. The light had already done its damage.

Ray's skin seemed to be melting. His whole face

sagged, then fell, dropping off his skull.

I stared into the circle of white light, unable to look away, as Ray's skin folded and drooped and melted away. As the bone underneath was revealed, his eyeballs rolled out of their sockets and fell silently to the ground.

Josh, frozen in horror, somehow held the bright light steady, and we both stared at the grinning skull, its dark craters staring back at us.

"Oh!" I shrieked as Ray took a step toward me.

But then I realized that Ray wasn't walking. He was falling.

I jumped aside as he crumpled to the ground. And gasped as his skull hit the top of the marble gravestone, and cracked open with a sickening *splat*.

"Come on!" Josh shouted. "Amanda — come *on!*" He grabbed my hand and tried to pull me away.

But I couldn't stop staring down at Ray, now a pile of bones inside a puddle of crumpled clothes.

"Amanda, come on!"

Then, before I even realized it, I was running, running beside Josh as fast as I could down the long row of graves toward the street. The light flashed against the blur of gravestones as we ran, slipping on the soft, dew-covered grass, gasping in the still, hot air.

"We've got to tell Mom and Dad. Got to get *away* from here!" I cried.

97

"They — they won't believe it!" Josh said, as we reached the street. We kept running, our sneakers thudding hard against the pavement. "I'm not sure I believe it myself!"

"They've *got* to believe us!" I told him. "If they don't, we'll *drag* them out of that house."

The white beam of light pointed the way as we ran through the dark, silent streets. There were no streetlights, no lights on in the windows of the houses we passed, no car headlights.

Such a dark world we had entered.

And now it was time to get out.

We ran the rest of the way home. I kept looking back to see if we were being followed. But I didn't see anyone. The neighborhood was still and empty.

I had a sharp pain in my side as we reached home. But I forced myself to keep running, up the gravel driveway with its thick blanket of dead leaves, and onto the front porch.

I pushed open the door and both Josh and I started to scream. "Mom! Dad! Where are you?"

Silence.

We ran into the living room. The lights were all off.

"Mom? Dad? Are you here?"

Please be here, I thought, my heart racing, the pain in my side still sharp. Please be here.

We searched the house. They weren't home.

"The potluck party," Josh suddenly remembered. "Can they still be at that party?"

We were standing in the living room, both of us breathing hard. The pain in my side had let up just a bit. I had turned on all the lights, but the room still felt gloomy and menacing.

I glanced at the clock on the mantel. Nearly two in the morning.

"They should be home by now," I said, my voice shaky and weak.

"Where did they go? Did they leave a number?" Josh was already on his way to the kitchen.

I followed him, turning on lights as we went. We went right to the memo pad on the counter where Mom and Dad always leave us notes.

Nothing. The pad was blank.

"We've *got* to find them!" Josh cried. He sounded very frightened. His wide eyes reflected his fear. "We have to get away from here."

What if something has happened to them?

That's what I started to say. But I caught myself just in time. I didn't want to scare Josh any more than he was already.

Besides, he'd probably thought of that, too.

"Should we call the police?" he asked, as we walked back to the living room and peered out the front window into the darkness.

"I don't know," I said, pressing my hot forehead against the cool glass. "I just don't know *what* to do. I want them to be home. I want them here so we can all leave."

"What's your hurry?" a girl's voice said from behind me.

Josh and I both cried out and spun around.

Karen Somerset was standing in the center of the room, her arms crossed over her chest.

"But — you're *dead*!" I blurted out.

She smiled, a sad smile, a bitter smile.

And then two more kids stepped in from the hallway. One of them clicked off the lights. "Too bright in here," he said. They moved next to Karen.

And another kid, Jerry Franklin — another dead kid — appeared by the fireplace. And I saw the girl with short black hair, the one I had seen on the stairs, move beside me by the curtains.

They were all smiling, their eyes glowing dully in the dim light, all moving in on Josh and me.

"What do you *want*?" I screamed in a voice I didn't even recognize. "What are you going to do?"

"We used to live in your house," Karen said softly.

"Huh?" I cried.

"We used to live in your house," George said.

"And now, guess what?" Jerry added. *"Now we're dead in your house!"*

The others started to laugh, crackling, dry laughs, as they all closed in on Josh and me.

15

"They're going to kill us!" Josh cried.

I watched them move forward in silence. Josh and I had backed up to the window. I looked around the dark room for an escape route.

But there was nowhere to run.

"Karen — you seemed so nice," I said. The words just tumbled out. I hadn't thought before I said them.

Her eyes glowed a little brighter. "I *was* nice," she said in a glum monotone, "until I moved here."

"We were all nice," George Carpenter said in the same low monotone. "But now we're dead."

"Let us go!" Josh cried, raising his hands in front of him as if to shield himself. "Please — let us go."

They laughed again, the dry, hoarse laughter. Dead laughter.

"Don't be scared, Amanda," Karen said. "Soon you'll be with us. That's why they invited you to this house."

"Huh? I don't understand," I cried, my voice shaking.

"This is the Dead House. This is where everyone lives when they first arrive in Dark Falls. When they're still alive."

This seemed to strike the others as funny. They all snickered and laughed.

"But our great-uncle — " Josh started.

Karen shook her head, her eyes glowing with amusement. "No. Sorry, Josh. No great-uncle. It was just a trick to bring you here. Once every year, someone new has to move here. Other years, it was us. We lived in this house — until we died. This year, it's your turn."

"We need new blood," Jerry Franklin said, his eyes glowing red in the dim light. "Once a year, you see, we need new blood."

Moving forward in silence, they hovered over Josh and me.

I took a deep breath. A last breath, perhaps. And shut my eyes.

And then I heard the knock on the door.

A loud knock, repeated several times.

I opened my eyes. The ghostly kids all vanished.

The air smelled sour.

Josh and I stared at each other, dazed, as the loud knocking started again.

"It's Mom and Dad!" Josh cried.

We both ran to the door. Josh stumbled over

102

the coffee table in the dark, so I got to the door first.

"Mom! Dad!" I cried, pulling open the door. "Where have you been?"

I reached out my arms to hug them both — and stopped with my arms in the air. My mouth dropped open and I uttered a silent cry.

"Mr. Dawes!" Josh exclaimed, coming up beside me. "We thought — "

"Oh, Mr. Dawes, I'm so glad to see you!" I cried happily, pushing open the screen door for him.

"Kids — you're okay?" he asked, eyeing us both, his handsome face tight with worry. "Oh, thank God!" he cried. "I got here in time!"

"Mr. Dawes — " I started, feeling so relieved, I had tears in my eyes. "I — "

He grabbed my arm. "There's no time to talk," he said, looking behind him to the street. I could see his car in the driveway. The engine was running. Only the parking lights were on. "I've got to get you kids out of here while there's still time."

Josh and I started to follow him, then hesitated.

What if Mr. Dawes was one of them?

"Hurry," Mr. Dawes urged, holding open the screen door, gazing nervously out into the darkness. "I think we're in terrible danger."

"But — " I started, staring into his frightened eyes, trying to decide if we could trust him.

"I was at the party with your parents," Mr.

Dawes said. "All of a sudden, they formed a circle. Everyone. Around your parents and me. They — they started to close in on us."

Just like when the kids started to close in on Josh and me, I thought.

"We broke through them and ran," Mr. Dawes said, glancing to the driveway behind him. "Somehow the three of us got away. Hurry. We've all got to get away from here — *now*!"

"Josh, let's go," I urged. Then I turned to Mr. Dawes. "Where are Mom and Dad?"

"Come on. I'll show you. They're safe for now. But I don't know for how long."

We followed him out of the house and down the driveway to his car. The clouds had parted. A sliver of moon shone low in a pale, early morning sky.

"There's something wrong with this whole town," Mr. Dawes said, holding the front passenger door open for me as Josh climbed into the back.

I slumped gratefully into the seat, and he slammed the door shut. "I know," I said, as he slid behind the wheel. "Josh and I. We both — "

"We've got to get as far away as we can before they catch up with us," Mr. Dawes said, backing down the drive quickly, the tires sliding and squealing as he pulled onto the street.

"Yes," I agreed. "Thank goodness you came.

My house — it's filled with kids. Dead kids and — "

"So you've seen them," Mr. Dawes said softly, his eyes wide with fear. He pushed down harder on the gas pedal.

As I looked out into the purple darkness, a low, orange sun began to show over the green treetops. "Where are our parents?" I asked anxiously.

"There's a kind of outdoor theater next to the cemetery," Mr. Dawes said, staring straight ahead through the windshield, his eyes narrow, his expression tense. "It's built right into the ground, and it's hidden by a big tree. I left them there. I told them not to move. I think they'll be safe. I don't think anyone'll think to look there."

"We've seen it," Josh said. A bright light suddenly flashed on in the backseat.

"What's that?" Mr. Dawes asked, looking into the rearview mirror.

"My flashlight," Josh answered, clicking it off. "I brought it just in case. But the sun will be up soon. I probably won't need it."

Mr. Dawes hit the brake and pulled the car to the side of the road. We were at the edge of the cemetery. I climbed quickly out of the car, eager to see my parents.

The sky was still dark, streaked with violet now. The sun was a dark orange balloon just barely poking over the trees. Across the street, beyond the jagged rows of gravestones, I could see the dark outline of the leaning tree that hid the mysterious amphitheater.

"Hurry," Mr. Dawes urged, closing his car door quietly. "I'm sure your parents are desperate to see you."

We headed across the street, half-walking, half-jogging, Josh swinging the flashlight in one hand.

Suddenly, at the edge of the cemetery grass, Josh stopped. "Petey!" he cried.

I followed his gaze, and saw our white terrier walking slowly along a slope of gravestones.

"Petey!" Josh yelled again, and began running to the dog.

My heart sank. I hadn't had a chance to tell Josh what Ray had revealed to me about Petey. "No — Josh!" I called.

Mr. Dawes looked very alarmed. "We don't have time. We have to hurry," he said to me. Then he began shouting for Josh to come back.

"I'll go get him," I said, and took off, running as fast as I could along the rows of graves, calling to my brother. "Josh! Josh, wait up! Don't! Don't! go after him! Josh — Petey is *dead*!"

Josh had been gaining on the dog, which was ambling along, sniffing the ground, not looking up, not paying any attention to Josh. Then suddenly, Josh tripped over a low grave marker.

He cried out as he fell, and the flashlight flew out of his hand and clattered against a gravestone.

I quickly caught up with him. "Josh — are you okay?"

He was lying on his stomach, staring straight ahead.

"Josh — answer me. Are you okay?"

I grabbed him by the shoulders and tried to pull him up, but he kept staring straight ahead, his mouth open, his eyes wide.

"Josh?"

"Look," he said finally.

I breathed a sigh of relief, knowing that Josh wasn't knocked out or something.

"Look," he repeated, and pointed to the gravestone he had tripped over.

I turned and squinted at the grave. I read the inscription, silently mouthing the words as I read:

COMPTON DAWES. R.I.P. 1950–1980.

My head began to spin. I felt dizzy. I steadied myself, holding onto Josh.

COMPTON DAWES.

It wasn't his father or his grandfather. He had told us he was the only Compton in his family.

So Mr. Dawes was dead, too.

Dead. Dead. Dead.

Dead as everyone else.

He was one of them. One of the dead ones.

Josh and I stared at each other in the purple darkness. Surrounded. Surrounded by the dead.

Now what? I asked myself.

Now what?

16

"Get up, Josh," I said, my voice a choked whisper. "We've got to get away from here."

But we were too late.

A hand grabbed me firmly by the shoulder.

I spun around to see Mr. Dawes, his eyes narrowing as he read the inscription on his own gravestone.

"Mr. Dawes — you, too!" I cried, so disappointed, so confused, so . . . scared.

"Me, too," he said, almost sadly. "All of us." His eyes burned into mine. "This was a normal town once. And we were normal people. Most of us worked in the plastics factory on the outskirts of town. Then there was an accident. Something escaped from the factory. A yellow gas. It floated over the town. So fast we didn't see it . . . didn't realize. And then, it was too late, and Dark Falls wasn't a normal town anymore. We were all dead, Amanda. Dead and buried. But we couldn't rest.

We couldn't sleep. Dark Falls was a town of living dead."

"What — what are you going to do to us?" I managed to ask. My knees were trembling so hard, I could barely stand. A dead man was squeezing my shoulder. A dead man was staring hard into my eyes.

Standing this close, I could smell his sour breath. I turned my head, but the smell already choked my nostrils.

"Where are Mom and Dad?" Josh asked, climbing to his feet and standing rigidly across from us, glaring accusingly at Mr. Dawes.

"Safe and sound," Mr. Dawes said with a faint smile. "Come with me. It's time for you to join them."

I tried to pull away from him, but his hand was locked on my shoulder. "Let go!" I shouted.

His smile grew wider. "Amanda, it doesn't hurt to die," he said softly, almost soothingly. "Come with me."

"No!" Josh shouted. And with sudden quickness, he dived to the ground and picked up his flashlight.

"Yes!" I cried. "Shine it on him, Josh!" The light could save us. The light could defeat Mr. Dawes, as it had Ray. The light could destroy him. "Quick — shine it on him!" I pleaded.

Josh fumbled with the flashlight, then pointed

it toward Mr. Dawes's startled face, and clicked it on.

Nothing.

No light.

"It — it's broken," Josh said. "I guess when it hit the gravestone. . . ."

My heart pounding, I looked back at Mr. Dawes. The smile on his face was a smile of victory.

17

"Nice try," Mr. Dawes said to Josh. The smile faded quickly from his face.

Close up, he didn't look so young and handsome. His skin, I could see, was dry and peeling and hung loosely beneath his eyes.

"Let's go, kids," he said, giving me a shove. He glanced up at the brightening sky. The sun was raising itself over the treetops.

Josh hesitated.

"I *said* let's go," Mr. Dawes snapped impatiently. He loosened his grip on my shoulder and took a menacing step toward Josh.

Josh glanced down at the worthless flashlight. Then he pulled his arm back and heaved the flashlight at Mr. Dawes's head.

The flashlight hit its target with a sickening *crack*. It hit Mr. Dawes in the center of his forehead, splitting a large hole in the skin.

Mr. Dawes uttered a low cry. His eyes widened in surprise. Dazed, he reached a hand up to the hole where a few inches of gray skull poked through.

"Run, Josh!" I cried.

But there was no need to tell him that. He was already zigzagging through the rows of graves, his head ducked low. I followed him, running as fast as I could.

Glancing back, I saw Mr. Dawes stagger after us, still holding his ripped forehead. He took several steps, then abruptly stopped, staring up at the sky.

It's too bright for him, I realized. He has to stay in the shade.

Josh had ducked down behind a tall marble monument, old and slightly tilted, cracked down the middle. I slid down beside him, gasping for breath.

Leaning on the cool marble, we both peered around the sides of the monument. Mr. Dawes, a scowl on his face, was heading back toward the amphitheater, keeping in the shadows of the trees.

"He — he's not chasing us," Josh whispered, his chest heaving as he struggled to catch his breath and stifle his fear. "He's going back."

"The sun is too bright for him," I said, holding onto the side of the monument. "He must be going to get Mom and Dad."

"That stupid flashlight," Josh cried.

"Never mind that," I said, watching Mr. Dawes

until he disappeared behind the big leaning tree. "What are we going to do now? I don't know — "

"Shhh. Look!" Josh poked me hard on the shoulder, and pointed. "Who's that?"

I followed his stare and saw several dark figures hurrying through the rows of tombstones. They seemed to have appeared from out of nowhere.

Did they rise out of the graves?

Walking quickly, seeming to float over the green, sloping ground, they headed into the shadows. All were walking in silence, their eyes straight ahead. They didn't stop to greet one another. They strode purposefully toward the hidden amphitheater, as if they were being drawn there, as if they were puppets being pulled by hidden strings.

"Whoa. Look at them all!" Josh whispered, ducking his head back behind the marble monument.

The dark, moving forms made all the shadows ripple. It looked as if the trees, the gravestones, the entire cemetery had come to life, had started toward the hidden seats of the amphitheater.

"There goes Karen," I whispered, pointing. "And George. And all the rest of them."

The kids from our house were moving quickly in twos and threes, following the other shadows, as silent and businesslike as everyone else.

Everyone was here except Ray, I thought.

Because we killed Ray.

We killed someone who was already dead.

"Do you think Mom and Dad are really down in that weird theater?" Josh asked, interrupting my morbid thoughts, his eyes on the moving shadows.

"Come on," I said, taking Josh's hand and pulling him away from the monument. "We've got to find out."

We watched the last of the dark figures float past the enormous leaning tree. The shadows stopped moving. The cemetery was still and silent. A solitary crow floated high above in the clear blue, cloudless sky.

Slowly, Josh and I edged our way toward the amphitheater, ducking behind gravestones, keeping low to the ground.

It was a struggle to move. I felt as if I weighed five hundred pounds. The weight of my fear, I guess.

I was desperate to see if Mom and Dad were there.

But at the same time, I didn't want to see.

I didn't want to see them being held prisoner by Mr. Dawes and the others.

I didn't want to see them . . . killed.

The thought made me stop. I reached out an arm and halted Josh.

We were standing behind the leaning tree, hidden by its enormous clump of upraised roots. Beyond the tree, down in the theater below, I could hear the low murmur of voices.

"Are Mom and Dad there?" Josh whispered. He started to poke his head around the side of the bent tree trunk, but I cautiously pulled him back.

"Be careful," I whispered. "Don't let them see you. They're practically right beneath us."

"But I've *got* to know if Mom and Dad are really here," he whispered, his eyes frightened, pleading.

"Me, too," I agreed.

We both leaned over the massive trunk. The bark felt smooth under my hands as I gazed into the deep shadows cast by the tree.

And then I saw them.

Mom and Dad. They were tied up, back-to-back, standing in the center of the floor at the bottom of the amphitheater in front of everyone.

They looked so uncomfortable, so terrified. Their arms were tied tightly down at their sides. Dad's face was bright red. Mom's hair was all messed up, hanging wildly down over her forehead, her head bowed.

Squinting into the darkness cast by the tree, I saw Mr. Dawes standing beside them along with another, older man. And I saw that the rows of long benches built into the ground were filled with people. Not a single empty space.

Everyone in town must be here, I realized.

Everyone except Josh and me.

"They're going to kill Mom and Dad," Josh whispered, grabbing my arm, squeezing it in fear. "They're going to make Mom and Dad just like them."

"Then they'll come after us," I said, thinking out loud, staring through the shadows at my poor parents. Both of them had their heads bowed now as they stood before the silent crowd. Both of them were awaiting their fates.

"What are we going to do?" Josh whispered.

"Huh?" I was staring so hard at Mom and Dad, I guess I momentarily blanked out.

"What are we going to do?" Josh repeated urgently, still holding desperately to my arm. "We can't just stand here and — "

I suddenly knew what we were going to do.

It just came to me. I didn't even have to think hard.

"Maybe we can save them," I whispered, backing away from the tree. "Maybe we *can* do something."

Josh let go of my arm. He stared at me eagerly.

"We're going to push this tree over," I whispered with so much confidence that I surprised myself. "We're going to push the tree over so the sunlight will fill the amphitheater."

"Yes!" Josh cried immediately. "Look at this tree. It's practically down already. We can do it!"

I *knew* we could do it. I don't know where my confidence came from. But I *knew* we could do it.

And I knew we had to do it fast.

Peering over the top of the trunk again, struggling to see through the shadows, I could see that everyone in the theater had stood up. They were all starting to move forward, down toward Mom and Dad.

"Come on, Josh," I whispered. "We'll take a running jump, and push the tree over. Come on!"

Without another word, we both took several steps back.

We just had to give the trunk a good, hard push, and the tree would topple right over. The roots were already almost entirely up out of the ground, after all.

One hard push. That's all it would take. And the sunlight would pour into the theater. Beautiful, golden sunlight. Bright, bright sunlight.

The dead people would all crumble.

And Mom and Dad would be saved.

All four of us would be saved.

"Come on, Josh," I whispered. "Ready?"

He nodded, his face solemn, his eyes frightened.

"Okay. Let's *go*!" I cried.

We both ran forward, digging our sneakers into the ground, moving as fast as we could, our arms outstretched and ready.

In a second, we hit the tree trunk and pushed with all of our strength, shoving it with our hands and then moving our shoulders into it, pushing . . . pushing . . . pushing . . .

It didn't budge.

18

"Push!" I cried. "Push it again!"

Josh let out an exasperated, defeated sigh. "I can't, Amanda. I can't move it."

"Josh — " I glared at him.

He backed up to try again.

Below, I could hear startled voices, angry voices.

"Quick!" I yelled. *"Push!"*

We hurtled into the tree trunk with our shoulders, both of us grunting from the effort, our muscles straining, our faces bright red.

"Push! Keep pushing!"

The veins at my temples felt about to pop.

Was the tree moving?

No.

It gave a little, but bounced right back.

The voices from below were getting louder.

"We can't do it!" I cried, so disappointed, so frustrated, so terrified. "We can't move it!"

Defeated, I slumped over onto the tree trunk,

and started to bury my face in my hands.

I pulled back with a gasp when I heard the soft cracking sound. The cracking sound grew louder until it was a rumble, then a roar. It sounded as if the ground were ripping apart.

The old tree fell quickly. It didn't have far to fall. But it hit with a thundering crash that seemed to shake the ground.

I grabbed Josh and we both stood in amazement and disbelief as bright sunlight poured into the amphitheater.

The cries went up instantly. Horrified cries. Angry cries. Frantic cries.

The cries became howls. Howls of pain, of agony.

The people in the amphitheater, the living dead caught in the golden light, began scrambling over one another, screeching, pulling, climbing, pushing, trying to claw their way to shade.

But it was too late.

Their skin began to drop off their bones and, as I stared open-mouthed, they crumbled to powder and dissolved to the ground, their clothes disintegrating along with them.

The painful cries continued to ring out as the bodies fell apart, the skin melted away, the dry bones collapsed. I saw Karen Somerset staggering across the floor. I saw her hair fall to the ground in a heap, revealing the dark skull underneath. She cast a glance up at me, a longing look, a look of regret. And then her eyeballs rolled out of their sockets, and she opened her toothless mouth, and she cried, "Thank you, Amanda! Thank you!" and collapsed.

Josh and I covered our ears to shut out the ghastly cries. We both looked away, unable to keep watching the entire town fall in agony and crumble to powder, destroyed by the sun, the clear, warm sun.

When we looked back, they had all disappeared.

Mom and Dad were standing right where they had been, tied back-to-back, their expressions a mixture of horror and disbelief.

"Mom! Dad!" I cried.

I'll never forget their smiles as Josh and I ran forward to free them.

It didn't take our parents long to get us packed up and to arrange for the movers to take us back to our old neighborhood and our old house. "I guess it's lucky after all that we couldn't sell the old place," Dad said, as we eagerly piled into the car to leave.

Dad backed down the driveway and started to roar away.

"Stop!" I cried suddenly. I'm not sure why, but I had a sudden, powerful urge to take one last look at the old house.

As both of my parents called out to me in confusion, I pushed open the door and jogged back to the driveway. Standing in the middle of the yard, I stared up at the house, silent, empty, still covered in thick layers of blue-gray shadows.

I found myself gazing up at the old house as if I were hypnotized. I don't know how long I stood there.

The crunch of tires on the gravel driveway snapped me out of my spell. Startled, I turned to see a red station wagon parked in the driveway.

Two boys about Josh's age jumped out of the back. Their parents followed. Staring up at the house, they didn't seem to notice me.

"Here we are, kids," the mother said, smiling at them. "Our new house."

"It doesn't look new. It looks old," one of the boys said.

And then his brother's eyes widened as he noticed me. "Who are *you*?" he demanded.

The other members of his family turned to stare at me.

"Oh. I . . . uh . . ." His question caught me by surprise. I could hear my dad honking his horn impatiently down on the street. "I . . . uh . . . used to live in your house," I found myself answering.

And then I turned and ran full speed down to the street.

Wasn't that Mr. Dawes standing at the porch, clipboard in hand? I wondered, catching a glimpse of a dark figure as I ran to the car.

No, it couldn't be Mr. Dawes up there waiting for them, I decided.

It just couldn't be.

I didn't look back. I slammed the car door behind me, and we sped away.

STAY OUT OF THE BASEMENT

1

"Hey, Dad — catch!"

Casey tossed the Frisbee across the smooth, green lawn. Casey's dad made a face, squinting into the sun. The Frisbee hit the ground and skipped a few times before landing under the hedge at the back of the house.

"Not today. I'm busy," Dr. Brewer said, and abruptly turned and loped into the house. The screen door slammed behind him.

Casey brushed his straight blond hair back off his forehead. "What's *his* problem?" he called to Margaret, his sister, who had watched the whole scene from the side of the redwood garage.

"You know," Margaret said quietly. She wiped her hands on the legs of her jeans and held them both up, inviting a toss. "I'll play Frisbee with you for a little while," she said.

"Okay," Casey said without enthusiasm. He walked slowly over to retrieve the Frisbee from under the hedge.

Margaret moved closer. She felt sorry for Casey. He and their dad were really close, always playing ball or Frisbee or Nintendo together. But Dr. Brewer didn't seem to have time for that anymore.

Jumping up to catch the Frisbee, Margaret realized she felt sorry for herself, too. Dad hadn't been the same to her, either. In fact, he spent so much time down in the basement, he barely said a word to her.

He doesn't even call me Princess anymore, Margaret thought. It was a nickname she hated. But at least it was a nickname, a sign of closeness.

She tossed the red Frisbee back. A bad toss. Casey chased after it, but it sailed away from him. Margaret looked up to the golden hills beyond their backyard.

California, she thought.

It's so weird out here. Here it is, the middle of winter, and there isn't a cloud in the sky, and Casey and I are out in jeans and T-shirts as if it were the middle of summer.

She made a diving catch for a wild toss, rolling over on the manicured lawn and raising the Frisbee above her head triumphantly.

"Show off," Casey muttered, unimpressed.

"You're the hot dog in the family," Margaret called.

"Well, you're a dork."

"Hey, Casey — you want me to play with you or not?"

He shrugged.

Everyone was so edgy these days, Margaret realized.

It was easy to figure out why.

She made a high toss. The Frisbee sailed over Casey's head. "*You* chase it!" he cried angrily, putting his hands on his hips.

"No, *you!*" she cried.

"*You!*"

"Casey — you're eleven years old. Don't act like a two-year-old," she snapped.

"Well, you act like a *one*-year-old," was his reply as he grudgingly went after the Frisbee.

It was all Dad's fault, Margaret realized. Things had been so tense ever since he started working at home. Down in the basement with his plants and weird machines. He hardly ever came up for air.

And when he did, he wouldn't even catch a Frisbee.

Or spend two minutes with either of them.

Mom had noticed it, too, Margaret thought, running full-out and making another grandstand catch just before colliding with the side of the garage.

Having Dad home has made Mom really tense, too. She pretends everything is fine. But I can tell she's worried about him.

"Lucky catch, Fatso!" Casey called.

Margaret hated the name Fatso even more than she hated Princess. People in her family jokingly called her Fatso because she was so thin, like her father. She also was tall like him, but she had her mother's straight brown hair, brown eyes, and dark coloring.

"Don't call me that." She heaved the red disc at him. He caught it at his knees and flipped it back to her.

They tossed it back and forth without saying much for another ten or fifteen minutes. "I'm getting hot," Margaret said, shielding her eyes from the afternoon sun with her hand. "Let's go in."

Casey tossed the Frisbee against the garage wall. It dropped onto the grass. He came trotting over to her. "Dad always plays longer," he said peevishly. "And he throws better. You throw like a girl."

"Give me a break," Margaret groaned, giving him a playful shove as she jogged to the back door. "You throw like a chimpanzee."

"How come Dad got fired?" he asked.

She blinked. And stopped running. The question had caught her by surprise. "Huh?"

His pale, freckled face turned serious. "You

know. I mean, why?" he asked, obviously uncomfortable.

She and Casey had never discussed this in the four weeks since Dad had been home. Which was unusual since they were pretty close, being only a year apart.

"I mean, we came all the way out here so he could work at PolyTech, right?" Casey asked.

"Yeah. Well . . . he got fired," Margaret said, half-whispering in case her dad might be able to hear.

"But why? Did he blow up the lab or something?" Casey grinned. The idea of his dad blowing up a huge campus science lab appealed to him.

"No, he didn't blow anything up," Margaret said, tugging at a strand of dark hair. "Botanists work with plants, you know. They don't get much of a chance to blow things up."

They both laughed.

Casey followed her into the narrow strip of shade cast by the low ranch-style house.

"I'm not sure exactly what happened," Margaret continued, still half-whispering. "But I overheard Dad on the phone. I think he was talking to Mr. Martinez. His department head. Remember? The quiet little man who came to dinner that night the barbecue grill caught fire?"

Casey nodded. "Martinez fired Dad?"

"Probably," Margaret whispered. "From what

I overheard, it had something to do with the plants Dad was growing, some experiments that had gone wrong or something."

"But Dad's real smart," Casey insisted, as if Margaret were arguing with him. "If his experiments went wrong, he'd know how to fix them."

Margaret shrugged. "That's all I know," she said. "Come on, Casey. Let's go inside. I'm dying of thirst!" She stuck her tongue out and moaned, demonstrating her dire need of liquid.

"You're gross," Casey said. He pulled open the screen door, then dodged in front of her so he could get inside first.

"Who's gross?" Mrs. Brewer asked from the sink. She turned to greet the two of them. "Don't answer that."

Mom looks very tired today, Margaret thought, noticing the crisscross of fine lines at the corners of her mother's eyes and the first strands of gray in her mother's shoulder-length brown hair. "I hate this job," Mrs. Brewer said, turning back to the sink.

"What are you doing?" Casey asked, pulling open the refrigerator and removing a box of juice.

"I'm deveining shrimp."

"Yuck!" Margaret exclaimed.

"Thanks for the support," Mrs. Brewer said dryly. The phone rang. Wiping her shrimpy hands with a dish towel, she hurried across the room to pick up the phone.

Margaret got a box of juice from the fridge, popped the straw into the top, and followed Casey into the front hallway. The basement door, usually shut tight when Dr. Brewer was working down there, was slightly ajar.

Casey started to close it, then stopped. "Let's go down and see what Dad is doing," he suggested.

Margaret sucked the last drops of juice through the straw and squeezed the empty box flat in her hand. "Okay."

She knew they probably shouldn't disturb their father, but her curiosity got the better of her. He had been working down there for four weeks now. All kinds of interesting equipment, lights, and plants had been delivered. Most days he spent at least eight or nine hours down there, doing whatever it was he was doing. And he hadn't shown it to them once.

"Yeah. Let's go," Margaret said. It was *their* house, too, after all.

Besides, maybe their dad was just waiting for them to show some interest. Maybe he was hurt that they hadn't bothered to come downstairs in all this time.

She pulled the door open the rest of the way,

and they stepped onto the narrow stairway. "Hey, Dad — " Casey called excitedly. "Dad — can we see?"

They were halfway down when their father appeared at the foot of the stairs. He glared up at them angrily, his skin strangely green under the fluorescent light fixture. He was holding his right hand, drops of red blood falling onto his white lab coat.

"*Stay out of the basement!*" he bellowed, in a voice they'd never heard before.

Both kids shrank back, surprised to hear their father scream like that. He was usually so mild and soft-spoken.

"*Stay out of the basement,*" he repeated, holding his bleeding hand. "Don't *ever* come down here — I'm warning you."

2

"Okay. All packed," Mrs. Brewer said, dropping her suitcases with a thud in the front hallway. She poked her head into the living room where the TV was blaring. "Do you think you could stop the movie for one minute to say good-bye to your mother?"

Casey pushed a button on the remote control, and the screen went blank. He and Margaret obediently walked to the hallway to give their mother hugs.

Margaret's friend, Diane Manning, who lived just around the corner, followed them into the hallway. "How long are you going to be gone, Mrs. Brewer?" she asked, her eyes on the two bulging suitcases.

"I don't know," Mrs. Brewer replied fretfully. "My sister went into the hospital in Tucson this morning. I guess I'll have to stay until she's able to go home."

"Well, I'll be glad to baby-sit for Casey and

Margaret while you're away," Diane joked.

"Give me a break," Margaret said, rolling her eyes. "I'm older than you are, Diane."

"And I'm smarter than both of you," Casey added with typical modesty.

"I'm not worried about you kids," Mrs. Brewer said, glancing nervously at her watch. "I'm worried about your father."

"Don't worry," Margaret told her seriously. "We'll take good care of him."

"Just make sure that he eats something once in a while," Mrs. Brewer said. "He's so obsessed with his work, he doesn't remember to eat unless you tell him."

It's going to be really lonely around here without Mom, Margaret thought. Dad hardly ever comes up from the basement.

It had been two weeks since he yelled at Casey and her to stay out of the basement. They had been tiptoeing around ever since, afraid to get him angry again. But in the past two weeks, he had barely spoken to them, except for the occasional "good morning" and "good night."

"Don't worry about anything, Mom," she said, forcing a smile. "Just take good care of Aunt Eleanor."

"I'll call as soon as I get to Tucson," Mrs. Brewer said, nervously lowering her eyes to her watch again. She took three long strides to the basement door, then shouted down, "Michael — time to take me to the airport!"

After a long wait, Dr. Brewer called up a reply. Then Mrs. Brewer turned back to the kids. "Think he'll even notice I'm gone?" she asked in a loud whisper. She meant it to be a light remark, but her eyes revealed some sadness.

A few seconds later, they heard footsteps on the basement stairs, and their dad appeared. He pulled off his stained lab coat, revealing tan slacks and a bright yellow T-shirt, and tossed the lab coat onto the banister. Even though it was two weeks later, his right hand, the hand that had been bleeding, was still heavily bandaged.

"Ready?" he asked his wife.

Mrs. Brewer sighed. "I guess." She gave Margaret and Casey a helpless look, then moved quickly to give them each one last hug.

"Let's go, then," Dr. Brewer said impatiently. He picked up the two bags and groaned. "Wow. How long are you planning to stay? A year?" Then he headed out the front door with them, not waiting for an answer.

"Bye, Mrs. Brewer," Diane said, waving. "Have a good trip."

"How can she have a good trip?" Casey asked sharply. "Her sister's in the hospital."

"You know what I mean," Diane replied, tossing back her long red hair and rolling her eyes.

They watched the station wagon roll down the driveway, then returned to the living room. Casey picked up the remote control and started the movie.

Diane sprawled on the couch and picked up the bag of potato chips she'd been eating.

"Who picked this movie?" Diane asked, crinkling the foil bag noisily.

"I did," Casey said. "It's neat." He had pulled a couch cushion down to the living room carpet and was lying on it.

Margaret was sitting cross-legged on the floor, her back against the base of an armchair, still thinking about her mother and her aunt Eleanor. "It's neat if you like to see a lot of people blown up and their guts flying all over," she said, making a face for Diane's benefit.

"Yeah. It's neat," Casey said, not taking his eyes off the glowing TV screen.

"I've got so much homework. I don't know why I'm sitting here," Diane said, reaching her hand into the potato chip bag.

"Me, too," Margaret sighed. "I guess I'll do it after dinner. Do you have the math assignment? I think I left my math book at school."

"Sshhh!" Casey hissed, kicking a sneakered foot in Margaret's direction. "This is a good part."

"You've seen this tape before?" Diane shrieked.

"Twice," Casey admitted. He ducked, and the

138

sofa pillow Diane threw sailed over his head.

"It's a pretty afternoon," Margaret said, stretching her arms above her head. "Maybe we should go outside. You know. Ride bikes or something."

"You think you're still back in Michigan? It's *always* a pretty afternoon here," Diane said, chewing loudly. "I don't even notice it anymore."

"Maybe we should do the math assignment together," Margaret suggested hopefully. Diane was much better in math than she was.

Diane shrugged. "Yeah. Maybe." She crinkled up the bag and set it on the floor. "Your dad looked kind of nervous, you know?"

"Huh? What do you mean?"

"Just nervous," Diane said. "How's he doing?"

"Sshhh," Casey insisted, picking up the potato chip bag and tossing it at Diane.

"You know. Being laid off and all."

"I guess he's okay," Margaret said wistfully. "I don't know, really. He spends all his time down in the basement with his experiments."

"Experiments? Hey — let's go take a look." Tossing her hair back behind her shoulders, Diane jumped up from the chrome and white leather couch.

Diane was a science freak. Math and science. The two subjects Margaret hated.

She should have been in the Brewer family,

Margaret thought with a trace of bitterness. Maybe Dad would pay some attention to her since she's into the same things he is.

"Come on — " Diane urged, bending over to pull Margaret up from the floor. "He's a botanist, right? What's he doing down there?"

"It's complicated," Margaret said, shouting over the explosions and gunfire on the TV. "He tried to explain it to me once. But — " Margaret allowed Diane to pull her to her feet.

"Shut up!" Casey yelled, staring at the movie, the colors from the TV screen reflecting over his clothes.

"Is he building a Frankenstein monster or something?" Diane demanded. "Or some kind of RoboCop? Wouldn't that be cool?"

"Shut up!" Casey repeated shrilly as Arnold Schwarzenegger bounded across the screen.

"He's got all these machines and plants down there," Margaret said uncomfortably. "But he doesn't want us to go down there."

"Huh? It's like top secret?" Diane's emerald green eyes lit up with excitement. "Come on. We'll just take a peek."

"No, I don't think so," Margaret told her. She couldn't forget the angry look on her father's face two weeks before when she and Casey had tried to pay a visit. Or the way he had screamed at them never to come down to the basement.

140

"Come on. I dare you," Diane challenged. "Are you chicken?"

"I'm not afraid," Margaret insisted shrilly. Diane was always daring her to do things she didn't want to do. Why is it so important for Diane to think she's so much braver than everyone else? Margaret wondered.

"Chicken," Diane repeated. Tossing her mane of red hair behind her shoulder, she strode quickly toward the basement door.

"Diane — stop!" Margaret cried, following after her.

"Hey, wait!" Casey cried, clicking off the movie. "Are we going downstairs? Wait for me!" He climbed quickly to his feet and enthusiastically hurried to join them at the basement door.

"We can't — " Margaret started, but Diane clamped a hand over her mouth.

"We'll take a quick peek," Diane insisted. "We'll just look. We won't touch anything. And then we'll come right back upstairs."

"Okay. I'll go first," Casey said, grabbing for the doorknob.

"Why do you want to do this?" Margaret asked her friend. "Why are you so eager to go down there?"

Diane shrugged. "It beats doing our math," she replied, grinning.

Margaret sighed, defeated. "Okay, let's go. But

remember — just looking, no touching."

Casey pulled open the door and led the way onto the stairway. Stepping onto the landing, they were immediately engulfed in hot, steamy air. They could hear the buzz and hum of electronic machinery. And off to the right, they could see the glare of the bright white lights from Dr. Brewer's workroom.

This is kind of fun, Margaret thought as the three of them made their way down the linoleum-covered stairway.

It's an adventure.

There's no harm in taking a peek.

So why was her heart pounding? Why did she have this sudden tingle of fear?

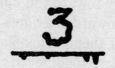

3

"Yuck! It's so hot in here!"

As they stepped away from the stairs, the air became unbearably hot and thick.

Margaret gasped. The sudden change in temperature was suffocating.

"It's so moist," Diane said. "Good for your hair and skin."

"We studied the rain forest in school," Casey said. "Maybe Dad's building a rain forest."

"Maybe," Margaret said uncertainly.

Why did she feel so strange? Was it just because they were invading their father's domain? Doing something he had told them not to do?

She held back, gazing in both directions. The basement was divided into two large, rectangular rooms. To the left, an unfinished rec room stood in darkness. She could barely make out the outlines of the Ping-Pong table in the center of the room.

The workroom to the right was brightly lit, so

bright they had to blink and wait for their eyes to adjust. Beams of white light poured down from large halogen lamps on tracks in the ceiling.

"Wow! Look!" Casey cried, his eyes wide as he stepped excitedly toward the light.

Reaching up toward the lights were shiny, tall plants, dozens of them, thick-stalked and broad-leafed, planted close together in an enormous, low trough of dark soil.

"It's like a jungle!" Margaret exclaimed, following Casey into the white glare.

The plants, in fact, resembled jungle plants — leafy vines and tall, treelike plants with long, slender tendrils, fragile-looking ferns, plants with gnarled, cream-colored roots poking up like bony knees from the soil.

"It's like a swamp or something," Diane said. "Did your father really grow these things in just five or six weeks?"

"Yeah. I'm pretty sure," Margaret replied, staring at the enormous red tomatoes on a slender, yellow stalk.

"Ooh. Feel this one," Diane said.

Margaret glanced over to find her friend rubbing her hand over a large, flat leaf the shape of a teardrop. "Diane — we shouldn't touch — "

"I know, I know," Diane said, not letting go of the leaf. "But just rub your hand on it."

Margaret reluctantly obeyed. "It doesn't feel like a leaf," she said as Diane moved over to examine a large fern. "It's so smooth. Like glass."

The three of them stood under the bright, white lights, examining the plants for several minutes, touching the thick stalks, running their hands over the smooth, warm leaves, surprised by the enormous size of the fruits some of the plants had produced.

"It's too hot down here," Casey complained. He pulled his T-shirt off over his head and dropped it onto the floor.

"What a bod!" Diane teased him.

He stuck out his tongue at her. Then his pale blue eyes grew wide and he seemed to freeze in surprise. "Hey!"

"Casey — what's the matter?" Margaret asked, hurrying over to him.

"This one — " He pointed to a tall, treelike plant. "It's *breathing*!"

Diane laughed.

But Margaret heard it, too. She grabbed Casey's bare shoulder and listened. Yes. She could hear breathing sounds, and they seemed to be coming from the tall, leafy tree.

"What's your problem?" Diane asked, seeing the amazed expressions on Casey's and Margaret's faces.

"Casey's right," Margaret said softly, listening to the steady, rhythmic sound. "You can hear it breathing."

Diane rolled her eyes. "Maybe it has a cold. Maybe its vine is stuffed up." She laughed at her own joke, but her two companions didn't join in. "I don't hear it." She moved closer.

All three of them listened.

Silence.

"It — stopped," Margaret said.

"Stop it, you two," Diane scolded. "You're not going to scare me."

"No. Really," Margaret protested.

"Hey — look at this!" Casey had already moved on to something else. He was standing in front of a tall glass case that stood on the other side of the plants. It looked a little like a phone booth, with a shelf inside about shoulder-high, and dozens of wires attached to the back and sides.

Margaret's eyes followed the wires to a similar glass booth a few feet away. Some kind of electrical generator stood between the two booths and appeared to be connected to both of them.

"What could that be?" Diane asked, hurrying over to Casey.

"Don't touch it," Margaret warned, giving the breathing plant one final glance, then joining the others.

But Casey reached out to the glass door on the

front of the booth. "I just want to see if this opens," he said.

He grabbed the glass — and his eyes went wide with shock.

His entire body began to shake and vibrate. His head jerked wildly from side to side. His eyes rolled up in his head.

"Oh, help!" he managed to cry, his body vibrating and shaking harder and faster. "Help me! I — can't stop!"

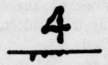

4

"Help me!"

Casey's whole body shook as if an electrical current were charging through him. His head jerked on his shoulders, and his eyes looked wild and dazed.

"Please!"

Margaret and Diane stared in open-mouthed horror. Margaret was the first to move. She lunged at Casey, and reached out to try to pull him away from the glass.

"Margaret — don't!" Diane screamed. "Don't touch him!"

"But we have to do something!" Margaret cried.

It took both girls a while to realize that Casey had stopped shaking. And was laughing.

"Casey?" Margaret asked, staring at him, her terrified expression fading to astonishment.

He was leaning against the glass, his body still now, his mouth wrapped in a broad, mischievous grin.

"Gotcha!" he declared. And then began to laugh even harder, pointing at them and repeating the phrase through his triumphant laughter. "Gotcha! Gotcha!"

"That wasn't funny!" Margaret screamed.

"You were faking it?! I don't believe it!" Diane cried, her face as pale as the white lights above them, her lower lip trembling.

Both girls leapt onto Casey and pushed him to the floor. Margaret sat on top of him while Diane held his shoulders down.

"Gotcha! Gotcha!" he continued, stopping only when Margaret tickled his stomach so hard he couldn't talk.

"You rat!" Diane cried. "You little rat!"

The free-for-all was brought to a sudden halt by a low moan from across the room. All three kids raised their heads and stared in the direction of the sound.

The large basement was silent now except for their heavy breathing.

"What was that?" Diane whispered.

They listened.

Another low moan, a mournful sound, muffled, like air through a saxophone.

The tendrils of a treelike plant suddenly drooped, like snakes lowering themselves to the ground.

Another low, sad moan.

"It's — the plants!" Casey said, his expression frightened now. He pushed his sister off him and climbed to his feet, brushing back his disheveled blond hair as he stood up.

"Plants don't cry and moan," Diane said, her eyes on the vast trough of plants that filled the room.

"These do," Margaret said.

Tendrils moved, like human arms shifting their position. They could hear breathing again, slow, steady breathing. Then a sigh, like air escaping.

"Let's get out of here," Casey said, edging toward the stairs.

"It's definitely creepy down here," Diane said, following him, her eyes remaining on the shifting, moaning plants.

"I'm sure Dad could explain it," Margaret said. Her words were calm, but her voice trembled, and she was backing out of the room, following Diane and Casey.

"Your dad is weird," Diane said, reaching the doorway.

"No, he isn't," Casey quickly insisted. "He's doing important work here."

A tall treelike plant sighed and appeared to bend toward them, raising its tendrils as if beckoning to them, calling them back.

"Let's just get out of here!" Margaret exclaimed.

All three of them were out of breath by the time they ran up the stairs. Casey closed the door tightly, making sure it clicked shut.

"Weird," Diane repeated, playing nervously with a strand of her long red hair. "Definitely weird." It was her word of the day. But Margaret had to admit it was appropriate.

"Well, Dad warned us not to go down there," Margaret said, struggling to catch her breath. "I guess he knew it would look scary to us, and we wouldn't understand."

"I'm getting out of here," Diane said, only half-kidding. She stepped out of the screen door and turned back toward them. "Want to go over the math later?"

"Yeah. Sure," Margaret said, still thinking about the moaning, shifting plants. Some of them had seemed to be reaching out to them, crying out to them. But of course that was impossible.

"Later," Diane said, and headed at a trot down the drive.

Just as she disappeared, their father's dark blue station wagon turned the corner and started up the drive. "Back from the airport," Margaret said. She turned from the door back to Casey a few yards behind her in the hallway. "Is the basement door closed?"

"Yeah," Casey replied, looking again to make sure. "No way Dad will know we — "

He stopped. His mouth dropped open, but no sound came out.

His face went pale.

"My T-shirt!" Casey exclaimed, slapping his bare chest. "I left it in the basement!"

5

"I've got to get it," Casey said. "Otherwise Dad'll know — "

"It's too late," Margaret interrupted, her eyes on the driveway. "He's already pulled up the drive."

"It'll only take a second," Casey insisted, his hand on the basement doorknob. "I'll run down and run right up."

"No!" Margaret stood tensely in the center of the narrow hallway, halfway between the front door and the basement door, her eyes toward the front. "He's parked. He's getting out of the car."

"But he'll know! He'll know!" Casey cried, his voice high and whiny.

"So?"

"Remember how mad he got last time?" Casey asked.

"Of course I remember," Margaret replied. "But he's not going to kill us, Casey, just because we took a peek at his plants. He's — "

Margaret stopped. She moved closer to the screen door. "Hey, wait."

"What's going on?" Casey asked.

"Hurry!" Margaret turned and gestured with both hands. "Go! Get downstairs — fast! Mr. Henry from next door. He stopped Dad. They're talking about something in the drive."

With a loud cry, Casey flung open the basement door and disappeared. Margaret heard him clumping rapidly down the stairs. Then she heard his footsteps fade as he hurried into their father's workroom.

Hurry, Casey, she thought, standing guard at the front door, watching her father shielding his eyes from the sun with one hand as he talked with Mr. Henry.

Hurry.

You know Dad never talks for long with the neighbors.

Mr. Henry seemed to be doing all the talking. Probably asking Dad some kind of favor, Margaret thought. Mr. Henry wasn't handy at all, not like Dr. Brewer. And so he was always asking Margaret's dad to come over and help repair or install things.

Her father was nodding now, a tight smile on his face.

Hurry, Casey.

Get back up here. Where are you?

Still shielding his eyes, Dr. Brewer gave Mr. Henry a quick wave. Then both men spun around and began walking quickly toward their houses.

Hurry, Casey.

Casey — he's coming! Hurry! Margaret urged silently.

It doesn't take this long to pick your T-shirt up from the floor and run up the stairs.

It *shouldn't* take this long.

Her dad was on the front walk now. He spotted her in the doorway and waved.

Margaret returned the wave and looked back through the hallway to the basement door. "Casey — where are you?" she called aloud.

No reply.

No sound from the basement.

No sound at all.

Dr. Brewer had paused outside to inspect the rosebushes at the head of the front walk.

"Casey?" Margaret called.

Still no reply.

"Casey — hurry!"

Silence.

Her father was crouching down, doing something to the soil beneath the rosebushes.

With a feeling of dread weighing down her entire body, Margaret realized she had no choice.

She had to go downstairs and see what was keeping Casey.

6

Casey ran down the steps, leaning on the metal banister so that he could jump down two steps at a time. He landed hard on the cement basement floor and darted into the bright white light of the plant room.

Stopping at the entranceway, he waited for his eyes to adjust to the brighter-than-day light. He took a deep breath, inhaling the steamy air, and held it. It was so hot down here, so sticky. His back began to itch. The back of his neck tingled.

The jungle of plants stood as if at attention under the bright white lights.

He saw his T-shirt, lying crumpled on the floor a few feet from a tall, leafy tree. The tree seemed to lean toward the T-shirt, its long tendrils hanging down, loosely coiled on the soil around its trunk.

Casey took a timid step into the room.

Why am I so afraid? he wondered.

It's just a room filled with strange plants.

Why do I have the feeling that they're watching me? Waiting for me?

He scolded himself for being so afraid and took a few more steps toward the crumpled T-shirt on the floor.

Hey — wait.

The breathing.

There it was again.

Steady breathing. Not too loud. Not too soft, either.

Who could be breathing? *What* could be breathing?

Was the big tree breathing?

Casey stared at the shirt on the floor. So near. What was keeping him from grabbing it and running back upstairs? What was holding him back?

He took a step forward. Then another.

Was the breathing growing louder?

He jumped, startled by a sudden, low moan from the big supply closet against the wall.

It sounded so human, as if someone were in there, moaning in pain.

"Casey — where are you?"

Margaret's voice sounded so far away, even though she was just at the head of the stairs.

"Okay so far," he called back to her. But his voice came out in a whisper. She probably couldn't hear him.

He took another step. Another.

The shirt was about three yards away.

A quick dash. A quick dive, and he'd have it.

Another low moan from the supply closet. A plant seemed to sigh. A tall fern suddenly dipped low, shifting its leaves.

"Casey?" He could hear his sister from upstairs, sounding very worried. "Casey — hurry!"

I'm trying, he thought. I'm trying to hurry.

What was holding him back?

Another low moan, this time from the other side of the room.

He took two more steps, then crouched low, his arms straight out in front of him.

The shirt was almost within reach.

He heard a groaning sound, then more breathing.

He raised his eyes to the tall tree. The long, ropy tendrils had tensed. Stiffened. Or had he imagined it?

No.

They had been drooping loosely. Now they were taut. Ready.

Ready to grab him?

"Casey — hurry!" Margaret called, sounding even farther away.

He didn't answer. He was concentrating on the shirt. Just a few feet away. Just a few feet. Just a foot.

The plant groaned again.

"Casey? Casey?"

The leaves quivered all the way up the trunk. Just a foot away. Almost in reach.

"Casey? Are you okay? *Answer* me!"

He grabbed the shirt.

Two snakelike tendrils swung out at him.

"Huh?" he cried out, paralyzed with fear. "What's happening?"

The tendrils wrapped themselves around his waist.

"Let go!" he cried, holding the T-shirt tightly in one hand, grabbing at the tendrils with the other.

The tendrils hung on, and gently tightened around him.

Margaret? Casey tried calling, but no sound came out of his mouth. Margaret?

He jerked violently, then pulled straight ahead.

The tendrils held on.

They didn't squeeze him. They weren't trying to strangle him. Or pull him back.

But they didn't let go.

They felt warm and wet against his bare skin. Like animal arms. Not like a plant.

Help! He again tried to shout. He pulled once more, leaning forward, using all his strength.

No good.

He ducked low, hit the floor, tried to roll away.

The tendrils hung on.

The plant uttered a loud sigh.

"Let go!" Casey cried, finally finding his voice.

And then suddenly Margaret was standing beside him. He hadn't heard her come down the stairs. He hadn't seen her enter the room.

"Casey!" she cried. "What's — "

Her mouth dropped open and her eyes grew wide.

"It — won't let go!" he told her.

"No!" she screamed. And grabbed one of the tendrils with both hands. And tugged with all her strength.

The tendril resisted for only a moment, then went slack.

Casey uttered a joyful cry and spun away from the remaining tendril. Margaret dropped the tendril and grabbed Casey's hand and began running toward the stairs.

"Oh!"

They both stopped short at the bottom of the stairway.

Standing at the top was their father, glaring down at them, his hands balled into tight fists at his sides, his face rigid with anger.

7

"Dad — the plants!" Margaret cried.

He stared down at them, his eyes cold and angry, unblinking. He was silent.

"One grabbed Casey!" Margaret told him.

"I just went down to get my shirt," Casey said, his voice trembling.

They stared up at him expectantly, waiting for him to move, to unball his fists, to relax his hard expression, to speak. But he glared down at them for the longest time.

Finally, he said, "You're okay?"

"Yeah," they said in unison, both of them nodding.

Margaret realized she was still holding Casey's hand. She let go of it and reached for the banister.

"I'm very disappointed in you both," Dr. Brewer said in a low, flat voice, cool but not angry.

"Sorry," Margaret said. "We knew we shouldn't — "

162

"We didn't touch anything. Really!" Casey exclaimed.

"Very disappointed," their father repeated.

"Sorry, Dad."

Dr. Brewer motioned for them to come upstairs, then he stepped into the hallway.

"I thought he was going to yell at us," Casey whispered to Margaret as he followed her up the steps.

"That's not Dad's style," Margaret whispered back.

"He sure yelled at us the *last* time we started into the basement," Casey replied.

They followed their father into the kitchen. He motioned for them to sit down at the white Formica table, then dropped into a chair across from them.

His eyes went from one to the other, as if studying them, as if seeing them for the first time. His expression was totally flat, almost robotlike, revealing no emotion at all.

"Dad, what's with those plants?" Casey asked.

"What do you mean?" Dr. Brewer asked.

"They're — so weird," Casey said.

"I'll explain them to you some day," he said flatly, still staring at the two of them.

"It looks very interesting," Margaret said, struggling to say the right thing.

Was their dad *trying* to make them feel uncomfortable? she wondered. If so, he was doing a good job of it.

This wasn't like him. Not at all. He was always a very direct person, Margaret thought. If he was angry, he said he was angry. If he was upset, he'd tell them he was upset.

So why was he acting so strange, so silent, so . . . cold?

"I asked you not to go in the basement," he said quietly, crossing his legs and leaning back so that the kitchen chair tilted back on two legs. "I thought I made it clear."

Margaret and Casey glanced at each other. Finally, Margaret said, "We won't do it again."

"But can't you take us down there and tell us what you're doing?" Casey asked. He still hadn't put the T-shirt on. He was holding it in a ball between his hands on the kitchen table.

"Yeah. We'd really like to understand it," Margaret added enthusiastically.

"Some day," their father said. He returned the chair to all four legs and then stood up. "We'll do it soon, okay?" He raised his arms above his head and stretched. "I've got to get back to work." He disappeared into the front hallway.

Casey raised his eyes to Margaret and shrugged. Their father reappeared carrying the lab coat he had tossed over the front banister.

"Mom got off okay?" Margaret asked.

He nodded. "I guess." He pulled on the lab coat over his head.

"I hope Aunt Eleanor is okay," Margaret said.

Dr. Brewer's reply was muffled as he adjusted the lab coat and straightened the collar. "Later," he said. He disappeared into the hallway. They heard him shut the basement door behind him.

"I guess he's not going to ground us or anything for going down there," Margaret said, leaning against the table and resting her chin in her hands.

"I guess," Casey said. "He sure is acting . . . weird."

"Maybe he's upset because Mom is gone," Margaret said. She sat up and gave Casey a push. "Come on. Get up. I've got work to do."

"I can't believe that plant grabbed me," Casey said thoughtfully, not budging.

"You don't have to push," Casey griped, but he climbed to his feet and stepped out of Margaret's way. "I'm going to have bad dreams tonight," he said glumly.

"Just don't think about the basement," Margaret advised. That's really lame advice, she told herself. But what else could she say?

She went up to her room, thinking about how she missed her mother already. Then the scene in the basement with Casey trying to pull himself free of the enormous, twining plant tendrils played once again through her mind.

With a shudder, she grabbed her textbook and threw herself onto her stomach on the bed, prepared to read.

But the words on the page blurred as the moaning, breathing plants kept creeping back into her thoughts.

At least we're not being punished for going down there, she thought.

At least Dad didn't yell and frighten us this time.

And at least Dad has promised to take us downstairs with him soon and explain to us what he's working on down there.

That thought made Margaret feel a lot better.

She felt better until the next morning when she awoke early and went downstairs to make some breakfast. To her surprise, her father was already at work, the basement door was shut tight, and a lock had been installed on the door.

The next Saturday afternoon, Margaret was up in her room, lying on top of the bed, talking to her mom on the phone. "I'm really sorry about Aunt Eleanor," she said, twisting the white phone cord around her wrist.

"The surgery didn't go as well as expected," her mother said, sounding very tired. "The doctors say she may have to have more surgery. But they have to build up her strength first."

"I guess this means you won't be coming home real soon," Margaret said sadly.

Mrs. Brewer laughed. "Don't tell me you actually miss me!"

"Well . . . yes," Margaret admitted. She raised her eyes to the bedroom window. Two sparrows had landed outside on the window ledge and were chattering excitedly, distracting Margaret, making it hard to hear her mother over the crackling line from Tucson.

"How's your father doing?" Mrs. Brewer asked. "I spoke to him last night, but he only grunted."

"He doesn't even grunt to us!" Margaret complained. She held her hand over her ear to drown out the chattering birds. "He hardly says a word."

"He's working really hard," Mrs. Brewer replied. In the background, Margaret could hear some kind of loudspeaker announcement. Her mother was calling from a pay phone at the hospital.

"He never comes out of the basement," Margaret complained, a little more bitterly than she had intended.

"Your father's experiments are very important to him," her mother said.

"More important than *we* are?" Margaret cried. She hated the whiny tone in her voice. She wished she hadn't started complaining about her dad over the phone. Her mother had enough to worry about at the hospital. Margaret knew she shouldn't make her feel even worse.

"Your dad has a lot to prove," Mrs. Brewer said. "To himself, and to others. I think he's working so hard because he wants to prove to Mr. Martinez and the others at the university that they were wrong to fire him. He wants to show them that they made a big mistake."

"But we used to see him more *before* he was home all the time!" Margaret complained.

She could hear her mother sigh impatiently. "Margaret, I'm trying to explain to you. You're old enough to understand."

"I'm sorry," Margaret said quickly. She decided to change the subject. "He's wearing a baseball cap all of a sudden."

"Who? Casey?"

"No, Mom," Margaret replied. "Dad. He's wearing a Dodgers cap. He never takes it off."

"Really?" Mrs. Brewer sounded very surprised.

Margaret laughed. "We told him he looks really dorky in it, but he refuses to take it off."

Mrs. Brewer laughed, too. "Uh-oh. I'm being

168

called," she said. "Got to run. Take care, dear. I'll try to call back later."

A click, and she was gone.

Margaret stared up at the ceiling, watching shadows from trees in the front yard move back and forth. The sparrows had flown away, leaving silence behind.

Poor Mom, Margaret thought.

She's so worried about her sister, and I had to go and complain about Dad.

Why did I do that?

She sat up, listening to the silence. Casey was over at a friend's. Her dad was no doubt working in the basement, the door carefully locked behind him.

Maybe I'll give Diane a call, Margaret thought. She reached for the phone, then realized she was hungry. Lunch first, she decided. Then Diane.

She brushed her dark hair quickly, shaking her head at the mirror over her dressing table, then hurried downstairs.

To her surprise, her dad was in the kitchen. He was huddled over the sink, his back to her.

She started to call out to him, but stopped. What was he doing?

Curious, she pressed against the wall, gazing at him through the doorway to the kitchen.

Dr. Brewer appeared to be eating something. With one hand, he was holding a bag on the

169

counter beside the sink. As Margaret watched in surprise, he dipped his hand into the bag, pulled out a big handful of something, and shoved it into his mouth.

Margaret watched him chew hungrily, noisily, then pull out another handful from the bag and eat it greedily.

What on earth is he eating? she wondered. He never eats with Casey and me. He always says he isn't hungry. But he sure is hungry now! He acts as if he's starving!

She watched from the doorway as Dr. Brewer continued to grab handful after handful from the bag, gulping down his solitary meal. After a while, he crinkled up the bag and tossed it into the trash can under the sink. Then he wiped his hands off on the sides of his white lab coat.

Margaret quickly backed away from the door, tiptoed through the hall and ducked into the living room. She held her breath as her father came into the hall, clearing his throat loudly.

The basement door closed behind him. She heard him carefully lock it.

When she was sure that he had gone downstairs, Margaret walked eagerly into the kitchen. She had to know what her father had been eating so greedily, so hungrily.

She pulled open the sink cabinet, reached into

the trash, and pulled out the crinkled-up bag.

Then she gasped aloud as her eyes ran over the label.

Her father, she saw, had been devouring *plant food*.

Margaret swallowed hard. Her mouth felt dry as
cotton. She suddenly realized she was squeezing
the side of the counter so tightly, her hand ached.

Forcing herself to loosen her grip, she stared
down at the half-empty plant food bag, which she
had dropped onto the floor.

She felt sick. She couldn't get the disgusting
picture out of her mind. How could her dad eat
mud?

He didn't just eat it, she realized. He shoveled
it into his mouth and gulped it down.

As if he *liked* it.

As if he *needed* it.

Eating the plant food had to be part of his experiments, Margaret told herself. But what *kind*
of experiments? What was he trying to prove with
those strange plants he was growing?

The stuff inside the bag smelled sour, like fer-
tilizer. Margaret took a deep breath and held it.
She suddenly felt sick to her stomach. Staring at

the bag, she couldn't help but imagine what the disgusting muck inside must taste like.

Ohh.

She nearly gagged.

How could her own father shove this horrid stuff into his mouth?

Still holding her breath, she grabbed the nearly empty bag, wadded it up, and tossed it back into the trash. She started to turn away from the counter when a hand grabbed her shoulder.

Margaret uttered a silent cry and spun around. "Casey!"

"I'm home," he said, grinning at her. "What's for lunch?"

Later, after making him a peanut butter sandwich, she told Casey what she had seen.

Casey laughed.

"It isn't funny," she said crossly. "Our own dad was eating dirt."

Casey laughed again. For some reason, it struck him funny.

Margaret punched him hard on the shoulder, so hard that he dropped his sandwich. "Sorry," she said quickly, "but I don't see what you're laughing at. It's sick! There's something wrong with Dad. Something really wrong."

"Maybe he just had a craving for plant food," Casey cracked, still not taking her seriously. "You know. Like you get a craving for those honey-roasted peanuts."

"That's different," Margaret snapped. "Eating dirt is disgusting. Why won't you admit it?"

But before Casey could reply, Margaret continued, letting all of her unhappiness out at once. "Don't you see? Dad has changed. A lot. Even since Mom has been gone. He spends even more time in the basement — "

"That's because Mom isn't around," Casey interrupted.

"And he's so quiet all the time and so cold to us," Margaret continued, ignoring him. "He hardly says a word to us. He used to kid around all the time and ask us about our homework. He never says a human word. He never calls me Princess or Fatso the way he used to. He never — "

"You hate those names, Fatso," Casey said, giggling with a mouthful of peanut butter.

"I know," Margaret said impatiently. "That's just an example."

"So what are you trying to say?" Casey asked. "That Dad is out of his tree? That he's gone totally bananas?"

"I — I don't know," Margaret answered in frustration. "Watching him gulp down that disgusting plant food, I — I had this horrible thought that he's turning *into* a plant!"

Casey jumped up, causing his chair to scrape

174

back across the floor. He began staggering around the kitchen, zombielike, his eyes closed, his arms stretched out stiffly in front of him. "I am The Incredible Plant Man!" he declared, trying to make his voice sound bold and deep.

"Not funny," Margaret insisted, crossing her arms over her chest, refusing to be amused.

"Plant Man versus Weed Woman!" Casey declared, staggering toward Margaret.

"Not funny," she repeated.

He bumped into the counter, banging his knee. "Ow!"

"Serves you right," Margaret said.

"Plant Man kills!" he cried, and rushed at her. He ran right into her, using his head as a battering ram against her shoulder.

"Casey — will you stop it!" she screamed. "Give me a break!"

"Okay, okay." He backed off. "If you'll do me one favor."

"What favor?" Margaret asked, rolling her eyes.

"Make me another sandwich."

Monday afternoon after school, Margaret, Casey, and Diane were tossing a Frisbee back and forth in Diane's backyard. It was a warm, breezy day, the sky dotted with small, puffy white clouds.

Diane tossed the disc high. It sailed over

Casey's head into the row of fragrant lemon trees that stretched from behind the clapboard garage. Casey went running after it and tripped over an in-ground sprinkler that poked up just an inch above the lawn.

Both girls laughed.

Casey, on the run, flung the Frisbee toward Margaret. She reached for it, but the breeze sent it sailing from her hand.

"What's it like to have a mad scientist for a dad?" Diane asked suddenly.

"What?" Margaret wasn't sure she heard right.

"Don't just stand there. Throw it!" Casey urged from beside the garage.

Margaret tossed the Frisbee high in the air in her brother's general direction. He liked to run and make diving catches.

"Just because he's doing strange experiments doesn't mean he's a mad scientist," Margaret said sharply.

"Strange is right," Diane said, her expression turning serious. "I had a nightmare last night about those gross plants in your basement. They were crying and reaching for me."

"Sorry," Margaret said sincerely. "I've had nightmares, too."

"Look out!" Casey cried. He tossed a low one that Diane caught around her ankles.

Mad scientist, Margaret thought. Mad scientist. Mad scientist.

The words kept repeating in her mind.

Mad scientists were only in the movies — right?

"My dad was talking about your dad the other night," Diane said, flipping the disc to Casey.

"You didn't tell him about — going down in the basement? Did you?" Margaret asked anxiously.

"No," Diane replied, shaking her head.

"Hey, are these lemons ripe?" Casey asked, pointing at one of the low trees.

"Why don't you suck one to find out?" Margaret snapped, annoyed that he kept interrupting.

"Why don't *you*?" he predictably shot back.

"My dad said that your dad was fired from PolyTech because his experiments got out of control, and he wouldn't stop them," Diane confided. She ran along the smooth, closely cropped grass, chasing down the Frisbee.

"What do you mean?" Margaret asked.

"The university told him he had to stop whatever it was he was doing, and he refused. He said he couldn't stop. At least that's what my dad heard from a guy who came into the salesroom."

Margaret hadn't heard this story. It made her feel bad, but she thought it was probably true.

"Something really bad happened in your dad's

lab," Diane continued. "Someone got really hurt or killed or something."

"That's not true," Margaret insisted. "We would've heard if that happened."

"Yeah. Probably," Diane admitted. "But my dad said your dad was fired because he refused to stop his experiments."

"Well, that doesn't make him a mad scientist," Margaret said defensively. She suddenly felt she had to stick up for her father. She wasn't sure why.

"I'm just telling you what I heard," Diane said, brusquely tossing back her red hair. "You don't have to bite my head off."

They played for a few more minutes. Diane changed the subject and talked about some kids they knew who were eleven but were going steady. Then they talked about school for a while.

"Time to go," Margaret called to Casey. He picked the Frisbee up from the lawn and came running over. "Call you later," Margaret told Diane, giving her a little wave. Then she and Casey began to jog home, cutting through familiar backyards.

"We need a lemon tree," Casey said as they slowed to a walk. "They're cool."

"Oh, yeah," Margaret replied sarcastically. "That's just what we need at our house. Another plant!"

As they stepped through the hedges into their backyard, they were both surprised to see their dad. He was standing at the rose trellis examining clusters of pink roses.

"Hey, Dad!" Casey called. "Catch!" He tossed the Frisbee to his father.

Dr. Brewer turned around a little too slowly. The Frisbee glanced off his head, knocking the Dodgers cap off. His mouth opened wide in surprise. He raised his hands to cover his head.

But it was too late.

Margaret and Casey both shrieked in surprise as they saw his head.

At first, Margaret thought her father's hair had turned green.

But then she clearly saw that it wasn't hair on his scalp.

His hair was gone. It had all fallen out.

In place of hair, Dr. Brewer had bright green leaves sprouting from his head.

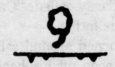

9

"Kids — it's okay!" Dr. Brewer called. He bent down quickly, picked up the baseball cap, and replaced it on his head.

A crow flew low overhead, cawing loudly. Margaret raised her eyes to follow the bird, but the sight of the hideous leaves sprouting from her father's head wouldn't go away.

Her whole head began to itch as she imagined what it must feel like to have leaves uncurling from your scalp.

"It's okay. Really," Dr. Brewer repeated, hurrying over to them.

"But, Dad — your head," Casey stammered. He suddenly looked very pale.

Margaret felt sick. She kept swallowing hard, trying to ride out the waves of nausea.

"Come here, you two," their father said softly, putting an arm around each of their shoulders. "Let's sit down in the shade over there and have a talk. I spoke to your mom on the phone this morning. She told me you're upset about my work."

"Your head — it's all green!" Casey repeated.

"I know," Dr. Brewer said, smiling. "That's why I put on the cap. I didn't want you two to worry."

He led them to the shade of the tall hedges that ran along the garage, and they sat down on the grass. "I guess you two think your dad has gotten pretty weird, huh?"

He stared into Margaret's eyes. Feeling uncomfortable, she looked away.

Cawing frantically, the crow flew over again, heading in the other direction.

"Margaret, you haven't said a word," her father said, squeezing her hand tenderly between his. "What's wrong? What do you want to say to me?"

Margaret sighed and still avoided her father's glance. "Come on. Tell us. Why do you have leaves growing out of your head?" she asked bluntly.

"It's a side effect," he told her, continuing to hold her hand. "It's only temporary. It'll go away soon and my hair will grow back."

"But how did it happen?" Casey asked, staring at his father's Dodgers cap. A few green leaves poked out from under the brim.

"Maybe you two would feel better if I explained what I'm trying to do down in the basement," Dr. Brewer said, shifting his weight and leaning back on his hands. "I've been so wrapped up in my experiments, I haven't had much time to talk to you."

"You haven't had *any* time," Margaret corrected him.

"I'm sorry," he said, lowering his eyes. "I really am. But this work I'm doing is so exciting and so difficult."

"Did you discover a new kind of plant?" Casey asked, crossing his legs beneath him.

"No, I'm trying to *build* a new kind of plant," Dr. Brewer explained.

"Huh?" Casey exclaimed.

"Have you ever talked about DNA in school?" their father asked. They shook their heads. "Well, it's pretty complicated," he continued. Dr. Brewer thought for a moment. "Let me try and put it in simple terms," he said, fiddling with the bandage around his hand. "Let's say we took a person who had a very high IQ. You know. Real brain power."

"Like me," Casey interrupted.

"Casey, shut up," Margaret said edgily.

"A real brain. Like Casey," Dr. Brewer said agreeably. "And let's say we were able to isolate the molecule or gene or tiny part of a gene that enabled the person to have such high intelligence. And then let's say we were able to transmit it into other brains. And then this brain power could be passed along from generation to generation. And lots of people would have a high IQ. Do you understand?" He looked first at Casey, then at Margaret.

"Yeah. Kind of," Margaret said. "You take a good quality from one person and put it into other people. And then they have the good quality, too, and they pass it on to their children, and on and on."

"Very good," Dr. Brewer said, smiling for the first time in weeks. "That's what a lot of botanists do with plants. They try to take the fruit-bearing building block from one plant and put it into another. Create a new plant that will bear five times as much fruit, or five times as much grain, or vegetables."

"And that's what you're doing?" Casey asked.

"Not exactly," their father said, lowering his voice. "I'm doing something a little more unusual. I really don't want to go into detail now. But I'll tell you that what I'm trying to do is build a kind of plant that has never existed and *could* never exist. I'm trying to build a plant that's *part animal*."

Casey and Margaret stared at their father in surprise. Margaret was the first to speak. "You mean you're taking cells from an animal and putting them into a plant?"

He nodded. "I really don't want to say more. You two understand why this must be kept secret." He turned his eyes on Margaret, then Casey, studying their reactions.

"How do you do it?" Margaret asked, thinking hard about everything he had just told them. "How do you get these cells from the animals to the plant?"

"I'm trying to do it by breaking them down electronically," he answered. "I have two glass booths connected by a powerful electron generator. You may have seen them when you were snooping around down there." He made a sour face.

"Yeah. They look like phone booths," Casey said.

"One booth is a sender, and one is a receiver," he explained. "I'm trying to send the right DNA, the right building blocks, from one booth to the other. It's very delicate work."

"And have you done it?" Margaret asked.

"I've come very close," Dr. Brewer said, a pleased smile crossing his face. The smile lasted only a few seconds. Then, his expression thoughtful, he abruptly climbed to his feet. "Got to get back to work," he said quietly. "See you two later." He started walking across the lawn, taking long strides.

"But, Dad," Margaret called after him. She and Casey climbed to their feet, too. "Your head. The leaves. You didn't explain it," she said as she and her brother hurried to catch up to him.

Dr. Brewer shrugged. "Nothing to explain," he said curtly. "Just a side effect." He adjusted his Dodgers cap. "Don't worry about it. It's only temporary. Just a side effect."

Then he hurried into the house.

Casey seemed really pleased by their dad's explanation of what was going on in the basement. "Dad's doing really important work," he said, with unusual seriousness.

But, as Margaret made her way into the house, she found herself troubled by what her dad had said. And even more troubled by what he *hadn't* said.

Margaret closed the door to her room and lay down on the bed to think about things. Her father hadn't really explained the leaves growing on his head. "Just a side effect" didn't explain much at all.

A side effect from what? What actually caused it? What made his hair fall out? When will his hair grow back?

It was obvious that he hadn't wanted to discuss it with them. He had certainly hurried back to his basement after telling them it was just a side effect.

185

A side effect.

It made Margaret feel sick every time she thought about it.

What must it feel like? Green leaves pushing up from your pores, uncurling against your head.

Yuck. Thinking about it made her itch all over. She knew she'd have hideous dreams tonight.

She grabbed her pillow and hugged it over her stomach, wrapping her arms tightly around it.

There were lots of other questions Casey and I should have asked, she decided. Like, why were the plants moaning down there? Why did some of them sound like they were breathing? Why did that plant grab Casey? What animal was Dad using?

Lots of questions.

Not to mention the one Margaret wanted to ask most of all: Why were you gulping down that disgusting plant food?

But she couldn't ask that one. She couldn't let her dad know she'd been spying on him.

She and Casey hadn't really asked any of the questions they'd wanted answered. They were just so pleased that their father had decided to sit down and talk with them, even for a few minutes.

His explanation was really interesting, as far as it went, Margaret decided. And it was good to know that he was close to doing something truly amazing, something that would make him really famous.

But what about the rest of it?

A frightening thought entered her mind: Could he have been lying to them?

No, she quickly decided. No. Dad wouldn't lie to us.

There are just some questions he hasn't answered yet.

She was still thinking about all of these questions late that night — after dinner, after talking to Diane on the phone for an hour, after homework, after watching a little TV, after going to bed. And she was still puzzling over them.

When she heard her father's soft footsteps coming up the carpeted stairs, she sat up in bed. A soft breeze fluttered the curtains across the room. She listened to her father's footsteps pass her room, heard him go into the bathroom, heard the water begin to run into the sink.

I've got to ask him, she decided.

Glancing at the clock, she saw that it was two-thirty in the morning.

But she realized she was wide awake.

I've got to ask him about the plant food.

Otherwise, it will drive me crazy. I'll think about it and think about it and think about it. Every time I see him, I'll picture him standing over the sink, shoving handful after handful into his mouth.

There's got to be a simple explanation, she told herself, climbing out of bed. There's got to be a *logical* explanation.

And I have to know it.

She padded softly down the hall, a sliver of light escaping through the bathroom door, which was slightly ajar. Water still ran into the sink.

She heard him cough, then heard him adjust the water.

I have to know the answer, she thought.

I'll just ask him point-blank.

She stepped into the narrow triangle of light and peered into the bathroom.

He was standing at the sink, leaning over it, his chest bare, his shirt tossed behind him on the floor. He had put the baseball cap on the closed toilet lid, and the leaves covering his head shone brightly under the bathroom light.

Margaret held her breath.

The leaves were so geeen, so thick.

He didn't notice her. He was concentrating on the bandage on his hand. Using a small scissors, he cut the bandage, then pulled it off.

The hand was still bleeding, Margaret saw.

Or was it?

What *was* that dripping from the cut on her father's hand?

Still holding her breath, she watched him wash it off carefully under the hot water. Then he examined it, his eyes narrowed in concentration.

After washing, the cut continued to bleed.

Margaret stared hard, trying to better focus her eyes.

It couldn't be blood — could it?

It couldn't be blood dripping into the sink.

It was bright green!

She gasped and started to run back to her room. The floor creaked under her footsteps.

"Who's there?" Dr. Brewer cried. "Margaret? Casey?"

He poked his head into the hallway as Margaret disappeared back into her room.

He saw me, she realized, leaping into bed.

He saw me — and now he's coming after me.

10

Margaret pulled the covers up to her chin. She realized she was trembling, her whole body shaking and chilled.

She held her breath and listened.

She could still hear water splashing into the bathroom sink.

But no footsteps.

He isn't coming after me, she told herself, letting out a long, silent sigh.

How could I have thought that? How could I have been so terrified — of my own father?

Terrified.

It was the first time the word had crossed her mind.

But sitting there in bed, trembling so violently, holding onto the covers so hard, listening for his approaching footsteps, Margaret realized that she was terrified.

Of her own father.

If only Mom were home, she thought.

Without thinking, she reached for the phone. She had the idea in her head to call her mother, wake her up, tell her to come home as fast as she could. Tell her something terrible was happening to Dad. That he was changing. That he was acting so weird. . . .

She glanced at the clock. Two-forty-three.

No. She couldn't do that. Her poor mother was having such a terrible time in Tucson trying to care for her sister. Margaret couldn't frighten her like that.

Besides, what could she say? How could she explain to her mother how she had become terrified of her own father?

Mrs. Brewer would just tell her to calm down. That her father still loved her. That he would never harm her. That he was just caught up in his work.

Caught up. . . .

He had leaves growing out of his head, he was eating dirt, and his blood was green.

Caught up. . . .

She heard the water in the sink shut off. She heard the bathroom light being clicked off. Then she heard her father pad slowly to his room at the end of the hall.

Margaret relaxed a little, slid down in the bed, loosened her grip on the blankets. She closed her eyes and tried to clear her mind.

She tried counting sheep.

That never worked. She tried counting to one thousand. At 375, she sat up. Her head throbbed. Her mouth was as dry as cotton.

She decided to go downstairs and get a drink of cold water from the refrigerator.

I'm going to be a wreck tomorrow, she thought, making her way silently through the hall and down the stairs.

It *is* tomorrow.

What am I going to do? I've got to get to sleep.

The kitchen floor creaked beneath her bare feet. The refrigerator motor clicked on noisily, startling her.

Be cool, she told herself. You've got to be cool.

She had opened the refrigerator and was reaching for the water bottle when a hand grabbed her shoulder.

"Aii!" She cried out and dropped the open bottle onto the floor. Ice-cold water puddled around her feet. She leapt back, but her feet were soaked.

"Casey — you scared me!" she exclaimed. "What are you doing up?"

"What are *you* doing up?" he replied, half asleep, his blond hair matted against his forehead.

"I couldn't sleep. Help me mop up this water."

"I didn't spill it," he said, backing away. "You mop it up."

"You *made* me spill it!" Margaret declared

shrilly. She grabbed a roll of paper towels off the counter and handed him a wad of them. "Come on. Hurry."

They both got down on their knees and, by the light from the refrigerator, began mopping up the cold water.

"I just keep thinking about things," Casey said, tossing a soaking wad of paper towel onto the counter. "That's why I can't sleep."

"Me, too," Margaret said, frowning.

She started to say something else, but a sound from the hallway stopped her. It was a plaintive cry, a moan filled with sadness.

Margaret gasped and stopped dabbing at the water. "What was that?"

Casey's eyes filled with fear.

They heard it again, such a sad sound, like a plea, a mournful plea.

"It — it's coming from the basement," Margaret said.

"Do you think it's a plant?" Casey asked very quietly. "Do you think it's one of Dad's plants?"

Margaret didn't answer. She crouched on her knees, not moving, just listening.

Another moan, softer this time but just as mournful.

"I don't think Dad told us the truth," she told Casey, staring into his eyes. He looked pale and frightened in the dim refrigerator light. "I don't

193

think a tomato plant would make a sound like that."

Margaret climbed to her feet, collected the wet clumps of paper towel, and deposited them in the trash can under the sink. Then she closed the refrigerator door, covering the room in darkness.

Her hand on Casey's shoulder, she guided him out of the kitchen and through the hall. They stopped at the basement door, and listened.

Silence now.

Casey tried the door. It was locked.

Another low moan, sounding very nearby now.

"It's so human," Casey whispered.

Margaret shuddered. What was going on down in the basement? What was *really* going on?

She led the way up the stairs and waited at her doorway until Casey was safely in his room. He gave her a wave, yawning silently, and closed the door behind him.

A few seconds later, Margaret was back in her bed, the covers pulled up to her chin despite the warmth of the night. Her mouth was still achingly dry, she realized. She had never managed to get a drink.

Somehow she drifted into a restless sleep.

Her alarm went off at seven-thirty. She sat up and thought about school. Then she remembered there was no school for the next two days because of some kind of teachers' conference.

She turned off the clock radio, slumped back onto her pillow, and tried to go back to sleep. But she was awake now, thoughts of the night before pouring back into her mind, flooding her with the fear she had felt just a few hours earlier.

She stood up and stretched, and decided to go talk to her father, to confront him first thing, to ask all the questions she wanted to ask.

If I don't, he'll disappear down to the basement, and I'll sit around thinking these frightening thoughts all day, she told herself.

I don't want to be terrified of my own father.

I don't.

She pulled a light cotton robe over her pajamas, found her slippers in the cluttered closet, and stepped out into the hallway. It was hot and stuffy in the hall, almost suffocating. Pale, morning light filtered down from the skylight overhead.

She stopped in front of Casey's room, wondering if she should wake him so that he could ask their father questions, too.

No, she decided. The poor guy was up half the night. I'll let him sleep.

Taking a deep breath, she walked the rest of the hall and stopped at her parents' bedroom. The door was open.

"Dad?"

No reply.

"Dad? Are you up?"

195

She stepped into the room. "Dad?"

He didn't seem to be there.

The air in here was heavy and smelled strangely sour. The curtains were drawn. The bedclothes were rumpled and tossed down at the foot of the bed. Margaret took a few more steps toward the bed.

"Dad?"

No. She had missed him. He was probably already locked in his basement workroom, she realized unhappily.

He must have gotten up very early and —

What was that in the bed?

Margaret clicked on a dresser lamp and stepped up beside the bed.

"Oh, no!" she cried, raising her hands to her face in horror.

The bedsheet was covered with a thick layer of dirt. Clumps of dirt.

Margaret stared down at it, not breathing, not moving.

The dirt was black and appeared to be moist.

And the dirt was moving.

Moving?

It can't be, Margaret thought. That's impossible.

She leaned down to take a closer look at the layer of dirt.

No. The dirt wasn't moving.

The dirt was filled with dozens of moving insects. And long, brown earthworms. All crawling through the wet, black clumps that lined her father's bed.

11

Casey didn't come downstairs until ten-thirty. Before his arrival, Margaret had made herself breakfast, managed to pull on jeans and a T-shirt, had talked to Diane on the phone for half an hour, and had spent the rest of the time pacing back and forth in the living room, trying to decide what to do.

Desperate to talk to her dad, she had banged a few times on the basement door, timidly at first and then loudly. But he either couldn't hear her or chose not to. He didn't respond.

When Casey finally emerged, she poured him a tall glass of orange juice and led him out to the backyard to talk. It was a hazy day, the sky mostly yellow, the air already stifling hot even though the sun was still hovering low over the hills.

Walking toward the block of green shade cast by the hedges, she told her brother about their dad's green blood and about the insect-filled dirt in his bed.

Casey stood open-mouthed, holding the glass of orange juice in front of him, untouched. He stared at Margaret, and didn't say anything for a very long time.

Finally, he set the orange juice down on the lawn and said, "What should we do?" in a voice just above a whisper.

Margaret shrugged. "I wish Mom would call."

"Would you tell her everything?" Casey asked, shoving his hands deep into the pockets of his baggy shorts.

"I guess," Margaret said. "I don't know if she'd believe it, but —"

"It's so scary," Casey said. "I mean, he's our dad. We've known him our whole lives. I mean —"

"I know," Margaret said. "But he's not the same. He's —"

"Maybe he can explain it all," Casey said thoughtfully. "Maybe there's a good reason for everything. You know. Like the leaves on his head."

"We asked him about that," Margaret reminded her brother. "He just said it was a side effect. Not much of an explanation."

Casey nodded, but didn't reply.

"I told some of it to Diane," Margaret admitted.

Casey looked up at her in surprise.

"Well, I had to tell *somebody*," she snapped

edgily. "Diane thought I should call the police."

"Huh?" Casey shook his head. "Dad hasn't done anything wrong — has he? What would the police do?"

"I know," Margaret replied. "That's what I told Diane. But she said there's got to be some kind of law against being a mad scientist."

"Dad isn't a mad scientist," Casey said angrily. "That's stupid. He's just — He's just —"

Just what? Margaret thought. What *is* he?

A few hours later, they were still in the backyard, trying to figure out what to do, when the kitchen door opened and their father called them to come in.

Margaret looked at Casey in surprise. "I don't believe it. He came upstairs."

"Maybe we can talk to him," Casey said.

They both raced into the kitchen. Dr. Brewer, his Dodgers cap in place, flashed them a smile as he set two soup bowls down on the table. "Hi," he said brightly. "Lunchtime."

"Huh? You made lunch?" Casey exclaimed, unable to conceal his astonishment.

"Dad, we've got to talk," Margaret said seriously.

"Afraid I don't have much time," he said, avoiding her stare. "Sit down. Try this new dish. I want to see if you like it."

Margaret and Casey obediently took their places at the table. "What *is* this stuff?" Casey cried.

The two bowls were filled with a green, pulpy substance. "It looks like green mashed potatoes," Casey said, making a face.

"It's something different," Dr. Brewer said mysteriously, standing over them at the head of the table. "Go ahead. Taste it. I'll bet you'll be surprised."

"Dad — you've never made lunch for us before," Margaret said, trying to keep the suspicion out of her voice.

"I just wanted you to try this," he said, his smile fading. "You're my guinea pigs."

"We have some things we want to ask you," Margaret said, lifting her spoon, but not eating the green mess.

"Your mother called this morning," their father said.

"When?" Margaret asked eagerly.

"Just a short while ago. I guess you were outside and didn't hear the phone ring."

"What did she say?" Casey asked, staring down at the bowl in front of him.

"Aunt Eleanor's doing better. She's been moved out of intensive care. Your mom may be able to come home soon."

"Great!" Margaret and Casey cried in unison.

"Eat," Dr. Brewer instructed, pointing to the bowls.

"Uh . . . aren't you going to have some?" Casey asked, rolling his spoon around in his fingers.

"No," their father replied quickly. "I already ate." He leaned with both hands against the tabletop. Margaret saw that his cut hand was freshly bandaged.

"Dad, last night —" she started.

But he cut her off. "Eat, will you? Try it."

"But what *is* it?" Casey demanded, whining. "It doesn't smell too good."

"I think you'll like the taste," Dr. Brewer insisted impatiently. "It should taste very sweet."

He stared at them, urging them to eat the green stuff.

Staring into the bowl at the mysterious substance, Margaret was suddenly frozen with fear. He's too eager for us to eat this, she thought, glancing up at her brother.

He's too desperate.

He's never made lunch before. Why did he make this?

And why won't he tell us what it is?

What's going on here? she wondered. And Casey's expression revealed that he was wondering the same thing.

Is Dad trying to do something to us? Is this

202

green stuff going to change us, or hurt us . . . or make us grow leaves, too?

What crazy thoughts, Margaret realized.

But she also realized that she was terrified of whatever this stuff was he was trying to feed them.

"What's the matter with you two?" their father cried impatiently. He raised his hand in an eating gesture. "Pick up your spoons. Come on. What are you waiting for?"

Margaret and Casey raised their spoons and dropped them into the soft, green substance. But they didn't raise the spoons to their mouths.

They couldn't.

"Eat! Eat!" Dr. Brewer screamed, pounding the table with his good hand. "What are you waiting for? Eat your lunch. Go ahead. Eat it!"

He's giving us no choice, Margaret thought.

Her hand was trembling as she reluctantly raised the spoon to her mouth.

12

"Go ahead. You'll like it," Dr. Brewer insisted, leaning over the table.

Casey watched as Margaret raised the spoon to her lips.

The doorbell rang.

"Who could that be?" Dr. Brewer asked, very annoyed at the interruption. "I'll be right back, kids." He lumbered out to the front hall.

"Saved by the bell," Margaret said, dropping the spoon back into the bowl with a sickening plop.

"This stuff is disgusting," Casey whispered. "It's some kind of plant food or something. Yuck!"

"Quick —" Margaret said, jumping up and grabbing the two bowls. "Help me."

They rushed to the sink, pulled out the wastebasket, and scooped the contents of both bowls into the garbage. Then they carried both bowls back to the table and set them down beside the spoons.

"Let's go see who's at the door," Casey said.

They crept into the hall in time to see a man carrying a black briefcase step into the front entranceway and greet their father with a short handshake. The man had a tanned bald head and was wearing large, blue-lensed sunglasses. He had a brown mustache and was wearing a navy blue suit with a red-and-white striped tie.

"Mr. Martinez!" their father exclaimed. "What a . . . surprise."

"That's Dad's old boss from PolyTech," Margaret whispered to Casey.

"I *know*," Casey replied peevishly.

"I said weeks ago I'd come check up on how your work is coming along," Martinez said, sniffing the air for some reason. "Wellington gave me a lift. My car is in the garage — for a change."

"Well, I'm not really ready," Dr. Brewer stammered, looking very uncomfortable even from Margaret's vantage point behind him. "I wasn't expecting anyone. I mean . . . I don't think this is a good time."

"No problem. I'll just have a quick look," Martinez said, putting a hand on Dr. Brewer's shoulder as if to calm him. "I've always been so interested in your work. You know that. And you know that it wasn't *my* idea to let you go. The board forced me. They gave me no choice. But

I'm not giving up on you. I promise you that. Come on. Let's see what kind of progress you're making."

"Well . . ." Dr. Brewer couldn't hide his displeasure at Mr. Martinez's surprise appearance. He scowled and tried to block the path to the basement steps.

At least, it seemed that way to Margaret, who watched silently beside her brother.

Mr. Martinez stepped past Dr. Brewer and pulled open the basement door. "Hi, guys." Mr. Martinez gave the two kids a wave, hoisting his briefcase as if it weighed two tons.

Their father looked surprised to see them there. "Did you kids finish your lunch?"

"Yeah, it was pretty good," Casey lied.

The answer seemed to please Dr. Brewer. Adjusting the brim of his Dodgers cap, he followed Mr. Martinez into the basement, carefully closing and locking the door behind him.

"Maybe he'll give Dad his job back," Casey said, walking back into the kitchen. He pulled open the refrigerator to look for something for lunch.

"Don't be stupid," Margaret said, reaching over him to pull out a container of egg salad. "If Dad really is growing plants that are part animal, he'll be famous. He won't need a job."

"Yeah, I guess," Casey said thoughtfully. "Is that all there is? Just egg salad?"

"I'll make you a sandwich," Margaret offered.

"I'm not really hungry," Casey replied. "That green stuff made me sick. Why do you think he wanted us to eat it?"

"I don't know," Margaret said. She put a hand on Casey's slender shoulder. "I'm really scared, Casey. I wish Mom were home."

"Me, too," he said quietly.

Margaret put the egg salad back into the refrigerator. She closed the door, then leaned her hot forehead against it. "Casey —"

"What?"

"Do you think Dad is telling us the truth?"

"About what?"

"About *anything*?"

"I don't know," Casey said, shaking his head. Then his expression suddenly changed. "There's one way to find out," he said, his eyes lighting up.

"Huh? What do you mean?" Margaret pushed herself away from the refrigerator.

"The first chance we get, the first time Dad is away," Casey whispered, "let's go back down in the basement and see for ourselves what Dad is doing."

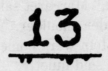

13

They got their chance the next afternoon when their father emerged from the basement, red metal toolchest in hand. "I promised Mr. Henry next door I'd help him install a new sink in his bathroom," he explained, adjusting his Dodgers cap with his free hand.

"When are you coming back?" Casey asked, glancing at Margaret.

Not very subtle, Casey, Margaret thought, rolling her eyes.

"It shouldn't take more than a couple of hours," Dr. Brewer said. He disappeared out the kitchen door.

They watched him cut through the hedges in the backyard and head to Mr. Henry's back door. "It's now or never," Margaret said, glancing doubtfully at Casey. "Think we can do this?" She tried the door. Locked, as usual.

"No problem," Casey said, a mischievous grin spreading across his face. "Go get a paper clip.

I'll show you what my friend Kevin taught me last week."

Margaret obediently found a paper clip on her desk and brought it to him. Casey straightened the clip out, then poked it into the lock. In a few seconds, he hummed a triumphant fanfare and pulled the door open.

"Now you're an expert lock picker, huh? Your friend Kevin is a good guy to know," Margaret said, shaking her head.

Casey grinned and motioned for Margaret to go first.

"Okay. Let's not think about it. Let's just do it," Margaret said, summoning her courage and stepping onto the landing.

A few seconds later, they were in the basement.

Knowing a little of what to expect down here didn't make it any less frightening. They were hit immediately by a blast of steamy, hot air. The air, Margaret realized, was so wet, so thick, that droplets immediately clung to her skin.

Squinting against the sudden bright light, they stopped in the doorway to the plant room. The plants seemed taller, thicker, more plentiful than the first time they had ventured down here.

Long, sinewy tendrils drooped from thick yellow stalks. Broad green and yellow leaves bobbed and trembled, shimmering under the white light. Leaves slapped against each other, making a soft, wet sound. A fat tomato plopped to the ground.

Everything seemed to shimmer. The plants all seemed to quiver expectantly. They weren't standing still. They seemed to be reaching up, reaching out, quaking with energy as they grew.

Long brown tendrils snaked along the dirt, wrapping themselves around other plants, around each other. A bushy fern had grown to the ceiling, curved, and started its way back down again.

"Wow!" Casey cried, impressed with this trembling, glistening jungle. "Are all these plants really brand-new?"

"I guess so," Margaret said softly. "They look prehistoric!"

They heard breathing sounds, loud sighing, a low moan coming from the direction of the supply closet against the wall.

A tendril suddenly swung out from a long stalk. Margaret pulled Casey back. "Look out. Don't get too close," she warned.

"I know," he said sharply, moving away from her. "Don't grab me like that. You scared me."

The tendril slid harmlessly to the dirt.

"Sorry," she said, squeezing his shoulder affectionately. "It's just . . . well, you remember last time."

"I'll be careful," he said.

Margaret shuddered.

She heard breathing. Steady, quiet breathing.

These plants are definitely not normal, she thought. She took a step back, letting her eyes roam over the amazing jungle of slithering, sighing plants.

She was still staring at them when she heard Casey's terrified scream.

"Help! It's got me! It's *got* me!"

14

Margaret uttered a shriek of terror and spun away from the plants to find her brother.

"Help!" Casey cried.

Gripped with fear, Margaret took a few steps toward Casey, then saw the small, gray creature scampering across the floor.

She started to laugh.

"Casey, it's a squirrel!"

"What?" His voice was several octaves higher than normal. "It — it grabbed my ankle and — "

"Look," Margaret said, pointing. "It's a squirrel. Look how scared it is. It must have run right into you."

"Oh." Casey sighed. The color began to return to his ash-gray face. "I thought it was a . . . plant."

"Right. A furry gray plant," Margaret said, shaking her head. Her heart was still thudding in her chest. "You sure gave me a scare, Casey."

The squirrel stopped several yards away,

turned, stood up on its hind legs, and stared back at them, quivering all over.

"How did a squirrel get down here?" Casey demanded, his voice still shaky.

Margaret shrugged. "Squirrels are always getting in," she said. "And remember that chipmunk we couldn't get rid of?" Then she glanced over to the small ground-level window at the top of the opposite wall. "That window — it's open," she told Casey. "The squirrel must have climbed in over there."

"Shoo!" Casey yelled at the squirrel. He started to chase it. The squirrel's tail shot right up in the air, and then it took off, running through the tangled plants. "Get out! Get out!" Casey screamed.

The terrified squirrel, with Casey in close pursuit, circled the plants twice. Then it headed to the far wall, leapt onto a carton, then onto a higher carton, then bounded out the open window.

Casey stopped running and stared up at the window.

"Good work," Margaret said. "Now, let's get out of here. We don't know what anything is. We have no idea what to look for. So we can't tell if Dad is telling the truth or not."

She started toward the stairs, but stopped when she heard the bumping sound. "Casey — did you hear that?" She searched for her brother, but he was hidden by the thick leaves of the plants. "Casey?"

"Yeah. I heard it," he answered, still out of her view. "It's coming from the supply closet."

The loud thumping made Margaret shudder. It sounded to her exactly like someone banging on the closet wall.

"Casey, let's check it out," she said.

No reply.

The banging got louder.

"Casey?"

Why wasn't he answering her?

"Casey — where *are* you? You're frightening me," Margaret called, moving closer to the shimmering plants. Another tomato plopped to the ground, so near her foot, it made her jump.

Despite the intense heat, she suddenly felt cold all over.

"Casey?"

"Margaret — come here. I've found something," he finally said. He sounded uncertain, worried.

She hurried around the plants and saw him standing in front of the worktable beside the supply closet. The banging from the closet had stopped.

"Casey, what's the matter? You scared me," Margaret scolded. She stopped and leaned against the wooden worktable.

"Look," her brother said, holding up a dark, folded-up bundle. "I found this. On the floor. Shoved under this worktable."

"Huh? What is it?" Margaret asked.

Casey unfolded it. It was a suit jacket. A blue suit jacket. A red-striped necktie was folded inside it.

"It's Mr. Martinez's," Casey said, squeezing the collar of the wrinkled jacket between his hands. "It's his jacket and tie."

Margaret's mouth dropped open into a wide O of surprise. "You mean he left it here?"

"If he left it, why was it bundled up and shoved back under the table?" Casey asked.

Margaret stared at the jacket. She ran her hand over the silky striped tie.

"Did you see Mr. Martinez leave the house yesterday afternoon?" Casey asked.

"No," Margaret answered. "But he *must* have left. I mean, his car was gone."

"He didn't drive, remember? He told Dad he got a lift."

Margaret raised her eyes from the wrinkled jacket to her brother's worried face. "Casey — what are you saying? That Mr. Martinez didn't leave? That he was eaten by a plant or something? That's ridiculous!"

"Then why were his coat and tie hidden like that?" Casey demanded.

Margaret didn't have a chance to respond.

They both gasped as they heard loud footsteps on the stairs.

Someone was hurrying down to the basement.

"Hide!" Margaret whispered.

"Where?" Casey asked, his eyes wide with panic.

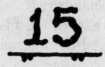

15

Margaret leapt up onto the carton, then pulled herself through the small, open window. A tight squeeze, but she struggled out onto the grass. Then she turned around to help Casey.

That squirrel turned out to be a friend, she thought, tugging her brother's arms as he scrambled out of the basement. It showed us the only escape route.

The afternoon air felt quite cool compared to the steamy basement. Breathing hard, they both squatted down to peer into the window. "Who is it?" Casey whispered.

Margaret didn't have to answer. They both saw their father step into the white light, his eyes searching the plant room.

"Why did Dad come back?" Casey asked.

"Sshhh!" Margaret held a finger to her lips. Then she climbed to her feet and pulled Casey toward the back door. "Come on. Hurry."

The back door was unlocked. They stepped into

the kitchen just as their father emerged from the basement, a concerned expression on his face. "Hey — *there* you are!" he exclaimed.

"Hi, Dad," Margaret said, trying to sound casual. "Why'd you come back?"

"Had to get more tools," he answered, studying their faces. He eyed them suspiciously. "Where *were* you two?"

"Out in the backyard," Margaret said quickly. "We came in when we heard the back door slam."

Dr. Brewer scowled and shook his head. "You never used to lie to me before," he said. "I know you went down into the basement again. You left the door wide open."

"We just wanted to look," Casey said quickly, glancing at Margaret, his expression fearful.

"We found Mr. Martinez's jacket and tie," Margaret said. "What happened to him, Dad?"

"Huh?" The question seemed to catch Dr. Brewer by surprise.

"Why did he leave his jacket and tie down there?" Margaret asked.

"I'm raising two snoops," her father griped. "Martinez got hot, okay? I have to keep the basement at a very high, tropical temperature with lots of humidity. Martinez became uncomfortable. He removed his jacket and tie and put them down on the worktable. Then he forgot them when he left."

Dr. Brewer chuckled. "I think he was in a state of shock from everything I showed him down there. It's no wonder he forgot his things. But I called Martinez this morning. I'm going to drive over and return his stuff when I finish at Mr. Henry's."

Margaret saw a smile break out on Casey's face. She felt relieved, too. It was good to know that Mr. Martinez was okay.

How awful to suspect my own father of doing something terrible to someone, she thought.

But she couldn't help herself. The fear returned every time she saw him.

"I'd better get going," Dr. Brewer said. Carrying the tools he had picked up, he started toward the back door. But he stopped at the end of the hall and turned around. "Don't go back in the basement, okay? It really could be dangerous. You could be very sorry."

Margaret listened to the screen door slam behind him.

Was that a warning — or a threat? she wondered.

16

Margaret spent Saturday morning biking up in the golden hills with Diane. The sun burned through the morning smog, and the skies turned blue. A strong breeze kept them from getting too hot. The narrow road was lined with red and yellow wildflowers, and Margaret felt as if she were traveling somewhere far, far away.

They had lunch at Diane's house — tomato soup and avocado salad — then wandered back to Margaret's house, trying to figure out how to spend the rest of a beautiful afternoon.

Dr. Brewer was just backing the station wagon down the drive as Margaret and Diane rode up on their bikes. He rolled down the window, a broad smile on his face. "Good news!" he shouted. "Your mom is on her way home. I'm going to the airport to get her!"

"Oh, that's great!" Margaret exclaimed, so happy she could almost cry. Margaret and Diane waved and pedaled up the driveway.

I'm so happy, Margaret thought. It'll be so good to have her back. Someone I can talk to. Someone who can explain . . . about Dad.

They looked through some old copies of *Sassy* and *People* in Margaret's room, listening to some tapes that Margaret had recently bought. At a little past three, Diane suddenly remembered that she had a make-up piano lesson that she was late for. She rushed out of the house in a panic, jumped on her bike, yelled, "Say hi to your mom for me!" and disappeared down the drive.

Margaret stood behind the house looking out at the rolling hills, wondering what to do next to make the time pass before her mother got home. The strong, swirling breeze felt cool against her face. She decided to get a book and go sit down with it under the shady sassafras tree in the middle of the yard.

She turned and pulled open the kitchen door, and Casey came running up. "Where are our kites?" he asked, out of breath.

"Kites? I don't know. Why?" Margaret asked. "Hey — " She grabbed his shoulder to get his attention. "Mom's coming home. She should be here in an hour or so."

"Great!" he cried. "Just enough time to fly some kites. It's so windy. Come on. Want to fly 'em with me?"

"Sure," Margaret said. It would help pass the

time. She thought hard, trying to remember where they put the kites. "Are they in the garage?"

"No," Casey told her. "I know. They're in the basement. On those shelves. The string, too." He pushed past her into the house. "I'll jimmy the lock and go down and get them."

"Hey, Casey — be careful down there," she called after him. He disappeared into the hallway. Margaret had second thoughts. She didn't want Casey down there by himself in the plant room. "Wait up," she called. "I'll come with you."

They made their way down the stairs quickly, into the hot, steamy air, into the bright lights.

The plants seemed to bend toward them, to reach out to them as they walked by. Margaret tried to ignore them. Walking right behind Casey, she kept her eyes on the tall metal shelves straight ahead.

The shelves were deep and filled with old, unwanted toys, games, and sports equipment, a plastic tent, some old sleeping bags. Casey got there first and started rummaging around on the lower shelves. "I know they're here somewhere," he said.

"Yeah. I remember storing them here," Margaret said, running her eyes over the top shelves.

Casey, down on his knees, started pulling boxes

off the bottom shelf. Suddenly, he stopped. "Whoa — Margaret."

"Huh?" She took a step back. "What is it?"

"Look at this," Casey said softly. He pulled something out from behind the shelves, then stood up with it bundled in his hands.

Margaret saw that he was holding a pair of black shoes. And a pair of blue trousers.

Blue suit trousers?

His face suddenly pale, his features drawn, Casey let the shoes drop to the floor. He unfurled the trousers and held them up in front of him.

"Hey — look in the back pocket," Margaret said, pointing.

Casey reached into the back pocket and pulled out a black leather wallet.

"I don't believe this," Margaret said.

Casey's hands trembled as he opened the wallet and searched inside. He pulled out a green American Express card and read the name on it.

"It belongs to Mr. Martinez," he said, swallowing hard. He raised his eyes to Margaret's. "This is Mr. Martinez's stuff."

17

"Dad lied," Casey said, staring in horror at the wallet in his hands. "Mr. Martinez might leave without his jacket. But he wouldn't leave without his pants and shoes."

"But — what *happened* to him?" Margaret asked, feeling sick.

Casey slammed the wallet shut. He shook his head sadly, but didn't reply.

In the center of the room, a plant seemed to groan, the sound startling the two kids.

"Dad lied," Casey repeated, staring down at the pants and shoes on the floor. "Dad lied to us."

"What are we going to *do*?" Margaret cried, panic and desperation in her voice. "We've got to tell someone what's happening here. But who?"

The plant groaned again. Tendrils snaked along the dirt. Leaves clapped against each other softly, wetly.

And then the banging began again in the supply closet next to the shelves.

Margaret stared at Casey. "That thumping. What is it?"

They both listened to the insistent banging sounds. A low moan issued from the closet, followed by a higher-pitched one, both mournful, both very human-sounding.

"I think someone's *in* there!" Margaret exclaimed.

"Maybe it's Mr. Martinez," Casey suggested, still gripping the wallet tightly in his hand.

Thud thud thud.

"Do you think we should open the closet?" Casey asked timidly.

A plant groaned as if answering.

"Yes. I think we should," Margaret replied, suddenly cold all over. "If it's Mr. Martinez in there, we've got to let him out."

Casey set the wallet down on the shelf. Then they moved quickly to the supply closet.

Across from them, the plants seemed to shift and move as the two kids did. They heard breathing sounds, another groan, scurrying noises. Leaves bristled on their stalks. Tendrils drooped and slid.

"Hey — look!" Casey cried.

"I see," Margaret said. The closet door wasn't just locked. A two-by-four had been nailed over it.

Thud thud. Thud thud thud.

225

"There's someone in there — I *know* it!" Margaret cried.

"I'll get the hammer," Casey said. Keeping close to the wall and as far away from the plants as he could, he edged his way toward the worktable.

A few seconds later, he returned with a claw hammer.

Thud thud.

Working together, they pried the two-by-four off the door. It clattered noisily to the floor.

The banging from inside the supply closet grew louder, more insistent.

"Now what do we do about the lock?" Margaret asked, staring at it.

Casey scratched his head. They both had perspiration dripping down their faces. The steamy, hot air made it hard to catch their breaths.

"I don't know how to unlock it," Casey said, stumped.

"What if we tried to pry the door off the way we pulled off the two-by-four?" Margaret asked.

Thud thud thud.

Casey shrugged. "I don't know. Let's try."

Working the claw of the hammer into the narrow crack, they tried prying the door on the side of the lock. When it wouldn't budge, they moved to the hinged side of the door and tried there.

"It's not moving," Casey said, mopping his forehead with his arm.

"Keep trying," Margaret said. "Here. Let's both push it."

Digging the claw in just above the lower hinge, they both pushed the handle of the hammer with all their strength.

"It — it moved a little," Margaret said, breathing hard.

They kept at it. The wet wood began to crack. They both pushed against the hammer, wedging the claw into the crack.

Finally, with a loud ripping sound, they managed to pull the door off.

"Huh?" Casey dropped the hammer.

They both squinted into the dark closet.

And screamed in horror when they saw what was inside.

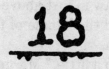

18

"Look!" Margaret cried, her heart thudding. She suddenly felt dizzy. She gripped the side of the closet to steady herself.

"I — don't believe this," Casey said quietly, his voice trembling as he stared into the long, narrow supply closet.

They both gaped at the weird plants that filled the closet.

Were they plants?

Under the dim ceiling bulb, they bent and writhed, groaning, breathing, sighing. Branches shook, leaves shimmered and moved, tall plants leaned forward as if reaching out to Margaret and Casey.

"Look at that one!" Casey cried, taking a step back, stumbling into Margaret. "It has an arm!"

"Ohh." Margaret followed Casey's stare. Casey was right. The tall, leafy plant appeared to have a green, human arm descending from its stalk.

Margaret's eyes darted around the closet. To her horror, she realized that several plants seemed to have human features — green arms, a yellow hand with three fingers poking from it, two stumpy legs where the stem should be.

She and her brother both cried out when they saw the plant with the face. Inside a cluster of broad leaves there appeared to grow a round, green tomato. But the tomato had a human-shaped nose and an open mouth, from which it repeatedly uttered the most mournful sighs and groans.

Another plant, a short plant with clusters of broad, oval leaves, had two green, nearly human faces partly hidden by the leaves, both wailing through open mouths.

"Let's get out of here!" Casey cried, grabbing Margaret's hand in fear and tugging her away from the closet. "This is — gross!"

The plants moaned and sighed. Green, finger-less hands reached out to Margaret and Casey. A yellow, sick-looking plant near the wall made choking sounds. A tall flowering plant staggered toward them, thin, tendril-like arms outstretched.

"Wait!" Margaret cried, pulling her hand out of Casey's. She spotted something on the closet floor behind the moaning, shifting plants. "Casey — what's that?" she asked, pointing.

She struggled to focus her eyes in the dim light of the closet. On the floor behind the plants, near the shelves on the back wall, were two human feet.

Margaret stepped cautiously into the closet. The feet, she saw, were attached to legs.

"Margaret — let's go!" Casey pleaded.

"No. Look. There's someone back there," Margaret said, staring hard.

"Huh?"

"A person. Not a plant," Margaret said. She took another step. A soft green arm brushed against her side.

"Margaret, what are you doing?" Casey asked, his voice high and frightened.

"I have to see who it is," Margaret said.

She took a deep breath and held it. Then, ignoring the moans, the sighs, the green arms reaching out to her, the hideous green-tomato faces, she plunged through the plants to the back of the closet.

"Dad!" she cried.

Her father was lying on the floor, his hands and feet tied tightly with plant tendrils, his mouth gagged by a wide strip of elastic tape.

"Margaret —" Casey was beside her. He lowered his eyes to the floor. "Oh, no!"

Their father stared up at them, pleading with

his eyes. "Mmmmm!" he cried, struggling to talk through the gag.

Margaret dived to the floor and started to untie him.

"No — stop!" Casey cried, and pulled her back by the shoulders.

"Casey, let go of me. What's wrong with you?" Margaret cried angrily. "It's Dad. He —"

"It can't be Dad!" Casey said, still holding her by the shoulders. "Dad is at the airport — remember?"

Behind them, the plants seemed to be moaning in unison, a terrifying chorus. A tall plant fell over and rolled toward the open closet door.

"Mmmmmmm!" their father continued to plead, struggling at the tendrils that imprisoned him.

"I've got to untie him," Margaret told her brother. "Let go of me."

"No," Casey insisted. "Margaret — look at his head."

Margaret turned her eyes to her father's head. He was bareheaded. No Dodgers cap. He had tufts of green leaves growing where his hair should be.

"We've already seen that," Margaret snapped. "It's a side effect, remember?" She reached down to pull at her father's ropes.

"No — don't!" Casey insisted.

"Okay, okay," Margaret said. "I'll just pull the tape off his mouth. I won't untie him."

She reached down and tugged at the elastic tape until she managed to get it off.

"Kids — I'm so glad to see you," Dr. Brewer said. "Quick! Untie me."

"How did you get in here?" Casey demanded, standing above him, hands on his hips, staring down at him suspiciously. "We saw you leave for the airport."

"That wasn't me," Dr. Brewer said. "I've been locked in here for days."

"Huh?" Casey cried.

"But we saw you —" Margaret started.

"It wasn't me. It's a plant," Dr. Brewer said. "It's a plant copy of me."

"Dad —" Casey said.

"Please. There's no time to explain," their father said urgently, raising his leaf-covered head to look toward the closet doorway. "Just untie me. Quick!"

"The father we've been living with? He's a plant?" Margaret cried, swallowing hard.

"Yes. Please — untie me!"

Margaret reached for the tendrils.

"No!" Casey insisted. "How do we know you're telling the truth?"

"I'll explain everything. I promise," he pleaded.

"Hurry. Our lives are at stake. Mr. Martinez is in here, too."

Startled, Margaret turned her eyes to the far wall. Sure enough, Mr. Martinez also lay on the floor, bound and gagged.

"Let me out — please!" her father cried.

Behind them, plants moaned and cried.

Margaret couldn't stand it anymore. "I'm untying him," she told Casey, and bent down to start grappling with the tendrils.

Her father sighed gratefully. Casey bent down and reluctantly began working at the tendrils, too.

Finally, they had loosened them enough so their father could slip out. He climbed to his feet slowly, stretching his arms, moving his legs, bending his knees. "Man, that feels good," he said, giving Margaret and Casey a grim smile.

"Dad — should we untie Mr. Martinez?" Margaret asked.

But, without warning, Dr. Brewer pushed past the two kids and made his way out of the closet.

"Dad — whoa! Where are you going?" Margaret called.

"You said you'd explain everything!" Casey insisted. He and his sister ran through the moaning plants, following their father.

"I will. I will." Breathing hard, Dr. Brewer strode quickly to the woodpile against the far wall.

Margaret and Casey both gasped as he picked up an axe.

He spun around to face them, holding the thick axe handle with both hands. His face frozen with determination, he started toward them.

"Dad — what are you *doing?*" Margaret cried.

19

Swinging the axe onto his shoulder, Dr. Brewer advanced on Margaret and Casey. He groaned from the effort of raising the heavy tool, his face reddening, his eyes wide, excited.

"Dad, please!" Margaret cried, gripping Casey's shoulder, backing up toward the jungle of plants in the center of the room.

"What are you *doing*?" she repeated.

"He's not our real father!" Casey cried. "I *told* you we shouldn't untie him!"

"He *is* our real father!' Margaret insisted. I *know* he is!" She turned her eyes to her father, looking for an answer.

But he stared back at them, his face filled with confusion — and menace, the axe in his hands gleaming under the bright ceiling lights.

"Dad — answer us!" Margaret demanded. "Answer us!"

Before Dr. Brewer could reply, they heard

loud, rapid footsteps clumping down the basement steps.

All four of them turned to the doorway of the plant room — to see an alarmed-looking Dr. Brewer enter. He grabbed the bill of his Dodgers cap as he strode angrily toward the two kids.

"What are you two doing down here?" he cried. "You promised me. Here's your mother. Don't you want to —?"

Mrs. Brewer appeared at his side. She started to call out a greeting, but stopped, freezing in horror when she saw the confusing scene.

"No!" she screamed, seeing the other Dr. Brewer, the capless Dr. Brewer, holding an axe in front of him with both hands. "No!" Her face filled with horror. She turned to the Dr. Brewer that had just brought her home.

He glared accusingly at Margaret and Casey. "What have you *done*? You let him escape?"

"He's our dad," Margaret said, in a tiny little voice she barely recognized.

"*I'm* your dad!" the Dr. Brewer at the doorway bellowed. "Not him! He's not your dad. He's not even human! He's a plant!"

Margaret and Casey both gasped and drew back in terror.

"*You're* the plant!" the bareheaded Dr. Brewer accused, raising the axe.

236

"He's dangerous!" the other Dr. Brewer exclaimed. "How could you have let him out?"

Caught in the middle, Margaret and Casey stared from one father to the other.

Who was their *real* father?

20

"That's not your father!" Dr. Brewer with the Dodgers cap cried again, moving into the room. "He's a copy. A plant copy. One of my experiments that went wrong. I locked him in the supply closet because he's dangerous."

"*You're* the copy!" the other Dr. Brewer accused, and raised the axe again.

Margaret and Casey stood motionless, exchanging terrified glances.

"Kids — what have you done?" Mrs. Brewer cried, her hands pressed against her cheeks, her eyes wide with disbelief.

"What *have* we done?" Margaret asked her brother in a low voice.

Staring wide-eyed from one man to the other, Casey seemed too frightened to reply.

"I — I don't know what to do," Casey managed to whisper.

What *can* we do? Margaret wondered silently, realizing that her entire body was trembling.

"He has to be destroyed!" the axe-wielding Dr. Brewer shouted, staring at his look-alike across the room.

Beside them, plants quivered and shook, sighing loudly. Tendrils slithered across the dirt. Leaves shimmered and whispered.

"Put down the axe. You're not fooling anyone," the other Dr. Brewer said.

"You have to be destroyed!" Dr. Brewer with no cap repeated, his eyes wild, his face scarlet, moving closer, the axe gleaming as if electrified under the white light.

Dad would *never* act like this, Margaret realized. Casey and I were idiots. We let him out of the closet. And now he's going to kill our real dad. And mom.

And then . . . us!

What can I do? she wondered, trying to think clearly even though her mind was whirring wildly out of control.

What can I do?

Uttering a desperate cry of protest, Margaret leapt forward and grabbed the axe from the imposter's hands.

He gaped in surprise as she steadied her grip on the handle. It was heavier than she'd imagined. "Get back!" she screamed. "Get back — now!"

"Margaret — wait!" her mother cried, still too frightened to move from the doorway.

The capless Dr. Brewer reached for the axe. "Give it back to me! You don't know what you're doing!" he pleaded, and made a wild grab for it.

Margaret pulled back and swung the axe. "Stay back. *Everyone*, stay back."

"Thank goodness!" Dr. Brewer with the Dodgers cap exclaimed. "We've got to get him back in the closet. He's very dangerous." He stepped up to Margaret. "Give *me* the axe."

Margaret hesitated.

"Give *me* the axe," he insisted.

Margaret turned to her mother. "What should I do?"

Mrs. Brewer shrugged helplessly. "I — I don't know."

"Princess — don't do it," the capless Dr. Brewer said softly, staring into Margaret's eyes.

He called me Princess, Margaret realized.

The other one never had.

Does this mean that the Dad in the closet is my real dad?

"Margaret — give me the axe." The one in the cap made a grab for it.

Margaret backed away and swung the axe again.

"Get back! Both of you — stay back!" she warned.

"I'm warning you," Dr. Brewer in the cap

240

said. "He's dangerous. Listen to me, Margaret."

"Get back!" she repeated, desperately trying to decide what to do.

Which one is my real dad?

Which one? Which one? Which one?

Her eyes darting back and forth from one to the other, she saw that each of them had a bandage around his right hand. And it gave her an idea.

"Casey, there's a knife on the wall over there," she said, still holding the axe poised. "Get it for me — fast!"

Casey obediently hurried to the wall. It took him a short while to find the knife among all the tools hanging there. He reached up on tiptoes to pull it down, then hurried back to Margaret with it.

Margaret lowered the axe and took the long-bladed knife from him.

"Margaret — give me the axe," the man in the Dodgers cap insisted impatiently.

"Margaret, what are you doing?" the man from the supply closet asked, suddenly looking frightened.

"I — I have an idea," Margaret said hesitantly.

She took a deep breath.

Then she stepped over to the man from the supply closet and pushed the knife blade into his arm.

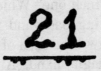

"Ow!" he cried out as the blade cut through the skin.

Margaret pulled the knife back, having made a tiny puncture hole.

Red blood trickled from the hole.

"He's our real dad," she told Casey, sighing with relief. "Here, Dad." She handed him the axe.

"Margaret — you're wrong!" the man in the baseball cap cried in alarm. "He's tricked you! He's *tricked* you!"

The capless Dr. Brewer moved quickly. He picked up the axe, took three steps forward, pulled the axe back, and swung with all his might.

The Dr. Brewer in the cap opened his mouth wide and uttered a hushed cry of alarm. The cry was choked off as the axe cut easily through his body, slicing him in two.

A thick green liquid oozed from the wound. And as the man fell, his mouth locking open in disbelief and horror, Margaret could see that his body was actually a stem. He had no bones, no human organs.

The body thudded to the floor. Green liquid puddled around it.

"Princess — we're okay!" Dr. Brewer cried, flinging the axe aside. "You guessed right!"

"It wasn't a guess," Margaret said, sinking into his arms. "I remembered the green blood. I saw it. Late at night. One of you was in the bathroom, bleeding green blood. I knew my real dad would have red blood."

"We're okay!" Mrs. Brewer cried, rushing into her husband's arms. "We're okay. We're all okay!"

All four of them rushed together in an emotional family hug.

"One more thing we have to do," their father said, his arms around the two kids. "Let's get Mr. Martinez out of the closet."

By dinnertime, things had almost returned to normal.

They had finally managed to welcome their mother home, and tried to explain to her all that had happened in her absence.

Mr. Martinez had been rescued from the supply closet, not too much the worse for wear. He and Dr. Brewer had had a long discussion about what had happened and about Dr. Brewer's work.

He expressed total bewilderment as to what Dr.

Brewer had accomplished, but he knew enough to realize that it was historic. "Perhaps you need the structured environment the lab on campus offers. I'll talk to the board members about getting you back on staff," Martinez said. It was his way of inviting their father back to work.

After Mr. Martinez was driven home, Dr. Brewer disappeared into the basement for about an hour. He returned grim-faced and exhausted. "I destroyed most of the plants," he explained, sinking into an armchair. "I had to. They were suffering. Later, I'll destroy the rest."

"Every single plant?" Mrs. Brewer asked.

"Well . . . there are a few normal ones that I can plant out back in the garden," he replied. He shook his head sadly. "Only a few."

At dinner, he finally had the strength to explain to Margaret, Casey, and Mrs. Brewer what had happened down in the basement.

"I was working on a super plant," he said, "trying to electronically make a new plant using DNA elements from other plants. Then I accidentally cut my hand on a slide. I didn't realize it, but some of my blood got mixed in with the plant molecules I was using. When I turned on the machine, my molecules got mixed in with plant molecules — and I ended up with something that was part human, part plant."

"That's gross!" Casey exclaimed, dropping a forkful of mashed potatoes.

"Well, I'm a scientist," Dr. Brewer replied, "so I didn't think it was gross. I thought it was pretty exciting. I mean, here I was, inventing an entirely new kind of creature."

"Those plants with faces — " Margaret started.

Her father nodded. "Yes. Those were things I made by inserting human materials into plant materials. I kept putting them in the supply closet. I got carried away. I didn't know how far I could go, how human I could make the plants. I could see that my creations were unhappy, suffering. But I couldn't stop. It was too exciting."

He took a long drink of water from his glass.

"You didn't tell me any of this," Mrs. Brewer said, shaking her head.

"I couldn't," he said. "I couldn't tell anyone. I — I was too involved. Then one day, I went too far. I created a plant that was an exact copy of me in almost every way. He looked like me. He sounded like me. And he had my brain, my mind."

"But he still acted like a plant in some ways," Margaret said. "He ate plant food and — "

"He wasn't perfect," Dr. Brewer said, leaning forward over the dinner table, talking in a low, serious voice. "He had flaws. But he was strong enough and smart enough to overpower me, to lock me in the closet, to take my place — and to continue my experiments. And when Martinez arrived unexpectedly, he locked Martinez in the closet, too, so that his secret would be safe."

"Was the head full of leaves one of the flaws?" Casey asked.

Dr. Brewer nodded. "Yes, he was almost a perfect clone of me, almost a perfect human, but not quite."

"But, Dad," Margaret said, pointing, "you have leaves on your head, too."

He reached up and pulled one off. "I know," he said, making a disgusted face. "That's really gross, huh?"

Everyone agreed.

"Well, when I cut my hand, some of the plant materials mixed with my blood, got into my system," he explained. "And then I turned on the machine. The machine created a strong chemical reaction between the plant materials and my blood. Then, my hair fell out overnight. And the leaves immediately started to sprout. Don't worry, guys. The leaves are falling out already. I think my hair will grow back."

Margaret and Casey cheered.

"I guess things will return to normal around here," Mrs. Brewer said, smiling at her husband.

"Better than normal," he said, smiling back. "If Martinez convinces the board to give me my job back, I'll clear out the basement and turn it into the best game room you ever saw!"

Margaret and Casey cheered again.

"We're all alive and safe," Dr. Brewer said, hugging both kids at once. "Thanks to you two."

It was the happiest dinner Margaret could remember. After they had cleaned up, they all went out for ice cream. It was nearly ten o'clock when they returned.

Dr. Brewer headed for the basement.

"Hey — where are you going?" his wife called suspiciously.

"I'm just going down to deal with the rest of the plants," Dr. Brewer assured her. "I want to make sure that everything is gone, that this horrible chapter in our lives is over."

By the end of the week, most of the plants had been destroyed. A giant pile of leaves, roots, and stalks were burned in a bonfire that lasted for hours. A few tiny plants had been transplanted outside. All of the equipment had been dismantled and trucked to the university.

On Saturday, all four Brewers went to select a pool table for the new basement rec room. On Sunday, Margaret found herself standing in back by the garden, staring up at the golden hills.

It's so peaceful now, she thought happily.

So peaceful here. And so beautiful.

The smile faded from her face when she heard the whisper at her feet. "Margaret."

She looked down to see a small yellow flower nudging her ankle.

"Margaret," the flower whispered, "help me. Please — help me. I'm your father. Really! I'm your real father."

MONSTER BLOOD

1

"I don't want to stay here. Please don't leave me here."

Evan Ross tugged his mother's hand, trying to pull her away from the front stoop of the small, gray-shingled house. Mrs. Ross turned to him, an impatient frown on her face.

"Evan — you're twelve years old. Don't act like an infant," she said, freeing her hand from his grasp.

"I *hate* when you say that!" Evan exclaimed angrily, crossing his arms in front of his chest.

Softening her expression, she reached out and ran her hand tenderly through Evan's curly, carrot-colored hair. "And I *hate* when you do that!" he cried, backing away from her, nearly stumbling over a broken flagstone in the walk. "Don't touch my hair. I hate it!"

"Okay, so you hate me," his mother said with a shrug. She climbed up the two steps and knocked on the front door. "You still have to stay here till I get back."

"Why can't I come with you?" Evan demanded, keeping his arms crossed. "Just give me one good reason."

"Your sneaker is untied," his mother replied.

"So?" Evan replied unhappily. "I like 'em untied."

"You'll trip," she warned.

"Mom," Evan said, rolling his eyes in exasperation, "have you ever seen *anyone* trip over his sneakers because they were untied?"

"Well, no," his mother admitted, a smile slowly forming on her pretty face.

"You just want to change the subject," Evan said, not smiling back. "You're going to leave me here for weeks with a horrible old woman and — "

"Evan — that's *enough*!" Mrs. Ross snapped, tossing back her straight blonde hair. "Kathryn is not a horrible old woman. She's your father's aunt. Your great-aunt. And she's — "

"She's a total stranger," Evan cried. He knew he was losing control, but he didn't care. How could his mother do this to him? How could she leave him with some old lady he hadn't seen since he was two? What was he supposed to do here all by himself until his mother got back?

"Evan, we've discussed this a thousand times,"

his mother said impatiently, pounding on his aunt's front door again. "This is a family emergency. I really expect you to cooperate a little better."

Her next words were drowned out by Trigger, Evan's cocker spaniel, who stuck his tan head out of the back window of the rented car and began barking and howling.

"Now *he's* giving me a hard time, too!" Mrs. Ross exclaimed.

"Can I let him out?" Evan asked eagerly.

"I guess you'd better," his mother replied. "Trigger's so old, we don't want him to have a heart attack in there. I just hope he doesn't terrify Kathryn."

"I'm coming, Trigger!" Evan called.

He jogged to the gravel driveway and pulled open the car door. With an excited yip, Trigger leapt out and began running in wide circles around Kathryn's small, rectangular front yard.

"He doesn't *look* like he's twelve," Evan said, watching the dog run, and smiling for the first time that day.

"See. You'll have Trigger for company," Mrs. Ross said, turning back to the front door. "I'll be back from Atlanta in no time. A couple of weeks at the most. I'm sure your dad and I can find a house in that time. And then we'll be back before you even notice we're gone."

"Yeah. Sure," Evan said sarcastically.

The sun dipped behind a large cloud. A shadow fell over the small front yard.

Trigger wore himself out quickly and came panting up the walk, his tongue hanging nearly to the ground. Evan bent down and petted the dog's back.

He looked up at the gray house as his mother knocked on the front door again. It looked dark and uninviting. There were curtains drawn over the upstairs windows. One of the shutters had come loose and was resting at an odd angle.

"Mom — why are you knocking?" he asked, shoving his hands into his jeans pockets. "You said Aunt Kathryn was totally deaf."

"Oh." His mother's face reddened. "You got me so upset, Evan, with all your complaining, I completely forgot. Of *course* she can't hear us."

How am I going to spend two weeks with a strange old lady who can't even hear me? Evan wondered glumly.

He remembered eavesdropping on his parents two weeks earlier when they had made the plan. They were seated across from each other at the kitchen table. They thought Evan was out in the backyard. But he was in the hallway, his back pressed against the wall, listening.

His father, he learned, was reluctant to leave Evan with Kathryn. "She's a very stubborn old woman," Mr. Ross had said. "Look at her. Deaf for twenty years, and she's refused to learn sign language or to lip-read. How's she going to take care of Evan?"

"She took good care of you when *you* were a boy," Mrs. Ross had argued.

"That was thirty years ago," Mr. Ross protested.

"Well, we have no choice," Evan heard his mother say. "There's no one else to leave him with. Everyone else is away on vacation. You know, August is just the worst month for you to be transferred to Atlanta."

"Well, excuuuuse me!" Mr. Ross said sarcastically. "Okay, okay. Discussion closed. You're absolutely right, dear. We have no choice. Kathryn it is. You'll drive Evan there and then fly down to Atlanta."

"It'll be a good experience for him," Evan heard his mother say. "He needs to learn how to get along under difficult circumstances. You know, moving to Atlanta, leaving all his friends behind — that isn't going to be easy on Evan either."

"Okay. I said okay," Mr. Ross said impatiently. "It's settled. Evan will be fine. Kathryn is a bit weird, but she's perfectly harmless."

Evan heard the kitchen chairs scraping across the linoleum, indicating that his parents were getting up, their discussion ended.

His fate was sealed. Silently, he had made his

way out the front door and around to the backyard to think about what he had just overheard.

He leaned against the trunk of the big maple tree, which hid him from the house. It was his favorite place to think.

Why didn't his parents ever include *him* in their discussions? he wondered. If they were going to discuss leaving him with some old aunt he'd never seen before, shouldn't he at least have a say? He learned all the big family news by eavesdropping from the hallway. It just wasn't right.

Evan pulled a small twig off the ground and tapped it against the broad tree trunk.

Aunt Kathryn was weird. That's what his dad had said. She was so weird, his father didn't want to leave Evan with her.

But they had no choice. No choice.

Maybe they'll change their minds and take me to Atlanta with them, Evan thought. Maybe they'll realize they can't *do* this to me.

But now, two weeks later, he was standing in front of Aunt Kathryn's gray house, feeling very nervous, staring at the brown suitcase filled with his belongings, which stood beside his mother on the stoop.

There's nothing to be scared of, he assured himself.

It's only for two weeks. Maybe less.

But then the words popped out before he'd even

had a chance to think about them: "Mom — what if Aunt Kathryn is mean?"

"Huh?" The question caught his mother by surprise. "Mean? Why would she be mean, Evan?"

And as she said this, facing Evan with her back to the house, the front door was pulled open, and Aunt Kathryn, a large woman with startling black hair, filled the doorway.

Staring past his mother, Evan saw the knife in Kathryn's hand. And he saw that the blade of the knife was dripping with blood.

2

Trigger raised his head and began to bark, hopping backward on his hind legs with each bark.

Startled, Evan's mother spun around, nearly stumbling off the small stoop.

Evan gaped in silent horror at the knife.

A smile formed on Kathryn's face, and she pushed open the screen door with her free hand.

She wasn't anything like Evan had pictured. He had pictured a small, frail-looking, white-haired old lady. But Kathryn was a large woman, very robust, broad-shouldered, and tall.

She wore a peach-colored housedress and had straight black hair, pulled back and tied behind her head in a long ponytail that flowed down the back of the dress. She wore no makeup, and her pale face seemed to disappear under the striking black hair, except for her eyes, which were large and round, and steely blue.

"I was slicing beef," she said in a surprisingly deep voice, waving the blood-stained kitchen knife. She stared at Evan. "You like beef?"

"Uh . . . yeah," he managed to reply, his chest still fluttery from the shock of seeing her appear with the raised knife.

Kathryn held open the screen door, but neither Evan nor his mother made any move to go inside. "He's big," Kathryn said to Mrs. Ross. "A big boy. Not like his father. I used to call his father Chicken. Because he was no bigger than a chicken." She laughed as if she had cracked a funny joke.

Mrs. Ross, picking up Evan's suitcase, glanced uncomfortably back at him. "Yeah . . . he's big," she said.

Actually, Evan was one of the shortest kids in his class. And no matter how much he ate, he remained "as skinny as a spaghetti noodle," as his dad liked to say.

"You don't have to answer me," Kathryn said, stepping aside so that Mrs. Ross could get inside the house with the suitcase. "I can't hear you." Her voice was deep, as deep as a man's, and she spoke clearly, without the indistinct pronunciation that some deaf people have.

Evan followed his mother into the front hallway, Trigger yapping at his heels. "Can't you get that dog quiet?" his mother snapped.

"It doesn't matter. She can't hear it," Evan replied, gesturing toward his aunt, who was heading to the kitchen to put down the knife.

Kathryn returned a few seconds later, her blue eyes locked on Evan, her lips pursed, as if she were studying him. "So, you like beef?" she repeated.

He nodded.

"Good," she said, her expression still serious. "I always fixed beef for your father. But he only wanted pie."

"What kind of pie?" Evan asked, and then blushed when he remembered Kathryn couldn't hear him.

"So he's a good boy? Not a troublemaker?" Kathryn asked Evan's mother.

Mrs. Ross nodded, looking at Evan. "Where shall we put his suitcase?" she asked.

"I can tell by looking he's a good boy," Kathryn said. She reached out and grabbed Evan's face, her big hand holding him under the chin, her eyes examining him closely. "Good-looking boy," she said, giving his chin a hard squeeze. "He likes the girls?"

Still holding his chin, she lowered her face to his. "You've got a girlfriend?" she asked, her pale face right above his, so close he could smell her breath, which was sour.

Evan took a step back, an embarrassed grin crossing his face. "No. Not really."

"Yes?" Kathryn cried, bellowing in his ear. "Yes? I *knew* it!" She laughed heartily, turning her gaze to Evan's mother.

"The suitcase?" Mrs. Ross asked, picking up the bag.

"He likes the girls, huh?" Kathryn repeated, still chuckling. "I could tell. Just like his father. His father always liked the girls."

Evan turned desperately to his mother. "Mom, I can't stay here," he said, whispering even though he knew Kathryn couldn't hear. "Please — don't make me."

"Hush," his mother replied, also whispering. "She'll leave you alone. I promise. She's just trying to be friendly."

"He likes the girls," Kathryn repeated, leering at him with her cold blue eyes, again lowering her face close to Evan's.

"Mom — her breath smells like Trigger's!" Evan exclaimed miserably.

"Evan!" Mrs. Ross shouted angrily. "Stop it! I expect you to cooperate."

"I'm going to bake you a pie," Kathryn said, tugging at her black ponytail with one of her huge hands. "Would you like to roll out the dough? I'll bet you would. What did your father tell you about me, Evan?" She winked at Mrs. Ross. "Did he tell you I was a scary old witch?"

"No," Evan protested, looking at his mother.

"Well, I am!" Kathryn declared, and once again burst into her deep-throated laugh.

Trigger took this moment to begin barking ferociously and jumping on Evan's great-aunt. She glared down at the dog, her eyes narrowing, her expression becoming stern. "Look out or we'll put *you* in the pie, doggie!" she exclaimed.

Trigger barked even harder, darting boldly toward the tall, hovering woman, then quickly retreating, his stub of a tail whipping back and forth in a frenzy.

"We'll put him in the pie, won't we, Evan?" Kathryn repeated, putting a big hand on Evan's shoulder and squeezing it till Evan flinched in pain.

"Mom — " he pleaded when his aunt finally let go and, smiling, made her way to the kitchen. "Mom — please."

"It's just her sense of humor, Evan," Mrs. Ross said uncertainly. "She means well. Really. She's going to bake you a pie."

"But I don't want pie!" Evan wailed. "I don't like it here, Mom! She hurt me. She squeezed my shoulder so hard — "

"Evan, I'm sure she didn't mean to. She's just trying to joke with you. She wants you to like her. Give her a chance — okay?"

Evan started to protest, but thought better of it.

"I'm counting on you," his mother continued, turning her eyes to the kitchen. They could both see Kathryn at the counter, her broad back to them, hacking away at something with the big kitchen knife.

"But she's . . . weird!" Evan protested.

"Listen, Evan, I understand how you're feeling," his mother said. "But you won't have to spend all your time with her. There are a lot of kids in this neighborhood. Take Trigger for a walk. I'll bet you'll make some friends your age. She's an old woman, Evan. She won't want you hanging around all the time."

"I guess," Evan muttered.

His mother bent down suddenly and gave him a hug, pressing her cheek against his. The hug, he knew, was supposed to cheer him up. But it only made him feel worse.

"I'm counting on you," his mother repeated in his ear.

Evan decided to try and be braver about this. "I'll help you carry the suitcase up to my room," he said.

They carried it up the narrow staircase. His room was actually a study. The walls were lined with bookshelves filled with old hardcover books. A large mahogany desk stood in the center of the room. A narrow cot had been made up under the single, curtained window.

The window faced out onto the backyard, a long green rectangle with the gray-shingled garage to the left, a tall picket fence to the right. A small, fenced-in area stretched across the back of the yard. It looked like some sort of dog run.

The room smelled musty. The sharp aroma of mothballs invaded Evan's nose.

Trigger sneezed. He rolled onto his back, his legs racing in the air.

Trigger can't stand this place either, Evan thought. But he kept his thought to himself, smiling bravely at his mother, who quickly unpacked his suitcase, nervously checking her watch.

"I'm late. Don't want to miss my plane," she said. She gave him another hug, longer this time. Then she took a ten-dollar bill from her pocketbook and stuffed it into his shirt pocket. "Buy yourself a treat. Be good. I'll hurry back as fast as I can."

"Okay. Bye," he said, his chest feeling fluttery, his throat as dry as cotton. The smell of her perfume momentarily drowned out the mothballs.

He didn't want her to leave. He had such a bad feeling.

You're just scared, he scolded himself.

"I'll call you from Atlanta," she shouted as she disappeared down the stairs to say good-bye to Kathryn.

Her perfume disappeared.

The mothballs returned.

Trigger uttered a low, sad howl, as if he knew what was happening, as if he knew they were being abandoned here in this strange house with the strange old woman.

Evan picked Trigger up and nose-kissed his cold, black nose. Putting the dog back down on the worn carpet, he made his way to the window.

He stood there for a long while, one hand holding the curtains aside, staring down at the small, green yard, trying to calm the fluttering in his chest. After a few minutes, he heard his mother's car back down the gravel drive. Then he heard it roll away.

When he could no longer hear it, he sighed and plopped down on the cot. "It's just you and me now, Trigger," he said glumly.

Trigger was busily sniffing behind the door.

Evan stared up at the walls of old books.

What am I going to do here all day? he asked himself, propping his head in his hands. No Nintendo. No computer. He hadn't even seen a TV in his great-aunt's small living room. What am I going to do?

Sighing again, he picked himself up and walked along the bookshelves, his eyes scanning the titles. There were lots of science books and textbooks, he saw. Books on biology and astronomy, ancient Egypt, chemistry texts, and medical books. Several shelves were filled with dusty, yellowed books. Maybe Kathryn's husband, Evan's great-uncle, had been some sort of scientist.

Nothing here for me to read, he thought glumly.

He pulled open the closet door.

"Oh!"

He cried out as something leapt out at him.

"Help! Please — help!"

Everything went black.

"Help! I can't see!" Evan screamed.

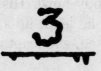

3

Evan staggered back in fear as the warm blackness crept over him.

It took him a few seconds to realize what it was. His heart still thudding in his chest, he reached up and pulled the screeching black cat off his face.

The cat dropped silently to the ground and padded to the doorway. Evan turned and saw Kathryn standing there, an amused grin on her face.

How long had she been standing there? he wondered.

"Sarabeth, how did you get in there?" she asked in a playfully scolding tone, bending down to speak to the cat. "You must have given the boy a fright."

The cat mewed and rubbed against Kathryn's bare leg.

"Did Sarabeth scare you?" Kathryn asked Evan, still smiling. "That cat has a strange sense of humor. She's evil. Pure evil." She chuckled as if she'd said something funny.

"I'm okay," Evan said uncertainly.

"Watch out for Sarabeth. She's evil," Kathryn repeated, bending down and picking the cat up by the scruff of the neck, holding her up in the air in front of her. "Evil, evil, evil."

Seeing the cat suspended in the air, Trigger uttered an unhappy howl. His stubby tail went into motion, and he leapt up at the cat, barking and yipping, missed, and leapt again, snapping at Sarabeth's tail.

"Down, Trigger! Get down!" Evan cried.

Struggling to get out of Kathryn's arms, the cat swiped a clawed black paw at her, screeching in anger and fear. Trigger barked and howled as Evan struggled to pull the excited cocker spaniel away.

Evan grabbed hold of Trigger as the cat swung to the floor and disappeared out the door. "Bad dog. Bad dog," Evan whispered. But he didn't really mean it. He was glad Trigger had scared the cat away.

He looked up to see Kathryn still filling the doorway, staring down at him sternly. "Bring the dog," she said in a low voice, her eyes narrowed, her pale lips pursed tightly.

"Huh?" Evan gripped Trigger in a tight hug.

"Bring the dog," Kathryn repeated coldly. "We can't have animals fighting in this house."

"But Aunt Kathryn — " Evan started to plead, then remembered she couldn't hear him.

"Sarabeth is a bad one," Kathryn said, not softening her expression. "We can't get her riled, can we?" She turned and started down the stairs. "Bring the dog, Evan."

Holding Trigger tightly by the shoulders with both hands, Evan hesitated.

"I have to take care of the dog," Kathryn said sternly. "Come."

Evan was suddenly filled with dread. What did she mean, *take care* of the dog?

A picture flashed into his mind of Kathryn standing at the doorway with the bloody kitchen knife in her hand.

"Bring the dog," Kathryn insisted.

Evan gasped. What was she going to *do* to Trigger?

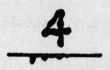

4

"I will take care of you, doggie," Kathryn repeated, frowning at Trigger. The dog whimpered in reply.

"Come, Evan. Follow me," she said impatiently.

Seeing that he had no choice, Evan obediently carried Trigger down the stairs and followed his aunt to the backyard. "I'm prepared," she said, turning to make sure he was following.

Despite her age — she was at least eighty — she walked with long, steady strides. "I knew you were bringing a dog, so I made sure I was prepared."

Trigger licked Evan's hand as they walked across the yard to the long, fenced-in area at the back. "It's a special place for your dog," Kathryn said, reaching up to grab one end of the rope that stretched across the run. "Attach this to the collar, Evan. Your dog will have fun here." She frowned disapprovingly at Trigger. "And there will be no problems with Sarabeth."

Evan felt very relieved that this was all Kathryn wanted to do to Trigger. But he didn't want to leave Trigger tied up in this prison in the back of the yard. Trigger was a house dog. He wouldn't be happy by himself out here.

But Evan knew he had no way of arguing with his aunt. Kathryn is smart in a way, he thought bitterly as he hooked Trigger's collar to the rope. Since she won't learn sign language and won't lipread, it means she gets to do whatever she wants, and no one can tell her no.

He bent down and gave Trigger's warm head a pat and looked up at the old woman. She had her arms crossed in front of her chest, her blue eyes glowing brightly in the sunlight, a cold smile of triumph on her face.

"That's a good boy," she said, waiting for Evan to get up before starting back to the house. "I knew when I looked at you. Come to the house, Evan. I have cookies and milk. You'll enjoy them." Her words were kind, but her voice was hard and cold.

Trigger sent up an unhappy howl as Evan followed Kathryn to the house. Evan turned, intending to go back and comfort the dog. But Kathryn grabbed his hand in an iron grip, and, staring straight ahead, led him to the kitchen door.

The kitchen was small and cluttered and very

warm. Kathryn motioned for him to sit at a small table against the wall. The table was covered with a plastic, checkered tablecloth. She frowned, her eyes studying him, as she brought over his snack.

He downed the oatmeal raisin cookies and milk, listening to Trigger howl in the backyard. Oatmeal raisin wasn't his favorite, but he was surprised to find that he was hungry. As he gobbled them down, Kathryn stood at the doorway, staring intently at him, a stern expression on her face.

"I'm going to take Trigger for a walk," he announced, wiping the milk mustache off his upper lip with the paper napkin she had given him.

Kathryn shrugged and wrinkled up her face.

Oh. Right. She can't hear me, Evan thought. Standing at the kitchen window, he pointed to Trigger, then made a walking motion with two fingers. Kathryn nodded.

Whew, he thought. This is going to be hard.

He waved good-bye and hurried to free Trigger from his backyard prison.

A few minutes later, Trigger was tugging at the leash, sniffing the flowers along the curb as Evan made his way up the block. The other houses on the street were about the same size as Kathryn's, he saw. And they all had small, neatly trimmed, square front yards.

He saw some little kids chasing each other around a birch tree. And he saw a middle-aged man in bright orange bathing trunks washing his car with a garden hose in his driveway. But he didn't see any kids his age.

Trigger barked at a squirrel and tugged the leash out of Evan's hand. "Hey — come back!" Evan called. Trigger, disobedient as always, took off after the squirrel.

The squirrel wisely climbed a tree. But Trigger, his eyesight not what it once was, continued the chase.

Running at full speed, calling the dog's name, Evan followed him around a corner and halfway down the block before Trigger finally realized he had lost the race.

Breathing hard, Evan grabbed the leash handle. "Gotcha," he said. He gave the leash a tug, trying to lead the panting dog back to Kathryn's street.

Trigger, sniffing around a dark tree trunk, pulled the other way. Evan was about to pick up the stubborn dog when he was startled by a hand grabbing his shoulder.

"Hey — who are *you*?" a voice demanded.

5

Evan spun around to find a girl standing behind him, staring at him with dark brown eyes. "Why'd you grab my shoulder like that?" he asked, his heart still pounding.

"To scare you," she said simply.

"Yeah. Well . . ." Evan shrugged. Trigger gave a hard tug at the leash and nearly pulled him over.

The girl laughed.

She was pretty, he thought. She had short, wavy brown hair, almost black, and flashing brown eyes, and a playful, teasing smile. She was wearing an oversized yellow T-shirt over black spandex leggings, and bright yellow Nikes.

"So who *are* you?" she demanded again.

She wasn't the shy type, he decided. "I'm me," he said, letting Trigger lead him around the tree.

"Did you move into the Winterhalter house?" she asked, following him.

He shook his head. "No. I'm just visiting."

She frowned in disappointment.

"For a couple of weeks," Evan added. "I'm staying with my aunt. Actually, she's my great-aunt."

"What's so great about her?" the girl cracked.

"Nothing," Evan replied without laughing. "For sure."

Trigger sniffed at a bug on a fat brown leaf.

"Is that your bike?" Evan asked, pointing to the red BMX bike lying on the grass behind her.

"Yeah," she replied.

"It's cool," he said. "I have one like it."

"I like your dog," she said, eyeing Trigger. "He looks real stupid. I like stupid dogs."

"Me, too. I guess." Evan laughed.

"What's his name? Does he have a stupid name?" She bent down and tried to pet Trigger's back, but he moved away.

"His name's Trigger," Evan said, and waited for her reaction.

"Yeah. That's pretty stupid," she said thoughtfully. "Especially for a cocker spaniel."

"Thanks," Evan said uncertainly.

Trigger turned to sniff the girl's hands, his tail wagging furiously, his tongue hanging down to the ground.

"I have a stupid name, too," the girl admitted. She waited for Evan to ask.

"What is it?" he said finally.

"Andrea," she said.

"That's not a stupid name."

"I hate it," she said, pulling a blade of grass off

275

her leggings. "Annndreeea." She stretched the name out in a deep, cultured voice. "It sounds so stuck up, like I should be wearing a corduroy jumper with a prim, white blouse, walking a toy poodle. So I make everyone call me Andy."

"Hi, Andy," Evan said, petting Trigger. "My name is — "

"Don't tell me!" she interrupted, clamping a hot hand over his mouth.

She certainly *isn't* shy, he thought.

"Let me guess," she said. "Is it a stupid name, too?"

"Yeah," he nodded. "It's Evan. Evan Stupid."

She laughed. "That's *really* a stupid name."

He felt glad that he made her laugh. She was cheering him up, he realized. A lot of the girls back home didn't appreciate his sense of humor. They thought he was silly.

"What are you doing?" she asked.

"Walking Trigger. You know. Exploring the neighborhood."

"It's pretty boring," she said. "Just a lot of houses. Want to go into town? It's only a few blocks away." She pointed down the street.

Evan hesitated. He hadn't told his aunt he was going into town. But, what the heck, he thought. She wouldn't care.

Besides, what could possibly happen?

6

"Okay," Evan said. "Let's check out the town."

"I have to go to a toy store and look for a present for my cousin," Andy said, hoisting her bike up by the handlebars.

"How old are you?" Evan asked, tugging Trigger toward the street.

"Twelve."

"Me, too," he said. "Can I try your bike?"

She shook her head as she climbed onto the narrow seat. "No, but I'll let you run alongside." She laughed.

"You're a riot," he said sarcastically, hurrying to keep up as she began to pedal.

"And you're stupid," she called back playfully.

"Hey, *Annnndreeeea* — wait up!" he called, stretching the name out to annoy her.

A few blocks later, the houses ended and they entered town, a three-block stretch of low two-story shops and offices. Evan saw a small brick post office, a barbershop with an old-fashioned barber pole out front, a grocery, a drive-through bank, and a hardware store with a large sign in the window proclaiming a sale on birdseed.

"The toy store is in the next block," Andy said, walking her bike along the sidewalk. Evan tugged Trigger's leash, encouraging him to keep up the pace. "Actually there are two toy stores, an old one and a new one. I like the old one best."

"Let's check it out," Evan said, examining the cluttered window display of the video store on the corner.

I wonder if Aunt Kathryn has a VCR, he thought. He quickly dismissed the idea. No way. . . .

The toy store was in an old clapboard building that hadn't been painted in many years. A small, hand-painted sign in the dust-smeared window proclaimed: WAGNER'S NOVELTIES & SUNDRIES. There were no toys on display.

Andy leaned her bike against the front of the building. "Sometimes the owner can be a little mean. I don't know if he'll let you bring your dog in."

"Well, let's give it a try," Evan said, pulling open the door. Tugging hard on his leash, Trigger led the way into the store.

Evan found himself in a dark, low-ceilinged, narrow room. It took awhile for his eyes to adjust to the dim light.

Wagner's looked more like a warehouse than a

store. There were floor-to-ceiling shelves against both walls, jammed with boxes of toys, and a long display counter that ran through the center of the store, leaving narrow aisles that even someone as skinny as Evan had to squeeze through.

At the front of the store, slumped on a tall stool behind an old-fashioned wooden cash register, sat a grumpy-looking man with a single tuft of white hair in the center of a red, bald head. He had a drooping white mustache that seemed to frown at Evan and Andy as they entered.

"Hi," Andy said timidly, giving the man a wave.

He grunted in reply and turned back to the newspaper he was reading.

Trigger sniffed the low shelves excitedly. Evan looked around at the stacks of toys. It appeared from the thick layer of dust that they'd been sitting there for a hundred years. Everything seemed tossed together, dolls next to building sets, art supplies mixed in with old action figures Evan didn't even recognize, a toy drum set underneath a pile of footballs.

He and Andy were the only customers in the store.

"Do they have Nintendo games?" Evan asked her, whispering, afraid to break the still silence.

"I don't think so," Andy whispered back. "I'll ask." She shouted up to the front, "Do you have Nintendo games?"

It took awhile for the man to answer. He

scratched his ear. "Don't carry them," he grunted finally, sounding annoyed by the interruption.

Andy and Evan wandered toward the back of the store. "Why do you like this place?" Evan whispered, picking up an old cap pistol with a cowboy holster.

"I just think it's neat," Andy replied. "You can find some real treasures here. It's not like other toy stores."

"That's for sure," Evan said sarcastically. "Hey — look!" He picked up a lunchbox with a cowboy dressed in black emblazoned on its side. "Hopalong Cassidy," he read. "Who's Hopalong Cassidy?"

"A cowboy with a stupid name," Andy said, taking the old lunchbox from him and examining it. "Look — it's made of metal, not plastic. Wonder if my cousin would like it. He likes stupid names, too."

"It's a pretty weird present," Evan said.

"He's a pretty weird cousin," Andy cracked. "Hey, look at this." She set down the old lunchbox and picked up an enormous box. "It's a magic set. 'Astound your friends. Perform one hundred amazing tricks,' " she read.

"That's a lot of amazing tricks," Evan said.

He wandered farther back into the dimly lit store, Trigger leading the way, sniffing furiously. "Hey — " To Evan's surprise, a narrow doorway led into a small back room.

This room, Evan saw, was even darker and dustier. Stepping inside, he saw worn-looking stuffed animals tossed into cartons, games in faded, yellowed boxes, baseball gloves with the leather worn thin and cracked.

Who would want this junk? he thought.

He was about to leave when something caught his eye. It was a blue can, about the size of a can of soup. He picked it up, surprised by how heavy it was.

Bringing it close to his face to examine it in the dim light, he read the faded label: MONSTER BLOOD. Below that, in smaller type, it read: SURPRISING MIRACLE SUBSTANCE.

Hey, this looks cool, he thought, turning the can around in his hand.

He suddenly remembered the ten dollars his mother had stuffed into his shirt pocket.

He turned to see the store owner standing in the doorway, his dark eyes wide with anger. "What are you *doing* back here?" he bellowed.

7

Trigger yipped loudly, startled by the man's booming voice.

Evan gripped the leash, pulled Trigger close. "Uh . . . how much is this?" he asked, holding up the can of Monster Blood.

"Not for sale," the owner said, lowering his voice, his mustache seeming to frown unpleasantly with the rest of his face.

"Huh? It was on the shelf here," Evan said, pointing.

"It's too old," the man insisted. "Probably no good anymore."

"Well, I'll take it, anyway," Evan said. "Can I have it for less since it's so old?"

"What is it?" Andy asked, appearing in the doorway.

"I don't know," Evan told her. "It looks cool. It's called Monster Blood."

"It's not for sale," the man insisted.

Andy pushed past him and took the can from Evan's hand. "Ooh, I want one, too," she said, turning the can around in her hand.

"There's only one," Evan told her.

"You sure?" She began searching the shelves.

"It's no good, I'm telling you," the owner insisted, sounding exasperated.

"I need one, too," Andy said to Evan.

"Sorry," Evan replied, taking the can back. "I saw it first."

"I'll buy it from you," Andy said.

"Why don't you two *share* it?" the owner suggested.

"You mean you'll sell it to us?" Evan asked eagerly.

The man shrugged and scratched his ear.

"How much?" Evan asked.

"You sure you don't have another one?" Andy demanded, going back to the shelf, pushing a pile of stuffed pandas out of her way. "Or maybe two? I could keep one and give one to my cousin."

"Two dollars, I guess," the man told Evan. "But I'm telling you, it's no good. It's too old."

"I don't care," Evan said, reaching into his shirt pocket for the ten-dollar bill.

"Well, don't bring it back to me complaining," the man said grumpily, and headed toward the cash register at the front of the store.

A few minutes later, Evan walked out into the bright daylight carrying the blue can. Trigger panted excitedly, wagging his stubby tail, pleased to be out of the dark, dusty store. Andy followed them out, an unhappy expression on her face.

"You didn't buy the lunchbox?" Evan asked.

"Don't change the subject," she snapped. "I'll pay you five dollars for it." She reached for the can of Monster Blood.

"No way," Evan replied. He laughed. "You really like to get your way, don't you!"

"I'm an only child," she said. "What can I tell you? I'm spoiled."

"Me, too," Evan said.

"I have an idea," Andy said, pulling her bike off the storefront wall. "Let's share it."

"Share it?" Evan said, shaking his head. "For sure. I'll share it the way you shared your bike."

"You want to ride the bike home? Here." She shoved it at him.

"No way," he said, pushing it back toward her. "I wouldn't ride your stupid bike now. It's a girl's bike, anyway."

"It is not," she insisted. "How is it a girl's bike?"

Evan ignored the question and, pulling at Trigger's leash to keep the old dog moving, started walking back toward his aunt's.

"How is it a girl's bike?" Andy repeated, walking the bike beside him.

"Tell you what," Evan said. "Let's go back to my aunt's house and open up the can. I'll let you mess with it for a while."

"Gee, swell," Andy said sarcastically. "You're a great guy, Evan."

"I know," he said, grinning.

Kathryn was seated in the big armchair in the living room when Evan and Andy arrived. Who is she talking to? he wondered, hearing her voice. She seemed to be arguing excitedly with someone.

Leading Andy into the room, Evan saw that it was just Sarabeth, the black cat. As Evan entered, the cat turned and haughtily walked out of the room.

Kathryn stared at Evan and Andy, a look of surprise on her face. "This is Andy," Evan said, gesturing to his new friend.

"What have you got there?" Kathryn asked, ignoring Andy and reaching a large hand out for the blue can of Monster Blood.

Evan reluctantly handed it to her. Frowning, she rolled it around in her hand, stopping to read the label, moving her lips as she read. She held the can for the longest time, seeming to study it carefully, then finally handed it back to Evan.

As Evan took it back and started to his room with Andy, he heard Kathryn say something to him in a low whisper. He couldn't quite hear what she had said. It sounded like, "Be careful." But he wasn't sure.

He turned to see Sarabeth staring at him from the doorway, her yellow eyes glowing in the dim light.

"My aunt is completely deaf," Evan explained to Andy as they climbed the stairs.

"Does that mean you can play your stereo as loud as you want?" Andy asked.

"I don't think Aunt Kathryn has a stereo," Evan said.

"That's too bad," Andy said, walking around Evan's room, pulling back the window curtains and looking down on Trigger, huddled unhappily in his pen.

"Is she really your great-aunt?" Andy asked. "She doesn't look very old."

"It's the black hair," Evan replied, setting the can of Monster Blood on the desk in the center of the room. "It makes her look young."

"Hey — look at all these old books on magic stuff!" Andy exclaimed. "I wonder why your aunt has all these."

She pulled one of the heavy, old volumes from the shelf and blew away a layer of dust from the top. "Maybe your aunt plans to come up here and cast a spell on you while you're sleeping, and turn you into a newt."

"Maybe," Evan replied, grinning. "What *is* a newt, anyway?"

Andy shrugged. "Some kind of lizard, I think." She flipped through the yellowed pages of the old book. "I thought you said there was nothing to do here," she told Evan. "You could read all these cool books."

"Thrills and chills," Evan said sarcastically.

Replacing the book on the shelf, Andy came over to the desk and stood next to Evan, her eyes on the can of Monster Blood. "Open it up. It's so old. It's probably all disgusting and rotten."

"I hope so," Evan said. He picked up the can and studied it. "No instructions."

"Just pull the top off," she said impatiently.

He tugged at it. It wouldn't budge.

"Maybe you need a can opener or something," she said.

"Very helpful," he muttered, studying the label again. "Look at this. No instructions. No ingredients. Nothing."

"Of course not. It's Monster Blood!" she exclaimed, imitating Count Dracula. She grabbed Evan's neck and pretended to strangle him.

He laughed. "Stop! You're not helping."

He slammed the can down on the desktop — and the lid popped off.

"Hey — look!" he cried.

She let go of his neck, and they both peered inside the can.

8

The substance inside the can was bright green. It shimmered like Jell-O in the light from the ceiling fixture.

"Touch it," Andy said.

But before Evan had a chance, she reached a finger in and poked it. "It's cold," she said. "Touch it. It's really cold."

Evan poked it with his finger. It was cold, thicker than Jell-O, heavier.

He pushed his finger beneath the surface. When he pulled his finger out, it made a loud sucking noise.

"Gross," Andy said.

Evan shrugged. "I've seen worse."

"I'll bet it glows in the dark," Andy said, hurrying over to the light switch by the door. "It looks like the green that glows in the dark."

She turned off the ceiling light, but late afternoon sunlight still poured in through the window curtains. "Try the closet," she instructed excitedly.

Evan carried the can into the closet. Andy followed and closed the door. "Yuck. Mothballs," she cried. "I can't breathe."

The Monster Blood definitely glowed in the dark. A circular ray of green light seemed to shine from the can.

"Wow. That's way cool," Andy said, holding her nose to keep out the pungent aroma of the mothballs.

"I've had other stuff that did this," Evan said, more than a little disappointed. "It was called Alien Stuff or Yucky Glop, something like that."

"Well, if you don't want it, I'll take it," Andy replied.

"I didn't say I didn't want it," Evan said quickly.

"Let's get out of here," Andy begged.

Evan pushed open the door and they rushed out of the closet, slamming the door shut behind them. Both of them sucked in fresh air for a few seconds.

"Whew, I hate that smell!" Evan declared. He looked around to see that Andy had taken a handful of Monster Blood from the can.

She squeezed it in her palm. "It feels even colder outside the can," she said, grinning at him. "Look. When you squeeze it flat, it pops right back."

"Yeah. It probably bounces, too," Evan said,

unimpressed. "Try bouncing it against the floor. All those things bounce like rubber."

Andy rolled the glob of Monster Blood into a ball and dropped it to the floor. It bounced back up into her hand. She bounced it a little harder. This time it rebounded against the wall and went flying out the bedroom door.

"It bounces really well," she said, chasing it out into the hall. "Let's see if it stretches." She grabbed it with both hands and pulled, stretching it into a long string. "Yep. It stretches, too."

"Big deal," Evan said. "The stuff I had before bounced and stretched really well, too. I thought this stuff was going to be different."

"It stays cold, even after it's been in your hand," Andy said, returning to the room.

Evan glanced at the wall and noticed a dark, round stain by the floorboard. "Uh-oh. Look, Andy. That stuff stains."

"Let's take it outside and toss it around," she suggested.

"Okay," he agreed. "We'll go out back. That way, Trigger won't be so lonely."

Evan held out the can, and Andy replaced the ball of Monster Blood. Then they headed downstairs and out to the backyard, where they were greeted by Trigger, who acted as if they'd been away for at least twenty years.

The dog finally calmed down, and sat down in the shade of a tree, panting noisily. "Good boy,"

Evan said softly. "Take it easy. Take it easy, old fella."

Andy reached into the can and pulled out a green glob. Then Evan did the same. They rolled the stuff in their hands until they had two ball-shaped globs. Then they began to play catch with them.

"It's amazing how they don't lose their shape," Andy said, tossing a green ball high in the air.

Evan shielded his eyes from the late afternoon sun and caught the ball with one hand. "All this stuff is the same," he said. "It isn't so special."

"Well, I think it's cool," Andy said defensively.

Evan's next toss was too high. The green ball of gunk sailed over Andy's outstretched hands.

"Whoa!" Andy cried.

"Sorry," Evan called.

They both stared as the ball bounced once, twice, then landed right in front of Trigger.

Startled, the dog jumped to his feet and lowered his nose to sniff it.

"No, boy!" Evan called. "Leave it alone. Leave it alone, boy!"

As disobedient as ever, Trigger lowered his head and licked the glowing green ball.

"No, boy! Drop! Drop!" Evan called, alarmed.

He and Andy both lunged toward the dog.

But they were too slow.

Trigger picked up the ball of Monster Blood in his teeth and began chewing it.

"No, Trigger!" Evan shouted. "Don't swallow it. Don't swallow!"

Trigger swallowed it.

"Oh, no!" Andy cried, balling her hands into fists at her sides. "Now there isn't enough left for us to share!"

But that wasn't what was troubling Evan. He bent down and pried apart the dog's jaws. The green blob was gone. Swallowed.

"Stupid dog," Evan said softly, releasing the dog's mouth.

He shook his head as troubling thoughts poured into his mind.

What if the stuff makes Trigger sick? Evan wondered.

What if the stuff is poison?

9

"Are we going to bake that pie today?" Evan asked his aunt, writing the question on a pad of lined yellow paper he had found on the desk in his room.

Kathryn read the question while adjusting her black ponytail. Her face was as white as cake flour in the morning sunlight filtering through the kitchen window.

"Pie? What pie?" she replied coldly.

Evan's mouth dropped open. He decided not to remind her.

"Go play with your friends," Kathryn said, still coldly, petting Sarabeth's head as the black cat walked by the breakfast table. "Why do you want to stay inside with an old witch?"

It was three days later. Evan had tried to be friendly with his aunt. But the more he tried, the colder she had become.

She's mean. She's really mean, he thought, as he ate the last spoonful of cereal from his bowl of shredded wheat. That was the only cereal she had. Evan struggled to choke it down every morning. Even with milk, the cereal was so dry and she wouldn't even let him put sugar on it.

"Looks like it might rain," Kathryn said, and took a long sip of the strong tea she had brewed. Her teeth clicked noisily as she drank.

Evan turned his eyes to the bright sunlight outside the window. What made her think it was going to rain?

He glanced back at her, seated across from him at the small kitchen table. For the first time, he noticed the pendant around her neck. It was cream-colored and sort of bone-shaped.

It *is* a bone, Evan decided.

He stared hard at it, trying to decide if it was a real bone, from some animal maybe, or a bone carved out of ivory. Catching his stare, Kathryn reached up with a large hand and tucked the pendant inside her blouse.

"Go see your girlfriend. She's a pretty one," Kathryn said. She took another long sip of tea, again clicking her teeth as she swallowed.

Yes. I've *got* to get out of here, Evan thought. He pushed his chair back, stood up, and carried his bowl to the sink.

I can't take much more of this, Evan thought miserably. She hates me. She really does.

He hurried up the stairs to his room, where he brushed his curly red hair. Staring into the mirror, he thought of the call he had received from his mother the night before.

She had called right after dinner, and he could tell immediately from her voice that things weren't going well down in Atlanta.

"How's it going, Mom?" he had asked, so happy to hear her voice, even though she was nearly a thousand miles away.

"Slowly," his mother had replied hesitantly.

"What do you mean? How's Dad? Did you find a house?" The questions seemed to pour out of him like air escaping a balloon.

"Whoa. Slow down," Mrs. Ross had replied. She sounded tired. "We're both fine, but it's taking a little longer to find a house than we thought. We just haven't found anything we like."

"Does that mean — " Evan started.

"We found one really nice house, very big, very pretty," his mother interrupted. "But the school you'd go to wasn't very good."

"Oh, that's okay. I don't have to go to school," Evan joked.

He could hear his father saying something in the background. His mother covered the receiver to reply.

"When are you coming to pick me up?" Evan asked eagerly.

It took his mother awhile to answer. "Well . . . that's the problem," she said finally. "We may need a few more days down here than we thought.

How's it going up there, Evan? Are you okay?"

Hearing the bad news that he'd have to stay even longer with Kathryn had made Evan feel like screaming and kicking the wall. But he didn't want to upset his mother. He told her he was fine and that he'd made a new friend.

His father had taken the phone and offered a few encouraging words. "Hang in there," he had said just before ending the conversation.

I'm hanging in, Evan had thought glumly.

But hearing his parents' voices had made him even more homesick.

Now it was the next morning. Putting down his hairbrush, he examined himself quickly in his dresser mirror. He was wearing denim cutoffs and a red Gap T-shirt.

Downstairs, he hurried through the kitchen, where Kathryn appeared to be arguing with Sarabeth, ran out the back door, then jogged to the backyard to get Trigger. "Hey, Trigger!"

But the dog was asleep, lying on his side in the center of his run, gently snoring.

"Don't you want to go to Andy's house?" Evan asked quietly.

Trigger stirred, but didn't open his eyes.

"Okay. See you later," Evan said. He made sure Trigger's water bowl was filled, then headed to the front of the house.

He was halfway down the next block, walking slowly, thinking about his parents so far away in

Atlanta, when a boy's voice called, "Hey — you!" And two boys stepped onto the sidewalk in front of him, blocking his way.

Startled, Evan stared from one boy to the other. They were twins. Identical twins. Both were big, beefy guys, with short, white-blond hair and round, red faces. They were both wearing dark T-shirts with the names of heavy-metal bands on the front, baggy shorts, and high-top sneakers, untied, without socks. Evan guessed they were about fourteen or fifteen.

"Who are *you*?" one of them asked menacingly, narrowing his pale gray eyes, trying to act tough. Both twins moved closer, forcing Evan to take a big step back.

These guys are twice my size, Evan realized, feeling a wave of fear sweep over him.

Are they just acting tough? Or do they really mean to give me trouble?

"I — I'm staying with my aunt," he stammered, shoving his hands into his pockets and taking another step back.

The twins flashed each other quick grins. "You can't walk on this block," one of them said, hovering over Evan.

"Yeah. You're not a resident," the other added.

"That's a big word," Evan cracked, then immediately wished he hadn't said it.

Why can't I ever keep my big mouth shut? he asked himself. His eyes surveyed the neighborhood, searching for someone who might come to his aid in case the twins decided to get rough.

But there was no one in sight. Front doors were closed. Yards were empty. Way down the block, he could see a mailman, heading the other way, too far away to shout to.

No one around. No one to help him.

And the two boys, their faces set, their eyes still menacing, began to move in on him.

10

"Where do you think you're going?" one of the twins asked. His hands were balled into fists at his sides. He stepped closer until he was just an inch or two from Evan, forcing Evan to take a few steps back.

"To see a friend," Evan replied uncertainly. Maybe these guys were just bluffing.

"Not allowed," the twin said quickly, grinning at his brother.

They both snickered and moved toward Evan, forcing him to back off the curb onto the street.

"You're not a resident," the other one repeated. He narrowed his eyes, trying to look tough.

"Hey, give me a break, guys," Evan said. He tried moving to the side, walking on the street, to get around them. But they both moved quickly to keep him from getting away.

"Maybe you could pay a toll," one of them said.

"Yeah," the other one quickly chimed in. "You could pay the nonresident toll. You know, to get temporary permission for walking on this block."

"I don't have any money," Evan said, feeling his fear grow.

He suddenly remembered he had eight dollars in his pocket. Were they going to rob him? Would they beat him up and *then* rob him?

"You have to pay the toll," one of them said, leering at him. "Let's just see what you've got."

They both moved quickly forward, making a grab for him.

He backed away. His legs suddenly felt heavy from fear.

Suddenly a voice cried out from down the sidewalk. "Hey — what's going on?"

Evan raised his eyes past the two hulking boys to see Andy speeding toward them on her bike along the curb. "Evan — hi!" she called.

The twins turned away from Evan to greet the new arrival. "Hi, Andy," one of them said in a mocking tone.

"How's it going, Andy?" the other one asked, imitating his brother.

Andy braked her bike and dropped both feet to the ground. She was wearing bright pink shorts and a yellow sleeveless undershirt top. Her face was red, her forehead beaded with perspiration from pedaling so hard.

"You two," she said, and made an unpleasant face. "Rick and Tony." She turned to Evan. "Were they getting on your case?"

"Well . . ." Evan started hesitantly.

"We were welcoming him to the neighborhood," the one named Rick said, grinning at his brother.

Tony started to add something, but Andy interrupted. "Well, leave him alone."

"Are you his *mother*?" Tony asked, snickering. He turned to Evan and made goo-goo baby noises.

"We'll leave him alone," Rick said, stepping toward Andy. "We'll borrow your bike and leave him alone."

"No way," Andy said heatedly.

But before Andy could move, Rick grabbed the handlebars. "Let go!" Andy cried, trying to pull the bike from his grasp.

Rick held tight. Tony shoved Andy hard.

She lost her balance and fell, and the bike toppled over on top of her.

"Ohhh."

Andy uttered a low cry as she hit her head on the concrete curb. She lay sprawled on the curb, her hands flailing, the bike on top of her.

Before she could get up, Tony reached down and grabbed the bike away. He swung his legs over the seat and began to pedal furiously. "Wait up!" his brother called, laughing as he ran alongside.

In seconds, the twins had disappeared around the corner with Andy's bike.

"Andy — are you okay?" Evan cried, hurrying to the curb. "Are you okay?"

He grabbed Andy's hand and pulled her to her feet. She stood up groggily, rubbing the back of her head. "I hate those creeps," she said. She brushed the dirt and grass off her shorts and legs. "Ow. That hurt."

"Who *are* they?" Evan asked.

"The Beymer twins," she answered, making a disgusted face. "Real heavy-duty dudes," she added sarcastically. She checked her leg to see if it was cut. It was just scraped. "They think they're so cool, but they're total creeps."

"What about your bike? Should we call the police or something?" Evan asked.

"No need," she said quietly, brushing back her dark hair. "I'll get it back. They've done this before. They'll leave it somewhere when they're finished."

"But shouldn't we — " Evan started.

"They just run wild," Andy interrupted. "There's no one home to check up on them. They live with their grandmother, but she's never around. Did they give you a hard time?"

Evan nodded. "I was afraid I was going to have to pound them," he joked.

Andy didn't laugh. "I'd like to pound them," she said angrily. "Just once. I'd like to pay them back. They pick on all the kids in the neighborhood. They think they can do whatever they want because they're so big, and because there are two of them."

"Your knee is cut," Evan said, pointing.

"I'd better go home and clean it up," she replied, rolling her eyes disgustedly. "See you later, okay? I have to go somewhere this afternoon, but maybe we can do something tomorrow."

She headed back to her house, rubbing the back of her head.

Evan returned to Kathryn's, walking slowly, thinking about the Beymer twins, daydreaming about fighting them, imagining himself beating them to a pulp in a fight as Andy watched, cheering him on.

Kathryn was dusting the front room as Evan entered. She didn't look up. He headed quickly up the stairs to his room.

Now what am I going to do? he wondered, pacing back and forth. The blue container of Monster Blood caught his eye. He walked over to the bookshelf and picked up the can from the middle shelf.

He pulled off the lid. The can was nearly full.

I guess Trigger didn't eat that much, he thought, feeling a little relieved.

Trigger!

He'd forgotten all about him. The poor dog must be hungry.

Putting down the Monster Blood, Evan bombed down the stairs, leaning against the banister and taking the stairs three at a time. Then, running full-out, he practically flew to the dog run at the back of the yard.

"Trigger! Hey — Trigger!" he called.

Halfway across the backyard, Evan could see that something was wrong.

Trigger's eyes were bulging. His mouth was wide open, his tongue flailing rapidly from side to side, white spittle running down his chin hair onto the ground.

"Trigger!"

The dog was gasping hoarsely, each breath a desperate, difficult struggle.

He's choking! Evan realized.

As Evan reached the dog run, Trigger's eyes rolled back, and the dog's legs collapsed under him, his stomach still heaving, the air filled with his loud, hideous gasps.

11

"Trigger — no!"

Evan dived to his knees beside the dog and began to tug at Trigger's collar. The collar, Evan saw, had become way too tight.

The dog's chest heaved. Thick white spittle flowed from his open mouth.

"Hold on, boy. Hold on!" Evan cried.

The dog's eyes rolled wildly in his head. He didn't seem to see or hear Evan.

"Hold on, fella! Just *hold on!*"

The collar wouldn't budge. It was buried tightly under the dog's fur.

His hands shaking, Evan struggled to pull the collar over Trigger's head.

Come loose, come loose, come *loose*, he begged.

Yes!

Trigger uttered a pained whimper as Evan finally managed to pull the collar away.

"Trigger — it's off! Are you okay?"

Still panting hard, the dog jumped immediately

to his feet. He licked Evan's face appreciatively, covering Evan's cheek with his thick saliva, whimpering as if he understood that Evan had just saved his life.

"Easy, boy! Easy, fella!" Evan repeated, but the dog continued to lick him gratefully.

Evan hugged the excited dog. This had been a close call, he knew. If he hadn't come along just then . . .

Well, he didn't want to think about it.

When Trigger finally calmed down, Evan examined the collar. "What made this collar shrink like that, boy?" he asked Trigger.

The dog had walked over to the fence and was frantically slurping water from his bowl.

This is plain weird, Evan thought. The collar couldn't have shrunk. It's made of leather. There was no reason for it to shrink.

Then why did it suddenly start choking Trigger?

Evan turned to Trigger, studying him as the dog lapped greedily at the water, breathing hard. He turned and glanced back at Evan for a second, then returned to his frantic water slurping.

He's *bigger*, Evan decided.

He's definitely bigger.

But Trigger was twelve years old, eighty-four in human years. Older than Aunt Kathryn.

Trigger was too old for a late growth spurt.

It must be my eyes, Evan decided, tossing the collar to the ground. This place must be making me see things.

Kathryn was at the kitchen door, calling Evan to lunch. He poured out a bowl of dry food, shouted good-bye to Trigger, who didn't look up from the water dish, and hurried to the house.

The next morning, an overcast morning with an autumn chill in the air, Evan made his way to Andy's house. He found her huddled under a big maple tree in the neighbor's front yard. "What's going on?" he called.

Then he saw that she was leaning over something, her hands working quickly. "Come help me!" she cried, not looking up.

Evan came jogging over. "Whoa!" he cried out when he saw that Andy was struggling to free a calico cat that had been tied to the tree trunk.

The cat screeched and swiped its paw at Andy. Andy dodged the claws and continued to pull at the big knots in the rope.

"The Beymer twins did this. I know it," she said loudly, over the shrilly protesting cat. "This poor cat was probably tied up here all night."

The cat, in a panic, shrieked with amazingly human-sounding cries.

"Stand still, cat," Evan said as the terrified cat

swiped its claws at Andy again. "Can I help?"

"No. I've almost got it," she replied, tugging at the knot. "I'd like to tie Rick and Tony to this tree."

"Poor, frightened cat," Evan said quietly.

"There," Andy said triumphantly, pulling the rope loose.

The cat gave one last cry of protest, its tail standing straight up. Then it darted away, running at full speed, and disappeared under a tall hedge without looking back.

"Not very polite," Evan muttered.

Andy stood up and sighed. She was wearing faded denim jeans and a pale green, oversized T-shirt that came down nearly to her knees. She lifted the bottom of the shirt to examine a hole the cat had managed to snag in it.

"I can't believe those two creeps," she said, shaking her head.

"Maybe we should call the police or the ASPCA or something," Evan suggested.

"The twins would just deny it," Andy said glumly, shaking her head. Then she added, "And the cat's not a very good witness."

They both laughed.

Evan led the way back to his aunt's house. All the way back, they talked about how they'd like to teach the Beymer twins a lesson. But neither of them had any good ideas.

They found Kathryn concentrating on a jigsaw puzzle at the dining room table.

She looked up when they entered, squinting at them. "You like jigsaw puzzles? I like to keep my mind active, you know. That's why I like puzzles. Your mind can get flabby when you get to be my age. A hundred and twelve."

She slapped the table gleefully at her own wit. Evan and Andy both flashed her agreeable smiles. Then she returned to her puzzle without waiting for a reply.

"She's going to drive me bananas!" Evan exclaimed.

"Evan — she'll hear you!" Andy protested, cupping a hand over his mouth.

"I told you, she's completely deaf. She can't hear me. She doesn't *want* to hear anyone. She *hates* everyone."

"I think she's sweet," Andy said. "Why does she wear a bone around her neck?"

"Probably thinks it's cool," Evan cracked.

"Let's go upstairs," Andy urged, pushing him toward the stairs. "I still feel weird talking about your aunt right in front of her."

"You're a crazy old coot," Evan called to Kathryn, a big smile on his face.

Kathryn looked up from her puzzle pieces to cast a cold stare his way.

"She heard you!" Andy cried, horrified.

"Don't be dumb," Evan said, and started up the stairs, nearly tripping over Sarabeth.

Up in Evan's room, Andy paced uncomfortably. "What do you want to do?"

"Well . . . we could read some of these great books," Evan said sarcastically, pointing to the dusty old books that lined the walls. "Maybe find a spell to cast on the Beymer twins. You know. Turn them into newts."

"Forget about newts," Andy said dryly. "Hey — where's the Monster Blood?" Before Evan could answer, she spotted it on one of the shelves.

They raced across the room for it. Andy got there first and grabbed the can. "Evan — look," she said, her eyes growing wide with surprise. "What's going on?"

She held up the can. The green gunk had pushed up the lid and was flowing up out of the can.

12

"Huh? Did the top break or something?" Evan asked.

He took the can from her and examined it. Sure enough, the lid had popped off. The gooey green substance was pushing up out of the can.

Evan pulled out a handful of the green gunk. "Weird," he exclaimed. "It's expanding," he said, squeezing it in his hand. "It's definitely growing."

"I guess so!" Andy exclaimed. "It grew right out of the can!"

"Hey — it's not cold anymore," Evan said. He balled it up and tossed it to Andy.

"It's really warm," she agreed. "Weird!"

She tried to toss it back to him, but it stuck to her palm. "It's getting sticky," she reported. "Are you sure this is the same stuff?"

"Of course," Evan replied.

"But it wasn't sticky before, remember?" she said.

He pulled another warm hunk of it from the

can. "I guess it just changes after the can has been opened."

He squeezed the stuff into a ball shape and tossed it to the floor. "Look — it stuck to the floor. It didn't bounce."

"Weird!" Andy repeated.

"Maybe I should throw it in the trash," Evan said, prying the sticky glob from the floor. "I mean, what good is it if it doesn't bounce?"

"Hey — no way," Andy said. "We've got to see what it does next."

A soft mewing sound made them both turn toward the door.

Evan was surprised to see Sarabeth standing there, her head cocked, her yellow eyes staring at him.

Or was she staring at the glob of Monster Blood in his hand?

"That cat looks so intelligent," Andy said.

"It's as stupid as every other cat," Evan muttered. "Look. She wants to play ball with the Monster Blood."

"Sorry, cat," Andy said. "It doesn't bounce."

As if she understood, Sarabeth mewed unhappily, turned, and padded silently from the room.

"Now where am I going to keep this stuff?" Evan asked. "It's too big for its can."

"Here. How about this?" Andy asked. She reached down to a low shelf and came up with an empty coffee can.

"Yeah. Okay." Evan tossed his hunk into the coffee can.

Andy squeezed hers into a flat pancake. "Look. It isn't glowing the way it used to, either," she said, holding the pancake up for Evan to see. "But it sure is warm. Almost hot."

"It's *alive!*" Evan screamed playfully. "Run for your life! It's *alive!*"

Andy laughed and began to chase Evan, menacing him with the flat, green pancake. "Come get your Monster Blood! Come and get it!"

He dodged away, then grabbed it from her hand. He squeezed it together, balling it up in one hand, then tossed it into the coffee can.

They both peered into the can. The green substance filled it up a little more than halfway.

"Go ahead. Taste it," Andy urged, poking the can in his face. "I dare you."

"Huh? No way. I double-dare you," Evan said, pushing the coffee can back to her.

"Double-darers have to go first," Andy insisted, grinning. "Go ahead. Taste it."

Evan made a disgusted face and shook his head. Then he grabbed a big hunk of it and heaved it at Andy. Laughing, she picked it up off the carpet and tossed it at his face. She threw high, and the green glob stuck to the wall.

Evan reached for another hunk.

They had a messy, hilarious Monster Blood battle till dinnertime. Then, as they tried to clean up, they both heard Trigger through the open window. He was barking loudly out in his pen.

Evan reached the window first. The sky was still gray and overcast. Trigger was leaning on the wooden fence, standing on his hind legs, barking his head off.

"Whoa, Trigger," Evan called, "chill out!"

"Hey — what's with Trigger?" Andy asked. "Is your dog still growing? He looks so big!"

Evan's mouth dropped open and he uttered a silent gasp, realizing that Andy was right.

Trigger had nearly doubled in size.

13

"Trigger — come back! Come *back*!"

The big dog continued to run, its giant paws thundering against the concrete.

"Come back!" Evan screamed, running with long, desperate strides, his heart thudding, his legs aching with each step as he tried to catch up with the galloping dog.

The night was dark and starless. The street glistened as if it had recently rained.

Trigger's paws hit the pavement, each step a loud thunderclap that seemed to echo forever. His giant ears flapped like wings, twin pennants caught on the wind. His big head bobbed up and down, but he didn't look back.

"Trigger! *Trigger!*"

Evan's voice seemed muffled by the gusting wind, pushed back in his face. He tried shouting louder, but no sound came out at all.

He knew he had to stop the dog from running away. He had to catch the dog and then get help.

Trigger was growing so fast, completely out of control. He was already the size of a pony, and getting larger by the minute.

"Trigger! Trigger! Stop, boy!"

Trigger didn't seem to hear him. Evan's voice didn't seem to carry beyond the gusting, swirling wind.

And still Evan ran, his chest pounding, every muscle aching. And as he ran, he suddenly realized there were others running, too.

Two large figures in front of the stampeding dog.

Two large figures Evan recognized as they fled at full speed, trying to get away from the on-rushing animal.

The Beymer twins. Rick and Tony.

Trigger was chasing them, Evan suddenly realized.

The boys turned a corner, onto an even darker street. Trigger followed, bounding after them. Evan continued to run, bringing up the rear of this dark, mysterious parade.

All was silent now, except for the steady, rhythmic thunder of Trigger's enormous padded paws.

Except for the *clapclapclap* of the Beymer twins' sneakers as they darted along the glistening pavement.

Except for the gasp of Evan's breathing as he struggled to keep up.

Suddenly, as Evan watched in horror, the dog raised up on his hind legs. He tilted his head to the sky and let out an ear-piercing howl. Not the howl of a dog. A creature howl.

And then Trigger's features began to transform. His forehead burst forward and enlarged. His eyes grew wide and round before sinking under the protruding forehead. Fangs slid from his gaping mouth, and he uttered another howl to the sky, louder and more chilling than the first.

"He's a monster! A monster!" Evan cried.

And woke up.

Woke up from his frightening dream.

And realized he was in bed, in the study upstairs in Kathryn's house.

It had all been a dream, a frightening, wild chase of a dream.

A harmless dream. Except that something still wasn't right.

The bed. It felt so uncomfortable. So cramped.

Evan sat up, alert, wide awake now.

And stared down at his giant feet. His giant hands. And realized how tiny the bed seemed beneath him.

Because he was a giant now.

Because he had grown so huge, so monstrously huge.

And when he saw how big he had become, he opened his mouth wide and began to scream.

14

His screams woke him up.

This time he really woke up.

And realized that, the first time, he had only dreamed that he was awake. Had only dreamed that he had become a giant.

Dreams upon dreams.

Was he really awake now?

He sat up, blinked, rubbed his eyes, struggled to focus.

Dripping with sweat.

His blankets tossed to the floor.

His pajamas damp, clinging to his prickly skin.

Nothing seemed familiar. It took awhile to shake off the dream, to remember where he was. That he was in his room at Kathryn's. Awake now. His normal size.

Tossed by the wind, the curtains brushed over him, then were noisily sucked out the window.

Evan sat up and, still feeling shaky, peered out the window.

Wisps of gray clouds floated over a pale half-moon. Trees tossed and whispered in the cool night wind.

Only a dream.

A frightening dream. A dream on top of a dream.

He could see Trigger sound asleep, curled up on himself, pressed against the fence wall.

Trigger wasn't a monster. But he was definitely bigger, Evan saw.

Maybe there's something wrong with him. The troubling thought pushed its way into Evan's mind as he stared down at the sleeping dog.

Maybe it's glands or something.

Maybe he's eating too much. Or maybe . . .

Evan yawned. He realized he was too sleepy to think clearly. Maybe the next morning he'd see if there was a vet in town.

Yawning again, he started to settle back into bed. But something caught his eye.

The coffee can on the bookshelf. The can where he had stored the Monster Blood.

"Hey — " he cried aloud.

The green gunk was bubbling, quivering up over the top of the coffee can.

15

"Your dog seems to be quite healthy for his age."
Dr. Forrest scratched Trigger gently under the
chin. "Look at all the white hairs," he said, bringing his face down close to the dog's. "You're a
good old dog, aren't you?"

Trigger licked the doctor's hand appreciatively.

Dr. Forrest grinned, pushing his black eye-
glasses up on his narrow nose, the ceiling light
reflecting off his shiny forehead. He wiped his
hand on the front of his white lab coat.

Evan and Andy stood across from Trigger in
the small, brightly lit office. They had both been
tense during the long examination the vet had
given the dog. But now, hearing the doctor's ver-
dict, they had relaxed expressions on their faces.

"So you think it's just a late growth spurt?"
Evan repeated.

Dr. Forrest nodded, returning to his desk in
the corner. "Highly unusual," he said softly, leaning over the desk to write a note on a pad. "Highly

unusual. We'll get a lab report in three or four days. It may tell us more. But the dog seems very healthy to me. I really wouldn't be alarmed."

"But do cocker spaniels usually get this big?" Evan asked, leaning down to scratch Trigger under the chin, the leash looped loosely in his hand.

Trigger wanted to leave. He pulled toward the door. Evan stood up and tugged hard at the leash to keep the dog in place. It took all of his strength. Trigger was not only bigger; he was much stronger than he had been a few days before.

"No. Not usually," the vet replied. "That's why I took the hormone tests and the blood and glandular samples. Maybe the lab will have an answer for us."

He finished writing and tore the sheet off the pad. "Here," he said, handing the paper to Evan. "I wrote down the name of a good dog food. Put Trigger on this, and see that he cuts down on his between-meal snacks." He chuckled at his own joke.

Evan thanked the doctor and allowed Trigger to pull him out of the office. Andy jogged after them. In the waiting room outside, a tiny Chihuahua cowered behind the couch, whimpering at the sight of the big cocker spaniel.

"I'm glad to be out of there," Evan exclaimed as they stepped out to the sidewalk.

"Trigger got a very good report," Andy said reassuringly, petting Trigger's head. "Hey, look

— his head is wider than my hand!"

"He's nearly as big as a sheepdog!" Evan said miserably. "And Dr. Forrest says he's perfectly okay."

"Don't exaggerate," Andy scolded. She glanced at her watch. "Oh, no! I don't believe it. Late for my piano lesson. Again! Mom'll *kill* me!"

She waved good-bye, turned, and ran full speed down the sidewalk, nearly colliding with an elderly couple coming slowly out of the small grocery store on the corner.

"Let's go, boy," Evan said, thinking about what Dr. Forrest had said. Tugging the leash, he headed out of the small, three-block town. Despite the vet's assurances, Evan was still plenty worried about Trigger.

He stopped outside the grocery. "Maybe an ice cream pop will help cheer me up." He tied Trigger's leash to the red fire hydrant across from the grocery's door. "Stay," he instructed.

Trigger, ignoring Evan, struggled to pull free.

"I'll only be a second," Evan said, and hurried into the store.

There were three or four people in the store, and it took a bit longer than Evan had expected. When he returned to the sidewalk ten minutes later, he discovered the Beymer twins busily untying Trigger.

"Hey — let go!" he cried angrily.

They both turned toward him, identical grins

on their beefy faces. "Look what we found," one of them teased. The other one successfully untied the leash from the hydrant.

"Hand me that," Evan insisted, holding his chocolate ice cream bar in one hand, reaching for the leash handle with the other.

The Beymer twin held the leash handle out to Evan — then quickly snapped it back out of his reach. "Gotcha!"

The brothers laughed gleefully and slapped each other a high five.

"Stop fooling around," Evan insisted. "Hand me the leash."

"Finders, keepers," one of them said. "Isn't that right, Tony?"

"Yeah," Tony replied, grinning. "It's an ugly dog. But it's *our* ugly dog now."

"Get your own dog, wimp," Rick said nastily. He stepped forward and punched the ice cream bar out of Evan's hand. It landed on the sidewalk with a *plop*.

The brothers started to laugh, but their laughter was cut short as Trigger suddenly uttered a low, warning growl. Pulling back his lips, he bared his teeth, and his growl became a snarl.

"Hey — " Rick cried, dropping the leash.

With a loud, angry roar, Trigger reared up and pounced on Rick, forcing him to stagger backward to the curb.

Tony had already started to run, his sneakers

pounding the pavement noisily as he headed at full speed past the vet's office, past the post office, and kept going.

"Wait up! Hey, Tony — wait up!" Rick stumbled, stood up, and took off after his brother.

Evan grabbed for Trigger's leash — and missed.

"Trigger — whoa! Stop!"

The dog took off after the fleeing twins, barking angrily, his enormous paws thudding loudly on the pavement, picking up speed as he closed in on them.

No, Evan thought, finding himself frozen there on the corner in front of the grocery.

No. No. No.

This *can't* be happening!

It's my dream.

Is it coming true?

Evan shuddered, remembering the rest of his dream, remembering how he, too, grew until he was twice his size.

Would that part of the dream also come true?

16

That afternoon, about an hour before dinnertime, Evan called Andy. "Can I come over?" he asked. "I have a small problem."

"Sounds like a big problem," Andy said.

"Yeah. Okay. A big problem," Evan snapped impatiently. "I'm not in the mood to kid around, okay?"

"Okay. Sorry," Andy replied quickly. "Any sign of Rick and Tony? They're not your problem, are they?"

"Not at the moment," he told her. "I told you, they were gone by the time I caught up with Trigger. Disappeared. Vanished. Trigger was still barking his head off. Somehow I dragged him home and got him in his pen."

"So what's your problem?" she asked.

"I can't tell you. I have to show you," he said. "I'll be right there. Bye."

He hung up the phone and hurried down the

325

stairs, carrying the bucket. Kathryn was in the kitchen, her back to him, chopping away at something with her big butcher knife. Evan hurried past and darted out the door.

Andy's house was a modern, redwood ranch style, with a low hedge of evergreens running along the front. Her dad, she said, was a fanatic about the lawn. It was clipped a perfect inch and a half above the ground, smooth as a carpet. A flower garden stretched along the front of the house, tall orange and yellow tiger lilies bobbing in the gentle breeze.

The front door was open. Evan knocked on the screen door.

"What's with the bucket?" was Andy's greeting as she let him in.

"Look," he said, out of breath from running all the way to her house. He held up the aluminum bucket he had taken from Kathryn's garage.

"Oh, wow," Andy exclaimed, raising her hands to her face as she stared into it wide-eyed.

"Yeah. Wow," he repeated sarcastically. "The Monster Blood. It's grown again. Look. It's almost filled this big bucket. What are we going to do?"

"What do you mean *we*?" Andy teased, leading him into the den.

"Not funny," he muttered.

"You didn't want to share it," she insisted.

"I'll share it now," he said eagerly. "In fact

. . . do you want it? I'll give it to you for a bargain price — free." He held the bucket toward her.

"Huh-uh." Andy shook her head, crossing her arms in front of her chest. "Put it down, will you?" She pointed to the corner behind the red leather couch. "Put it over there. It's giving me the creeps."

"Giving *you* the creeps!?" Evan cried. "What am I going to do? Every time I turn around, it grows some more. It's growing faster than Trigger!"

"Hey!" they both cried at once.

Both had the same thought, the same frightening memory. Both suddenly remembered that Trigger had eaten a ball of the green gunk.

"Do you think . . ." Evan started.

"Maybe . . ." Andy replied, not waiting for him to finish his thought. "Maybe Trigger's growing because he ate the Monster Blood."

"What am I going to *do*?" Evan wailed, pacing the room nervously, his hands shoved into his jeans pockets. "The stuff is getting bigger and bigger, and so is poor Trigger. I'm all alone here. There's no one who can help me. No one."

"What about your aunt?" Andy suggested, staring at the bucket on the floor in the corner. "Maybe Kathryn can think of something — "

"Are you kidding? She can't hear me. She doesn't *want* to hear me. She *hates* me. She just sits at her jigsaw puzzle and argues

327

with that horrible black cat all day."

"Okay. Forget the aunt," Andy said, making a dispirited face.

"Perhaps if you told Dr. Forrest — "

"Oh, yeah. For sure," Evan snapped. "He'd really believe that Trigger is turning into a giant because I let him eat Monster Blood."

He threw himself down on the couch. "I'm all alone here, Andy. There's no one to help me. No one I can even talk to about this."

"Except me?"

"Yeah," he said, locking his eyes on hers. "Except you."

She plopped down on the other end of the couch. "Well, what can I do?" she asked hesitantly.

He jumped up and carried the bucket over. "Take some of this. Let's split it up."

"Huh? Why don't we just toss it in the trash?" she asked, staring down at it. The green gunk was pushing up near the top of the bucket.

"Toss it? We can't," he said.

"Sure, we can. Come on. I'll show you." She reached for the bucket handle, but he shoved it out of her reach.

"What if it outgrows the trash can?" he asked. "What if it just keeps growing?"

Andy shrugged. "I don't know."

"Also, I *have* to save it," Evan continued excitedly. "If it's really the thing that's causing Trigger to grow, I'll need it as proof. You know. To show the doctors or whatever. So they can cure Trigger."

"Maybe we should call the police," Andy said thoughtfully, tugging at a strand of hair.

"Oh. Sure," Evan replied, rolling his eyes. "They'll really believe us. For sure. 'We bought this stuff in a toy store, officer, and now it's growing bigger and bigger and it's turning my dog into a giant monster.' "

"Okay, okay. You're right," Andy said. "We can't call the police."

"So, are you going to help me?" Evan demanded. "Will you take some of this stuff?"

"I guess," she said reluctantly. "But just a little." She climbed to her feet, carefully stepping around the bucket. "I'll be right back."

She left the room, then quickly returned, carrying an empty coffee can. "Fill 'er up," she said, smiling.

Evan stared at the coffee can. "That's *all* you're going to take?" he complained. Then he immediately softened his tone. "Okay. Okay. It's a help."

Andy crouched down and dipped the coffee can into the middle of the bucket. "Hey!" she cried out. Her hands flew up and she tumbled back onto the floor.

"What's wrong?" Evan hurried over to her.

"It was pulling the coffee can in," she said, her features tight with fear and surprise. "Sucking it. Look."

Evan peered into the bucket. The coffee can had disappeared under the surface. "Huh?"

"I could feel it pulling," Andy said shakily. She regained her perch over the bucket.

"Let's see," Evan said, and plunged both hands into the middle of the Monster Blood.

"Yuck," Andy said. "This is really gross."

"It's pulling. You're right," Evan agreed. "It feels like it's pulling my hands down. Wow. It's so warm. As if it's alive."

"Don't say that!" Andy cried with a shudder. "Just get the can out, okay?"

Evan had to tug hard, but he managed to pull up the coffee can, filled to the top with the quivering green substance. "Yuck."

"You sure I have to take this?" Andy asked, not reaching for it even though he was holding it out to her.

"Just for a little while," he said. "Till we think of a better plan."

"Maybe we could feed it to the Beymer twins," Andy suggested, finally taking the can.

"Then we'd have *giant* Beymer twins," Evan joked. "No, thank you."

"Seriously, you'd better watch out for them," Andy warned. "If Trigger scared them away this morning, they'll be looking to get back at you. They really think they're tough dudes, Evan. They can be vicious. They could really hurt you."

"Thanks for trying to cheer me up," Evan said

glumly. He was still pulling tiny, clinging clumps of the Monster Blood off his hands and tossing them into the bucket.

"I was watching a video before you came over. The first Indiana Jones movie. Want to watch it?"

Evan shook his head. "No. I'd better go. Aunt Kathryn was busy making dinner when I left. Chopping up some kind of meat. Another great dinner, sitting there in silence, being stared at by Aunt Kathryn and her cat."

"Poor Evan," Andy said, half teasing, half sympathetic.

He picked up the bucket, now only two-thirds full, and let her walk him to the front door. "Call me later, okay?" she asked.

He nodded and stepped outside. She closed the door behind him.

He was halfway to the sidewalk when the Beymer twins slipped out from behind the evergreen hedge, their hands balled into red, beefy fists.

17

The brothers stepped out of the shadows of the hedge. Their short blond hair caught the late afternoon sunlight. They were both grinning gleefully.

Evan stood frozen in place, staring from one to the other.

No one said a word.

One of the Beymers grabbed the bucket from Evan's hand and tossed it to the ground. The bucket hit with a heavy *thud*, and its thick, green contents oozed onto the grass, making disgusting sucking sounds.

"Hey — " Evan cried, breaking the tense silence.

He didn't have a chance to say more.

The other twin punched him hard in the stomach.

Evan felt the pain radiate through his body. The punch took his breath away. He gasped for air.

He didn't see the next punch. It landed on his cheek just below his right eye.

He howled in pain, and his hands flailed the air helplessly.

Both brothers were hitting him now. And then one of them gave Evan's shoulders a hard shove, and he went sprawling onto the cool, damp grass.

The pain swept over him, blanketing him, followed by a wave of nausea. He closed his eyes, gasping noisily, waiting for the sharp ache in his stomach to fade.

The ground seemed to tilt. He reached out and grabbed it, and held on tightly so he wouldn't fall off.

When he finally managed to raise his head, Andy was standing over him, her eyes wide with alarm. "Evan — "

He groaned and, pushing with both hands, tried to sit up. The dizziness, the spinning, tilting grass, forced him to lie back down.

"Are they gone?" he asked, closing his eyes, willing the dizziness away.

"Rick and Tony? I saw them run away," Andy said, kneeling beside him. "Are you okay? Should I call my mom?"

He opened his eyes. "Yeah. No. I don't know."

"What *happened*?" she demanded.

He raised a hand to his cheek. "Ow!" It was already swollen, too painful to touch.

"They beat you up?"

"Either that or I was hit by a truck," he groaned.

A few minutes later — it seemed like hours — he was back on his feet, breathing normally, rubbing his swollen cheek. "I've never been in a fight before," he told Andy, shaking his head. "Never."

"It doesn't look like it was much of a fight," she said, her expression still tight with concern.

He started to laugh, but it made his stomach hurt.

"We'll pay them back," Andy said bitterly. "We'll find a way to pay them back. The creeps."

"Oh. Look. The Monster Blood." Evan hurried over to it.

The bucket lay on its side. The green gunk had oozed onto the grass, forming a wide, thick puddle.

"I'll help you get it back in the bucket," Andy said, leaning over to stand the bucket up. "Hope it doesn't kill the grass. My dad'll have a cow if his precious lawn is hurt!"

"It's so heavy," Evan said, groaning as he tried to push the glob into the bucket. "It doesn't want to move."

"Let's try picking up handfuls," Andy suggested.

"Whoa. It doesn't want to come apart," Evan said in surprise. "Look. It sticks together."

"It's like taffy," Andy said. "Ever see them

make taffy in those taffy machines? The stuff just sticks together in one big glob."

"This isn't taffy," Evan muttered. "It's disgusting."

Working together, they managed to lift the entire green ball and drop it into the bucket. The stuff made a sickening sucking sound as it filled the bucket, and both Evan and Andy had trouble pulling their hands out of it.

"It's so sticky," Andy said, making a disgusted face.

"And warm," Evan added. He finally managed to free his hands from it. "It's like it's trying to swallow my hands," he said, wiping his hands on his T-shirt. "Sucking them in."

"Take it home," Andy said. She looked up to the house to see her mother motioning to her from the front window. "Uh-oh. Dinnertime. I've got to go." Her eyes stopped at his swollen cheek. "Wait till your aunt sees you."

"She probably won't even notice," Evan said glumly. He picked up the bucket by the handle. "What are we going to do with this stuff?"

"We'll take it back to the toy store tomorrow," Andy replied, taking long strides across the lawn to the house.

"Huh?"

"That's what we'll do. We'll simply take it back."

Evan didn't think it was such a hot idea. But he didn't have the strength to argue about it now. He watched Andy disappear into the house. Then he headed slowly back to Kathryn's, his head throbbing, his stomach aching.

Creeping along the wall of the house, he slipped into the garage through the side door to hide the bucket of Monster Blood. Sliding it behind an overturned wheelbarrow, he realized that the bucket was full to the top.

But I gave Andy a big hunk of it, he thought. The bucket had been only two-thirds full.

I'll have to find a bigger place to put it, he decided. Tonight. Maybe there's a box or something in the basement.

He crept into the house, determined to clean himself up before seeing Kathryn. She was still busy in the kitchen, he saw, leaning over the stove, putting the last touches on dinner. He tiptoed up the stairs and washed up. Unable to do much about his swollen, red cheek, he changed into a clean pair of baggy shorts and a fresh T-shirt, and carefully brushed his hair.

As they sat down at the dining room table, Kathryn's eyes fell on Evan's swollen cheek. "You been in a fight?" she asked, squinting suspiciously at him. "You're a little roughneck, aren't you? Just like your father. Chicken was always getting into scrapes, always picking on boys twice his size."

"I wasn't exactly picking on them," Evan muttered, spearing a chunk of beef from his stew with his fork.

All through dinner, Kathryn stared at his swollen cheek. But she didn't say another word.

She doesn't care if I'm hurt or not, Evan thought miserably.

She really doesn't care.

She didn't even ask if it hurts.

In a way, he was grateful. He didn't need her getting all upset, making a fuss because he was in a fight, maybe calling his parents in Atlanta and telling them.

Well . . . she couldn't call his parents. She couldn't use the phone, since she couldn't hear.

Evan downed his big plate of beef stew. It was pretty good, except for the vegetables.

The silence seemed so *loud*. He began thinking about his problem — the Monster Blood.

Should he tell Kathryn about it?

He could write down the whole problem on the yellow pad and hand it to her to read. It would feel so good to tell someone, to have an adult take over the problem and handle it.

But not his Aunt Kathryn, he decided.

She was too weird.

She wouldn't understand.

She wouldn't know what to do.

And she wouldn't care.

Andy was right. They had to carry the stuff back to the toy store. Give it back. Just get rid of it.

But in the meantime, he had to find something to keep it in.

Evan waited in his room until he heard Kathryn go to bed, a little after ten o'clock. Then he crept down the stairs and headed out to the garage.

18

It was a cool, clear night. Crickets sent up a relentless curtain of noise. The black sky glittered with tiny specks of stars.

The round beam of light from the flashlight in his hand darted across the driveway, leading Evan to the dark garage. As he entered, something scuttled across the floor near the back wall.

Maybe it was just a dead leaf, blown by the wind when I opened the door, he thought hopefully.

He moved the flashlight unsteadily, beaming it onto the overturned wheelbarrow. Then the light darted across the garage ceiling as he bent down, reached behind the wheelbarrow, and pulled out the bucket of Monster Blood.

He moved the light to the center of the bucket, and gasped.

The green substance was quivering up over the top.

It's growing much faster than before, he thought.

I've *got* to find something bigger to hide it in — just for tonight.

The bucket was too heavy to carry with one hand. Tucking the flashlight into his armpit, he gripped the bucket handle with both hands and hoisted the bucket off the floor.

Struggling to keep from spilling it, he made his way into the dark house. He paused at the door to the basement steps, silently setting the heavy bucket down on the linoleum floor.

He clicked the light switch on the wall. Somewhere downstairs a dim light flickered on, casting a wash of pale yellow light over the concrete floor.

There's got to be something to put this stuff in down there, Evan thought. Hoisting up the bucket, he made his way slowly, carefully down the steep, dark stairway, leaning his shoulder against the wall to steady himself.

Waiting for his eyes to adjust to the pale light, he saw that the basement was one large room, low-ceilinged and damp. It was cluttered with cartons, stacks of old newspapers and magazines, and old furniture and appliances covered in stained, yellowed bed sheets.

Something brushed his face as he stepped away from the stairs.

He uttered a silent cry and, dropping the bucket, raised his hands to swipe at the thick cobwebs that seemed to reach out for him. They clung to his skin, dry and scratchy, as he frantically pulled at them.

He suddenly realized it wasn't the web that was moving against his cheek.

It was a spider.

With a sharp intake of breath, he brushed it away. But even after he saw the insect scuttle across the floor, he could still feel its prickly feet moving on his face.

Moving quickly away from the wall, his heart pounding now, his eyes searching the open wooden shelves hidden in shadow against the far wall, he stumbled over something on the floor.

"Oh!" He fell headfirst over it, throwing his hands forward to break his fall.

A human body!

Someone lying there under him!

No.

Calm down, Evan. Calm down, he instructed himself.

He pulled himself shakily to his feet.

It was a dressmaker's dummy he had stumbled over. Probably a model of Kathryn when she was younger.

He rolled it out of the way as his eyes searched the shadowy room for a container to store the Monster Blood. What was that long, low object in front of the worktable?

Moving closer, he saw that it was an old bathtub, the insides stained and peeling. It's big enough, he realized, and quickly decided to store the green gunk inside it.

With a loud groan, he hoisted the bucket onto the side of the old tub. His stomach muscles were still sore from the punch he had taken, and the pain shot through his body.

He waited for the aching to fade, then tilted the bucket. The thick green substance rolled out of the bucket and hit the tub bottom with a sickening soft *plop*.

Evan set the bucket aside and stared down at the Monster Blood, watching it ooze, spreading thickly over the bottom of the bathtub. To his surprise, the tub appeared nearly half full.

How fast was this stuff growing?!

He was leaning over the tub, about to make his way back upstairs, when he heard the cat screech.

Startled, he let go of the side of the tub just as Sarabeth leapt onto his back. Evan didn't have time to cry out as he toppled forward, over the edge of the tub and into the thick, green gunk.

19

Evan landed hard on his elbows, but the thick Monster Blood softened the fall. He heard the cat screech again and pad away.

He sank into the ooze, his arms and legs flailing, trying to lift himself away. But the sticky substance was sucking him down, pulling him with surprising force.

His whole body seemed to be held by it, stuck as if in cement, and now it was quivering up, bubbling silently, rising up to his face. I'm going to suffocate, he realized.

It's trying to choke me.

The warmth of it spread across his body, invaded his chest, his legs, his throat.

I can't move.

I'm stuck.

It's trying to choke me.

No!

He pulled his head up just as the green gunk began to cover his face.

Then he struggled to twist his body, to twist himself around in it. With great effort, panting loudly, hoarse cries escaping his open lips, he pulled himself up into a sitting position.

The green substance rose up even higher, as if it were reaching up to him, reaching to drag him back down into it.

Evan gripped the side of the tub with both hands, held on to it tightly, and began to force himself up. Up, up from the clinging, pulling ooze. Up from the strange force that seemed to be drawing him back with renewed power.

Up. Up.

"No!" he managed to scream as the warm, green ooze slid over his shoulders.

"No!"

It was gripping his shoulders now, sliding around his neck, sucking him down, pulling him back into its sticky depths.

Down. Down.

It's got me, he realized.

It's got me now.

20

"No!" Evan screamed aloud as the green gunk bubbled up to his neck.

Pulling him. Pulling him down.

"No!"

Try again. Up.

Try again.

Up. Up.

Yes!

Gripping the sides of the tub, he was moving upward, pulling himself, hoisting himself, straining with all of his strength.

Yes! Yes! He was beating it.

He was stronger than it was. One more tug and he would be free.

With a relieved sigh, he dropped over the side of the tub onto the cool basement floor.

And lay there, pressed against the damp concrete, waiting to catch his breath.

When he looked up, Sarabeth stood a few feet away, her head cocked to one side, her yellow eyes peering into his, an expression of supreme satisfaction on her dark feline face.

The next morning, after a fitful, restless sleep, Evan brought the pad of yellow lined paper and a marker to the breakfast table.

"Well, well," Kathryn greeted him, placing a bowl of shredded wheat in front of him, "you certainly look like something the cat dragged in!" She laughed, shaking her head.

"Don't mention *cat* to me," Evan muttered. He shoved the bowl of cereal aside and pointed to the pad in his hand.

"Don't let your cereal get soggy," Kathryn scolded, reaching to push the bowl back to him. "You get more of the vitamins that way. And it's good roughage."

"I don't care about your stupid roughage," Evan said moodily, knowing she couldn't hear him. He pointed to the pad again, and then began to write, scribbling quickly in big, black letters.

His writing caught her interest. She moved around the table and stood behind him, her eyes on the pad as he wrote his desperate message.

I HAVE A PROBLEM, he wrote. I NEED YOUR HELP. THE BATHTUB DOWNSTAIRS IS OVERFLOWING WITH GREEN MONSTER BLOOD AND I CAN'T STOP IT.

He put down the marker and held the pad up close to her face.

Looking up at her from the chair, seeing her pale face in the morning sunlight as she leaned over him in her gray flannel bathrobe, Kathryn suddenly looked very old to him. Only her eyes, those vibrant, blue eyes running quickly over his words, seemed youthful and alive.

Her lips were pursed tightly in concentration as she read what he had written. Then, as Evan stared eagerly up at her, her mouth spread into a wide smile. She tossed back her head and laughed.

Completely bewildered by her reaction, Evan slid his chair back and jumped up. She rested a hand on his shoulder and gave him a playful shove.

"Don't kid an old woman!" she exclaimed, shaking her head. She turned and headed back to her side of the table. "I thought you were serious. I guess you're not like your father at all. He never played any dumb jokes or tricks. Chicken was always such a serious boy."

"*I don't care about Chicken!*" Evan shouted, losing control, and tossed the pad angrily onto the breakfast table.

His aunt burst out laughing. She didn't seem to notice that Evan was glaring at her in frustration, his hands tightened into fists at his sides.

"Monster Blood! What an imagination!" She wiped tears of laughter from her eyes with her fingers. Then suddenly, her expression turned serious. She grabbed his earlobe and squeezed it.

"I warned you," she whispered. "I warned you to be careful."

"Ow!"

When he cried out in pain, she let go of his ear, her eyes glowing like blue jewels.

I've got to get out of here, Evan thought, rubbing his tender earlobe. He turned and strode quickly from the kitchen and up to his room.

I knew she wouldn't be any help, he thought bitterly.

She's just a crazy old lady.

I should pull her down to the basement and *show* her the disgusting stuff, he thought, angrily tossing the clothes he had worn yesterday onto the floor.

But what's the point? She'd probably laugh at that, too.

She isn't going to help me.

He had only one person he could rely on, he knew.

Andy.

He called her, punching in her number with trembling fingers.

"Hi. You're right," he said, not giving her a chance to say anything. "We have to take the stuff back to the store."

"*If* we can carry it," Andy replied, sounding worried. "That hunk of Monster Blood you gave me — it outgrew the coffee can. I put it in my parents' ice bucket, but it's outgrowing that."

"How about a plastic garbage bag?" Evan suggested. "You know. One of the really big lawn bags? We can probably carry it in a couple of those."

"It's worth a try," Andy said. "This stuff is so disgusting. It's making all these sick noises, and it's really sticky."

"Tell me about it," Evan replied gloomily, remembering the night before. "I took a *swim* in it."

"Huh? You can explain later," she said impatiently. "The toy store opens at ten, I think. I can meet you on the corner in twenty minutes."

"Good deal." Evan hung up the phone and headed to the garage to get a plastic lawn bag.

Andy showed up with her plastic bag wrapped around the handlebars of her BMX bike. Once again. Evan had to go along beside her on foot. His plastic bag was bulging, and so heavy he had to drag it over the sidewalk. He couldn't lift it.

"The tub was nearly full to the top," he told Andy, groaning as he struggled to pull the bag over the curb. "I'm afraid it's going to burst out of this bag."

"Only two blocks to go," she said, trying to sound reassuring. A car rolled by slowly. The driver, a teenager with long black hair, stuck his head out the window, grinning. "What's in the bag? A dead body?"

"Just garbage," Evan told him.

"That's for sure," Andy muttered as the car rolled away.

Several people stopped to stare at them as they entered town. "Hi, Mrs. Winslow," Andy called to a friend of her mother's.

Mrs. Winslow waved, then gave Andy a curious stare, and headed into the grocery.

Andy climbed off her bike and walked it. Evan continued to drag his bulging bag behind him.

They made their way to the next block, then started to cross the street to the toy store.

But they both stopped short in the middle of the street.

And gaped in shock.

The door and window of the store were boarded up. A small, hand-printed sign tacked to the top of the door read: OUT OF BUSINESS.

21

Desperate to get rid of the disgusting contents of the garbage bags, Evan pounded on the door anyway.

"Come on — somebody! Somebody, open up!"

No reply.

He pounded with both fists.

Silence.

Finally, Andy had to pull him away.

"The store is closed," a young woman called from across the street. "It closed a few days ago. See? It's all boarded up and everything."

"Very helpful," Evan muttered under his breath. He slammed his hand angrily against the door.

"Evan — stop. You'll hurt yourself," Andy warned.

"Now what?" Evan demanded. "Got any more fantastic ideas, Andy?"

She shrugged. "It's your turn to come up with something brilliant."

Evan sighed miserably. "Maybe I could give it to Kathryn and tell her it's beef. Then she'd chop it up with that knife she's always carrying around."

"I don't think you're thinking too clearly right now," Andy said, putting a sympathetic hand on his shoulder.

They both stared down at the garbage bags. They appeared to be moving — expanding and contracting, as if the green globs inside were *breathing!*

"Let's go back to Kathryn's," Evan said, his voice trembling. "Maybe we'll think of something on the way."

Somehow they managed to drag the Monster Blood back to Kathryn's house. The sun had gotten high in the sky. As they headed to the backyard, Evan was drenched with sweat. His arms ached. His head throbbed.

"Now what?" he asked weakly, letting go of the bulging lawn bag.

Andy leaned her bike against the side of the garage. She pointed to the big aluminum trash can next to the garage door. "How about that? It looks pretty sturdy." She walked over to it to investigate. "And look — the lid clamps down."

"Okay," Evan agreed, wiping his forehead with the sleeve of his T-shirt.

Andy pulled off the lid of the big can. Then she

dumped in the contents of her bag. It hit the bottom with a sick, squishy sound. Then she hurried to help Evan.

"It's so heavy," Evan groaned, struggling to pull the bag up.

"We can do it," Andy insisted.

Working together, they managed to slide the Monster Blood from the plastic bag. It rolled out like a tidal wave, sloshing noisily against the sides of the can, raising up as if trying to escape.

With a loud sigh of relief, Evan slammed the metal lid down on top of it and clamped the handles down.

"Whoa!" Andy cried.

They both stared at the can for a long moment, as if expecting it to explode or burst apart. "Now what?" Evan asked, his features tight with fear.

Before Andy could reply, they saw Kathryn step out of the kitchen door. Her eyes searched the backyard until she spotted them. "Evan — good news!" she called.

Glancing back at the trash can, Evan and Andy came hurrying over. Kathryn was holding a yellow piece of paper in her hand. A telegram.

"Your mother is coming to pick you up this afternoon," Kathryn said, a wide smile on her face.

I think Kathryn is glad to get rid of me, was Evan's first thought.

And then, dismissing that thought, he leapt up and whooped for joy. It was the best news he'd ever received.

"I'm outta here!" he exclaimed after his aunt had returned to the house. "I'm outta here! I can't wait!"

Andy didn't appear to share his joy. "You're leaving your aunt a nice little surprise over there," she said, pointing to the trash can.

"I don't care! I'm outta here!" Evan repeated, raising his hand for Andy to slap him a high five.

She didn't cooperate. "Don't you think we have to tell someone about the Monster Blood? Or do something about it — before you leave?"

But Evan was too excited to think about that now. "Hey, Trigger!" he called, running to the dog's pen at the back of the yard. "Trigger — we're going home, boy!"

Evan pulled open the gate — and gasped.

22

"Trigger!"

The dog that came bounding toward him *looked* like Trigger. But the cocker spaniel was the size of a pony! He had *doubled* in size since the day before!

"No!" Evan had to hit the dirt as Trigger excitedly tried to jump on him. "Hey — wait!"

Before Evan could get up, Trigger began barking ferociously. The huge dog was already past the gate and thundering across the backyard toward the street.

"I don't believe it!" Andy cried, raising her hands to her face, staring in shock as the enormous creature bounded around the side of the house and out of sight. "He's so — big!"

"We've got to stop him! He might hurt someone!" Evan cried.

"Trigger! Trigger — come back!" Still off balance, Evan started to run, calling frantically. But he stumbled over Andy's bike and fell onto the trash can.

"No!" Andy shrieked, looking on helplessly as the metal can toppled over, with Evan sprawled on top of it. The can hit the driveway with a loud *clang*.

The lid popped off and rolled away.

The green gunk poured out.

It oozed away from the can, then stopped and appeared to stand up. Quivering, making loud sucking sounds, it righted itself, pulling itself up tall.

As the two kids stared in silent horror, the quivering green mass appeared to come to life, like a newly born creature pulling itself up, stretching, looking around.

Then, with a loud sucking sound, it arched toward Evan, who was still sprawled on the toppled can.

"Get up, Evan!" Andy cried. "Get up! It's going to roll right over you!"

23

"Noooooo!"

Evan uttered an animal cry, a sound he had never made before — and rolled away as the quivering green ball bounced toward him.

"Run, Evan!" Andy screamed. She grabbed his hand and pulled him to his feet. "It's alive!" she cried. "Run!"

The Monster Blood heaved itself against the garage wall. It seemed to stick there for a brief second. Then it peeled off, and came bouncing toward them with surprising speed.

"Help! Help!"

"Somebody — please — *help*!"

Screaming at the top of their lungs, Evan and Andy took off. Scrambling as fast as he could, his legs weak and rubbery from fear, Evan followed Andy down the driveway toward the front yard.

"Help! Oh, please! Help us!"

Evan's voice was hoarse from screaming. His heart thudded in his chest. His temples throbbed.

He turned and saw that the Monster Blood was right behind them, picking up speed as it bounced across the yard, making disgusting squishing noises with each bounce.

Plop. Plop. Plop.

A robin, pulling at a worm in the grass, didn't look up in time. The trembling green mass rolled over it.

"Oh!" Evan moaned, turning back to see the bird sucked into the green ball. Its wings flapping frantically, the bird uttered a final cry, then disappeared inside.

Plop. Plop. Plop.

The Monster Blood changed direction, still bouncing and quivering, and leaving white stains on the grass like enormous, round footsteps.

"It's alive!" Andy screamed, her hands pressed against her cheeks. "Oh, my God — it's *alive!*"

"What can we do? What can we do?" Evan didn't recognize his own terrified voice.

"It's catching up!" Andy screamed, pulling him by the hand. "Run!"

Gasping loudly, they made their way to the front of the house.

"Hey — what's happening?" a voice called.

"Huh?"

Startled by the voice, Evan stopped short. He looked to the sidewalk to see the Beymer twins, matching grins on their beefy faces.

"My favorite punching bag," one of them said

to Evan. He raised his fist menacingly.

They took a few steps toward Evan and Andy. Then their grins faded and their mouths dropped open in horror as the gigantic green mass appeared, heading down the drive, rolling as fast as a bicycle.

"Look out!" Evan screamed.

"Run!" Andy cried.

But the two brothers were too startled to move.

Their eyes bulging with fear, they threw their hands up as if trying to shield themselves.

Plop. Plop. Plop.

The enormous ball of Monster Blood picked up speed as it bounced forward. Evan shut his eyes as it hit the twins with a deafening *smack*.

"Ow!"

"No!"

Both brothers cried out, flailing their arms, struggling to pull themselves free.

"Help us! Please — help us!"

Their bodies twisted and writhed as they struggled.

But they were stuck tight. The green gunk oozed over them, covering them completely.

Then it pulled them inside with a loud sucking *pop*.

Andy shielded her eyes. "Sick," she muttered. "Oooh. Sick."

Evan gasped in helpless horror as the Beymer brothers finally stopped struggling.

Their arms went limp. Their faces disappeared into the quivering gunk.

The sucking sounds grew louder as the two boys were pulled deeper and deeper inside. Then the Monster Blood bounced high, turned, and started back up the drive.

Andy and Evan froze, unsure of which way to head.

"Split up!" Evan cried. "It can't go after us both!"

Andy returned his frightened stare. She opened her mouth, but no sound came out.

"Split up! Split up!" Evan repeated shrilly.

"But — " Andy started.

Before she could say anything, the front door of the house burst open, and Kathryn stepped out onto the stoop.

"Hey — what are you kids doing? What's *that*?" she cried, gripping the screen door, her eyes filling with horror.

Picking up speed, the giant ball bounded toward the stoop.

Kathryn tossed up her hands in fright. She stood frozen for a long moment, as if trying to make sense of what she was seeing. Then, leaving the front door wide open, she spun around and fled into the house.

Plop. Plop.

The Monster Blood hesitated at the front stoop.

It bounced in place once, twice, three times, as if considering what to do next.

Evan and Andy gaped in horror from across the lawn, trying to catch their breath.

A wave of nausea swept over Evan as he saw the Beymer twins, still visible deep within the quivering glob, faceless prisoners bouncing inside it.

Then suddenly, the Monster Blood bounced high and hurtled up the stairs of the stoop.

"No!" Evan screamed as it squeezed through the open doorway and disappeared into the house.

From the middle of the yard, Andy and Evan heard Kathryn's bloodcurdling scream.

"It's got Aunt Kathryn," Evan said weakly.

24

Evan reached the house first. He had run so fast, his lungs felt as if they were about to burst.

"What are you going to do?" Andy called, following close behind.

"I don't know," Evan replied. He grabbed on to the screen door and propelled himself into the house.

"Aunt Kathryn!" Evan screamed, bursting into the living room.

The enormous glob filled the center of the small room. The Beymer twins were outlined in its side as it bounced and quivered, oozing over the carpet, leaving its sticky footprints in its path.

It took Evan a few seconds to see his aunt. The bouncing hunk of Monster Blood had backed her against the fireplace.

"Aunt Kathryn — run!" Evan cried.

But even he could see that she had nowhere to run.

"Get out of here, kids!" Kathryn cried, her voice

shrill and trembling, suddenly sounding very old.

"But, Aunt Kathryn — "

"Get out of here — now!" the old woman insisted, her black hair wild about her head, her eyes, those blue, penetrating eyes, staring hard at the green glob as if willing it away.

Evan turned to Andy, uncertain of what to do.

Andy's hands tugged at the sides of her hair, her eyes wide with growing fear as the seething green glob made its way steadily closer to Evan's aunt.

"Get out!" Kathryn repeated shrilly. "Save your lives! I made this thing! Now I must die for it!"

Evan gasped.

Had he heard correctly?

What had his aunt just said?

The words repeated in his mind, clear now, so clear — and so frightening.

"I made this thing. Now I must die for it."

25

"No!"

Gaping in horror, as the sickening glob of Monster Blood pushed toward his aunt, Evan felt the room tilt and begin to spin. He gripped the back of Kathryn's armchair as pictures flooded his mind.

He saw the strange bone pendant Kathryn always wore around her neck.

The mysterious books that lined the walls of his bedroom.

Sarabeth, the black cat with the glowing yellow eyes.

The black shawl Kathryn always wrapped around her shoulders in the evening.

"I made this thing. Now I must die for it."

Evan saw it all now, and it began to come clear to him.

Evan pictured the day he and Andy brought home the can of Monster Blood from the toy store. Kathryn had insisted on seeing it.

On studying it.

On touching it.

He remembered the way she rolled the can around in her hands, examining it so carefully. Moving her lips silently as she read the label.

What had she been doing? What had she been saying?

A thought flashed into Evan's mind.

Had she been casting a spell on the can?

A spell to make the Monster Blood grow? A spell to terrify Evan?

But why? She didn't even know Evan.

Why did she want to frighten him? To . . . *kill* him?

"Be careful," she had called to him after handing the blue can back. "Be careful."

It was a real warning.

A warning against her spell.

"You did this!" Evan shouted in a voice he didn't recognize. The words burst out of him. He had no control over them.

"You did this! You cast a spell!" he repeated, pointing an accusing finger at his aunt.

He saw her blue eyes shimmer as they read his lips. Then her eyes filled with tears, tears that overflowed onto her pale cheeks.

"No!" she cried. "No!"

"You did something to the can! You did this, Aunt Kathryn!"

"No!" she cried, shouting over the sickening

grunts and *plop*s of the mountainous ball that nearly hid her from view.

"No!" Kathryn cried, her back pressed tightly against the mantelpiece. "I didn't do it! *She* did!"

And she pointed an accusing finger at Andy.

26

Andy?

Was Aunt Kathryn accusing *Andy*?

Evan spun around to confront Andy.

But Andy turned, too.

And Evan realized immediately that his aunt wasn't pointing at Andy. She was pointing past Andy to Sarabeth.

Standing in the doorway to the living room, the black cat hissed and arched her back, her yellow eyes flaring at Kathryn.

"She did it! She's the one!" Kathryn declared, pointing frantically.

The enormous glob of green Monster Blood bounced back, retreated a step, as if stung by Kathryn's words. Shadows shifted inside the glob as it quivered, catching the light filtering in through the living room window.

Evan stared at the cat, then turned his eyes to Andy. She shrugged, her face frozen in horror and bewilderment.

Aunt Kathryn is crazy, Evan thought sadly.

She's totally lost it.

She isn't making any sense.

None of this makes sense.

"She's the one!" Kathryn repeated.

The cat hissed in response.

The glob bounced in place, carrying the un-moving Beymer brothers inside.

"Oh — look!" Evan cried to Andy as the black cat suddenly raised up on its hind legs.

Andy gasped and squeezed Evan's arm. Her hand was as cold as ice.

Still hissing, the cat grew like a shadow against the wall. It raised its claws, swiping the air. Its eyes closed, and it became consumed in darkness.

No one moved.

The only sounds Evan could hear were the bubbling of the green glob and the pounding of his own heart.

All eyes were on the cat as it rose up, stretched, and grew. And as it grew, it changed its shape.

Became human.

With shadowy arms and legs in the eerie darkness.

And then the shadow stepped away from the darkness.

And Sarabeth was now a young woman with fiery red hair and pale skin and yellow eyes, the same yellow cat eyes that had haunted Evan since he'd arrived. The young woman was dressed in a swirling black gown down to her ankles.

She stood blocking the doorway, staring accusingly at Kathryn.

"You see? She's the one," Kathryn said, quietly now. And the next words were intended only for Sarabeth: "Your spell over me is broken. I will do no more work for you."

Sarabeth tossed her red hair behind a black-cloaked shoulder and laughed. "I'll decide what you will do, Kathryn."

"No," Kathryn insisted. "For twenty years, you have used me, Sarabeth. For twenty years you have imprisoned me here, held me in your spell. But now I will use this Monster Blood to escape."

Sarabeth laughed again. "There is no escape, fool. All of you must die now. *All* of you."

27

"All of you must die," Sarabeth repeated. Her smile revealed that she enjoyed saying those words.

Kathryn turned to Evan, her eyes reflecting her fear. "Twenty years ago, I thought she was my friend. I was all alone here. I thought I could trust her. But she cast a spell on me. And then another. Her dark magic made me deaf. She refused to let me lip-read or learn to sign. That was one way she kept me her prisoner."

"But, Aunt Kathryn — " Evan started.

She raised a finger to her lips to silence him.

"Sarabeth forced me to cast the spell on the can of Monster Blood. She had warned me that I was allowed no guests, you see. I was her slave. Her personal servant for all these years. She wanted me all to herself, to do her evil bidding.

"When you arrived," Kathryn continued, her back still pressed against the fireplace mantel, "she first decided to scare you away. But that was impossible. You had nowhere to go. Then she became desperate to get you out of the way. She was terrified that you would learn her secret, that you would somehow free me of her spell. So Sarabeth decided that you had to die."

Kathryn's eyes fell. She sighed. "I'm so sorry, Evan. I had no choice, no will of my own." She turned her eyes to Sarabeth. "But no more. No more. No more. As I plunge myself into this ghastly creation, Sarabeth, I will end your spell. I will end your hold over me."

"The children will still die," Sarabeth said quietly, coldly.

"What?" Kathryn's eyes filled with fury. "I will be gone, Sarabeth. You can let the children go. You have no reason to do them harm."

"They know too much," Sarabeth replied softly, crossing her slender arms in front of her, her yellow eyes aglow.

"We've got to get out of here," Evan whispered to Andy, staring at the seething green glob.

"But how?" Andy whispered back. "Sarabeth is blocking the doorway."

Evan's eyes darted around the small room, searching for an escape route.

Nothing.

Sarabeth raised one hand and drew it toward her slowly, as if summoning the green glob.

It quivered once, twice, then moved obediently in the direction of her hand.

"No! Sarabeth — stop!" Kathryn pleaded.

Ignoring Kathryn, Sarabeth gestured with her hand again.

The green gunk bubbled and rolled forward.

"Kill the children," Sarabeth commanded.

The enormous glob picked up speed as it rolled across the carpet toward Evan and Andy.

"Let's rush the door," Evan suggested to Andy, as they backed up away from the rolling Monster Blood.

"She'll never let us past," Andy cried.

"Kill the children!" Sarabeth repeated, raising both hands high above her head.

"Maybe one of us can get by her!" Evan cried.

"It's too late!" Andy shrieked.

The bouncing, pulsating, green glob was just a few feet away.

"We — we're going to be sucked in!" Evan screamed.

"Kill the children!" Sarabeth screamed triumphantly.

28

The glob rolled forward.

Evan sighed, feeling all hope sink. Frozen in place, he felt as if he weighed a thousand pounds.

Andy grabbed his hand.

They both closed their eyes and held their breath, and waited for the impact.

To their surprise, the Monster Blood emitted a deafening roar.

"Huh?"

Evan opened his eyes. Andy, he saw, was staring at the doorway, beyond Sarabeth.

The Monster Blood hadn't roared.

"Trigger!" Evan cried.

The huge dog bounded into the doorway, its deafening bark echoing off the low ceiling.

Sarabeth tried to get out of the dog's way. But she was too late.

Thrilled to see Evan, Trigger enthusiastically leapt at Sarabeth — and pushed her from behind.

Under the weight of the gigantic paws, Sarabeth staggered forward . . . forward . . . forward — raising her hands as she collided with the Monster Blood.

There was a wet *smack* as Sarabeth hit the surface of the green glob.

Then loud, disgusting sucking noises.

Her hands hit first. They disappeared quickly. And then Sarabeth was in up to her elbows.

And then the glob seemed to give a hard tug, and her body hit the surface. Then her face was pulled in, covered over.

Sarabeth never uttered a sound as she was pulled inside.

Whimpering with joy, completely unaware of what he had done, the dog loped into the room and headed for Evan.

"Down, boy! Down!" Evan cried, as Trigger happily leapt at him.

And as the dog jumped, he began to shrink.

"Trigger!" Evan called in astonishment, reaching out to hold the dog.

Trigger didn't seem to notice that he was changing. He licked Evan's face as Evan held on tightly.

In seconds, Trigger was back to normal cocker spaniel size.

"Look — the glob is shrinking, too!" Andy cried, squeezing Evan's shoulder.

Evan turned to see that the green glob was rapidly growing smaller.

As it shrunk, the Beymer brothers fell to the floor.

They didn't move. They lay facedown in a crumpled heap. Their open eyes stared lifelessly. They didn't appear to be breathing.

Then one blinked. The other blinked.

Their mouths opened and closed.

"Ohhh." One of them uttered a long, low groan.

Then, pulling themselves up slowly, they both looked around the room, dazed.

The trapped robin had also fallen to the floor. Chirping furiously, it flapped its wings wildly and fluttered about the room in a panic — until it found the open living room window and sailed out.

Andy held on to Evan as they stared at the Monster Blood, expecting Sarabeth to reappear, too.

But Sarabeth was gone.

Vanished.

The Monster Blood, shrunk to its original size, lay lifeless, inert, a dull green spot on the carpet, no bigger than a tennis ball.

The Beymer brothers stood up uncertainly, their eyes still reflecting terror and confusion. They stretched as if testing their arms and legs, seeing if their muscles still worked. Then they scrambled out of the house, slamming the screen door behind them.

"It's over," Kathryn said softly, moving forward to put an arm around Evan and Andy.

"Sarabeth is gone," Evan said, holding Trigger tightly in his arms, still staring at the tiny wedge of Monster Blood on the floor.

"And I can hear!" Kathryn said jubilantly, hugging them both. "Sarabeth *and* her spells are gone for good."

But as she said this, the screen door swung open and a shadowy figure stepped into the living room doorway.

29

"Mom!" Evan cried.

He set down Trigger and hurried to greet her, throwing his arms around her in a tight hug.

"What on earth is going on here?" Mrs. Ross asked. "Why did those two boys come bursting out like that? They looked scared to *death*!"

"It — it's a little hard to explain," Evan told her. "I'm so glad to see you!"

Trigger was glad, too. When he finally had finished jumping up and down and whimpering, Kathryn led Evan's mom to the kitchen. "I'll make some tea," she said. "I have a rather long story to tell you."

"I hope it isn't *too* long," Mrs. Ross said, glancing back questioningly at Evan. "We have a four o'clock plane to catch."

"Mom, I think you'll find this story interesting," Evan said, flashing Andy an amused look.

The two women disappeared into the kitchen.

377

Andy and Evan dropped down wearily onto the couch.

"I guess you're going forever," Andy said. "I mean, to Atlanta and everything — "

"I'd like to . . . uh . . . write to you," Evan said, suddenly feeling awkward.

"Yeah. Good," Andy replied, brightening. "And my dad has a phone credit card. Maybe I could get the number and . . . you know . . . call you."

"Yeah. Great," Evan said.

"Could I ask one small favor?" Andy asked.

"Yeah. Sure," Evan replied, curious.

"Well, it's going to sound strange," Andy said reluctantly. "But can I . . . uh . . . can I have the little bit of Monster Blood that's left? You know. Sort of as a memento or something?"

"Sure. Okay with me," Evan said.

They both turned their eyes to where it had come to rest on the carpet.

"Hey — " Andy cried in surprise.

It was gone.